ESCHER'S
LOOPS

Zoran Živković

Escher's Loops
Copyright © 2008 by Zoran Živković

FG-RS0019L2
ISBN: 978-4-908793-23-3

Cover: Youchan Ito, Togoru Art Works

Neoclassic Fleurons font used with permission of
Paulo W–Intellecta Design

Cadmus Press
cadmusmedia.org

ESCHER'S LOOPS

Zoran Živković

Translated from the Serbian
by
Alice Copple-Tošić

Cadmus Press
2018

Contents

The First Loop

The surgeon had just dried his hands in a stream of hot air from the hand dryer next to the wash basin, pulled on his gloves and headed for the operating room, when a sudden recollection made him stop in front of the double glass door. Even though he was urgently awaited inside, the thought disconcerted him so much that he was rooted to the spot.

Those who knew him better would certainly have assumed that he'd remembered the incident he most wanted to forget. It was the only stain on his career. He'd left a pair of surgical tweezers inside a patient. There was no excuse for this oversight. What could he say in his defense? That he'd been captivated by her face and couldn't keep his eyes off her? The anesthesia had seemed to bestow an angelic quality on the beautiful young woman. Mentioning this enchantment as the cause of his distraction would only have aggravated his position.

But the surgeon was not thinking of this mishap just then, although it had happened in the room he was about to enter. Something else, considerably less unpleasant, had flashed across his mind, although there was no obvious reason for it.

He had gone to a colleague's wedding because he hadn't been able to get out of it. He didn't like weddings and even preferred funerals to them. Had anyone asked him why, he wouldn't have been able to explain. He found weddings repugnant, a perversity that embarrassed him. Indeed, what opinion could a doctor have of himself when he gave death priority over life?

In order to hide his bad mood, he'd acted out of character. A smile was stuck permanently on his face and he was annoyingly affable. As the wedding party gathered in front of the church, he struck up intimate conversations with people he hardly knew. He inquired after their health and offered advice even to those without any complaints. Since he was a reputable surgeon, everyone was grateful to receive his free counsel, even those in the pink of health.

He was relieved when they started to enter the church because this gave him a break from his feigned good humor. His face darkened, but he knew that as soon as they came out he would have to reassume a cheerful mask and keep it until late in the evening. Engrossed in somber thoughts, he failed to notice that the ceremony was delayed.

He realized that something was wrong from the commotion around him. Heads drew together as people whispered to each other. Shorter guests behind him craned their necks to get a better look at the altar where the wedding couple, best man and maid of honor were standing. Although he was right up front, it took a few moments before he detected the cause of the trouble.

There was no trace of the priest. The bride's agitation was clearly apparent even from her back. The bridegroom shrugged his shoulders helplessly and turned this way and that, but there was no one to give him an explanation. Who knew how long the uneasy tension would have lasted if the bride hadn't suddenly raised her veil and stamped her foot on the stone floor.

The blow of her thin heel resounded like an explosion in the echoing church. Everyone suddenly fell silent. She turned around brusquely and for some reason fixed her eyes on the surgeon. Words were not necessary. As though receiving a strict military order, he practically ran to the back of the church to see what was holding things up.

The surgeon knocked but received no reply. He waited briefly, then entered uninvited. A completely unexpected sight awaited him in the priest's little office. Most of the space was taken up by a massive pool table. The priest was standing motionless, bent all the way over it, holding a cue aimed at the white ball. All he had on below the waist was chequered long johns, black knee socks and slippers. It was not until the surgeon cleared his throat that the priest snapped out of his paralysis. As he quickly put on his pants, surplice and shoes, he tried to justify his behaviour.

He always played a bit of pool before a wedding ceremony. By himself and half-dressed. It was the best way to relax. This was the only ceremony that gave him the jitters. Hitting just two or three balls into the pockets was enough to calm him down. This time, however, as he swung the cue for the third time he suddenly remembered something and went stiff.

There was no time to satisfy the surgeon's curiosity. The priest was to blame for the wedding ceremony's late start. As soon as he had tied his shoelaces, they rushed out of the room. As they approached the altar, the priest's face turned penitent. The bride's stamping heel rang ominously in the church.

He mumbled something unintelligible in apology.

The ceremony started at once and proceeded without a hitch. The bride's good mood returned as soon as she said "I do." On the way out of the church she was radiantly happy, as though there hadn't been any delay.

Had the surgeon known the priest better, no explanation would have been necessary. He would have assumed that the priest had recalled an event of twenty-six years ago, just after his appointment to this church. He was looking forward to the first wedding that was to install him officially in his duties. It had been scheduled before his arrival so he still hadn't had a chance to see the bride and groom.

When the wedding couple appeared before him he was thrown completely out of kilter. The face he glimpsed through the transparent veil took his breath away. He knew he shouldn't stare at the bride, but his eyes kept coming back to her. When the time came to start the ceremony, his memory failed him.

He stood there helplessly, mouth half-open, eyes fixed on the veil. Tension rose and his agony along with it, but he was unable to break the spell. When the bride, groom, best man and maid of honor started to look at each other in surprise, he finally managed to regain just enough control of himself to turn without a word and run to the priest's office.

Disaster was avoided owing to the fact that the recently retired former priest was in the church. He finished the ceremony that had barely started and then did his utmost to make allowances for his colleague. He ascribed the priest's disorientation to the jitters and lack of experience. When the wedding party left, he spent a long time consoling the young priest, telling him that something similar had happened to him as well at the beginning of his service.

The young priest felt better when he realized that no one had caught on to the cause of his embarrassment. He followed his colleague's advice about finding something to reduce his agitation before the ceremony. The retired priest, who used a pinball machine for the same purpose, saw nothing wrong with fulfilling the young man's wish to have a pool table in his office. He even used his influence to get a good price for a used table.

∽ 2 ∾

The memory of this distant embarrassment, however, was not what had now caused the priest to forget the bride, groom and wedding party awaiting him. He'd been held back by another memory that appeared out of the blue just as he was about to send the third ball into the pocket, then quickly get dressed and head toward the altar.

He'd remembered an incident at the theater that had almost turned into a scandal. The priest hadn't always been a theater buff. He would go occasionally to see a play when it seemed suitable to his calling. And then, suddenly, four-and-a-half years ago, he'd become a regular theatergoer. Sometimes he wouldn't miss a single performance the whole week long, even if the same play were given five times.

If anyone noticed the priest's sudden affinity for the theater, it aroused no suspicions. Why should it? Is there anything wrong with devotion to the theatrical arts stirring in a man of the cloth, even late in life? Had anyone taken a close look at what connected the plays he watched, they might have discovered that the priest's motives were not exactly above reproach. But who had any reason to undertake such an investigation?

Had there been a reason, the first thing to catch the eye was that the priest had warmed to the theater ever since a new young actress had started to play there. He watched only the plays in which she performed. He always sat in the same seat in the eleventh row, dressed in inconspicuous civvies. After every performance a bouquet of white roses awaited the actress in her dressing room, sent by a florist in the name of a fan who wanted to remain anonymous.

No investigation, however, would have ascertained what it was that bewitched the priest so much. The young actress was talented, but not exceptionally so. She was pretty too, although somewhat aloof. It might have been this detached beauty that attracted him, since priests are known for their unusual proclivities, but if someone could have penetrated the innermost corners of his mind, there where even he was unwilling to look, they would have discovered something else. The face hidden behind the veil was almost identical to that of the young actress. As though they were the same person. Such a similarity might be found, for example, in pictures of a mother and daughter taken when they were the same age.

Nothing indicated that something unusual would happen in the play. It was finely-tuned and had already been performed three times that week. At the beginning of the second act when the garden scene took place, the young actress was alone on the stage with an actor who was still cast in the role of a Don Juan even though he'd been dyeing his hair for years and wore a corset to fight his excess weight.

At his fiery declaration, "You must be mine," accompanied by an attempt to kiss her, she was supposed to push him away, slap him lightly and shout "What's come over you?" But she did none of that. She stood there without moving, staring over his shoulder into the audience as though struck dumb by something she saw there.

Those who hadn't seen the play before found nothing strange at first. The young woman was supposed to reject the courtship of her aggressive seducer, but this might be an unexpected turn that was characteristic of such plays. Indeed, he was holding her rather awkwardly, as though equally surprised by the lack of resistance. The priest, however, who knew the play perfectly, realized at once that something unusual was going on.

As the seconds passed tensely and the actress just stood there thunderstruck, the audience started to fidget. The priest felt panic creep over him, as though he himself were on the stage. At first he thought the young woman had forgotten her lines, although this had never happened before. Since he already knew most of her role by heart, he was tempted to call out the line to her from the gloom, but before he could do so, the prompter beat him to it and practically shouted, "What's come over you?"

The shout caused an even greater stir in the audience. Two low whistles were heard. It was certain that general discontent would be quick to follow, with the inevitable suspension of the play. Had the priest thought it over, he might have hesitated. Unwarranted public displays were certainly not suitable to his position and reputation. But now he had no choice.

He jumped up from his seat and briskly applauded. The audience turned their eyes from the stage to him. When they recognized him in the gloom, they hesitated just a moment and then joined his applause. Is there any better example to follow than that of a priest? If he doesn't know what should be done, who does?

As though the thundering sound had snapped her out of her paralysis, the young actress returned to her role more spiritedly than necessary. With the shrill cry, "What's come over you?" she slapped the actor and pushed him so violently that he, who was only holding her lightly, lost his balance and fell flat on his back with his long legs flying in the air. This brought an outburst of laughter that instantly erased the theatergoers' peevishness over the hitch of a moment before.

The play continued seamlessly with even greater inspiration than usual and in the end the actors were brought back on stage for seven curtain calls. For days afterwards rumors were spread about what had come over the young actress. For some mysterious reason she refused to offer any explanation. The theater's management did not insist on getting one owing to the favorable outcome.

The only apology the young woman gave was to her older colleague who didn't begrudge her very much for disgracing him since he'd turned the incident to his advantage. He soon stopped playing suitors and seducers, and turned to comic roles full of gags where he managed quite well and no longer had to dye his hair and wear a corset.

Most people supported the hypothesis that the empty third seat in the right front row was to blame for everything. Those sitting nearby remembered that an extremely handsome young man no one had seen before had been occupying that seat during the first act. Several of them claimed they'd seen the young actress glance towards him frequently, always with a fleeting smile, even when the role did not occasion it.

Why the young man did not return to the auditorium after the intermission remained a mystery. When the young woman noticed he was gone she'd turned completely numb. Was this to be held against her? Everyone knows how hard it is when your loved one spurns you, and this had been done in front of so many eyewitnesses. Everyone sympathized with her grief, which only increased her popularity.

∽ 3 ∾

The rumors went all the way to the young actress. She did not deny them, however, because this was not to her advantage. She shrewdly kept her mouth shut even though she knew there wasn't a grain of truth to any of it. First of all, even if she'd wanted to see someone in the audience, in the front row or any other, this was impossible because the stage lights practically blinded her. In addition, she wasn't in love with the handsome young man because she didn't even know who he was.

Finally, if she started to deny the story she would have to explain what had made her almost interrupt the performance, and this was something she certainly wanted to avoid. Among other things, there was nothing romantic about the real reason. Without that ingredient she would lose the public's sympathy and the management's regard.

What had completely thrown her out of the role she was playing was a memory that suddenly crossed her mind. She remembered a fire that had engulfed a two-story residential building in her neighborhood. She'd been nine-and-a-half at the time. Never before or after would she directly experience the horrors of an uncontrolled blaze. Standing at a safe distance, she watched the flames rise from the basement where something had caught fire. Water streaming from the firefighters' hoses seemed to have no effect.

Shouts were heard from all around when a window in the attic opened and a terrified old woman appeared. She was screaming for help, waving her arms. A ladder quickly sprang up from one of the fire trucks. Before it even reached the attic, a fully outfitted, heavyset firefighter grabbed hold of a rung.

He took hold of the woman around the waist. Nothing happened for a few moments. Her shaking head indicated that she was too afraid to go down. The firefighter had to take off his mask so she could hear him.

Everyone breathed a sigh of relief when she finally put her arms around his neck. He lifted her with ease and started down the ladder as the onlookers cheered. But everyone fell silent when he stopped unexpectedly about halfway down the ladder. His helmet and her gray head turned towards the window in the attic that was now empty. The firefighter took off his mask once again to calm her down as she held on with one hand and pointed up with the other.

He spent a good two minutes reassuring the woman before they started down again. When they reached the roof of the truck, the firefighter's colleagues took hold of her and he started up the ladder again. Even though the hoses were turned on full blast, the fire had devoured the first floor in the meantime and fiery tongues were flicking towards the second. But this did not deter the courageous firefighter.

He hastened inside when he reached the window and spent only a few moments there, although it seemed much longer to the crowd. When he reappeared he was carrying a cage with a small white parrot fluttering about in distress. Applause filled the air.

The firefighter had just straddled the window when he saw the old woman's arms waving to him from the ground. He couldn't make out what she was shouting in distress, but it seemed this was not even necessary. He hesitated briefly about what to do with the cage, then finally let it fall into the outstretched canvas out at the bottom of the ladder. Before he went back into the room he made sure that the parrot had survived the fall, even though the worn-out cage had broken to pieces.

This time it was not merely an impression. The firefighter was gone for a long time. During that time the fire spread to the second floor. Now the hoses were focused on the narrow space around the ladder to keep the fire at bay, but this would clearly not work for very long. A terrible roar had begun inside.

The commander of the fire brigade knew he had no choice. His hand was already raised to signal the truck to lower the ladder and move back when the firefighter appeared in a cloud of smoke pouring out of the attic window. Under his arm was a small chest of valuables.

Elated cheering mixed with shouts urging him to hurry. Just as he started to descend the ladder again the smoke above him turned red and flames darted out of the window. Luckily he was beyond their reach, but there was no time to lose. He had to get down as quickly as possible. The truck couldn't move while he was on the ladder.

As an experienced firefighter, he was certainly aware of this, but even so he stopped at approximately the same place as he had the first time he went down. When it became clear that this was not just a brief stop, all hell broke loose. The fire was now blazing from all the openings on the building and had already broken through the roof.

The other firefighters shouted at him to continue, but he just stood there motionless on the same rung. He must have been overcome by the heat and smoke in spite of the gas mask and protective suit. The hoses turned on him to cool him off and bring him back to his senses. This was all they could do. No one dared go up to him because it was already too dangerous.

As he stood there like a statue, the crowd was struck with horror. The building was about to collapse and he was sure to die. Many turned their heads away. The little girl, however, continued to watch. And not only that.

She started to sing. Quite softly, so that in the surrounding noise she couldn't even hear herself. Had anyone been watching they would have thought she was mouthing the words. But no one paid any attention to the little girl who, in any case, had no business to be there.

It must have been a coincidence. The firefighter on the ladder was the last person who could have heard her little tune. Nevertheless, as soon as she started, he suddenly came to his senses. Instead of climbing, he slid down in a flash. The little girl didn't stop until he was safely on the ground and the truck had withdrawn. The moment the inaudible song ended, the building collapsed with a tremendous crash and burst of flames.

The fire was finally put out an hour-and-a-half later, but the little girl left as soon as the firefighter was saved. After the men returned to the fire station, no one asked why he'd stopped on the ladder. They were all convinced they knew the answer. The glowing heat and smoke hadn't dazed him. The little chest was to blame.

The object the fireman went back to retrieve from the attic must have reminded him of a distant event that he'd mentioned only once to his colleagues in an unprecedented state of drunkenness at a fireman's ball and later, when he sobered up, refused to talk about again.

Before he became a firefighter he'd worked for over four years as a lighthouse keeper on a small island quite distant from land. One gray autumn morning he had a surprise waiting for him on the deserted rocky coast—a shipwrecked boat with no one inside. The ocean current must have brought it from far away.

Inside the boat was a wooden chest with metal studs. It measured about one meter by half a meter and reached up to his knees. A gold chain with an oval locket was attached to the large padlock. When he removed the chain, he noticed that the locket opened. Inside was a black and white picture of the most beautiful young woman he had ever seen. He couldn't tear his eyes away for a long time.

Finally he returned to the lighthouse and brought back his toolbox. He knew that he wasn't allowed to do anything on his own. The rules required that he radio the lighthouse management and wait for a maritime inspector, but the young woman's face seemed to have completely confused him. He simply had to open the chest, which he'd already ascertained was quite heavy. There was no way he could bring it to shore by himself.

It took quite a bit of effort before he finally forced the padlock. Kneeling next to the chest, he raised the lid halfway. All he did was stare for some time, oblivious to the rain that had started to drizzle. Then he closed the lid slowly and rummaged briefly through his tool-box until he found a new padlock. He put it in place of the broken one and attached the chain to it.

Then he brought a motor boat from the lighthouse harbor, tied a rope to the shipwrecked boat and headed out to open sea. When he thought he was far enough from the island, he stopped. Taking an axe from the motor boat, he got into the wrecked ship and start-ed breaking its hull without a second thought. When water started pouring in, he returned to his boat and untied the rope, then watched until the boat with the chest went under. On regaining the lighthouse, he in-formed his superiors that he was resigning. He would no longer do the job of a lighthouse keeper.

The firefighter's colleagues did everything they could to find out what he'd seen in the chest but he, in spite of his drunken state, had kept the secret to himself. Now that unfinished story had come in handy. He didn't have to explain what had come over him during his second descent from the attic with its near-tragic end.

4

What had come over him was a sudden flashback that had nothing to do with the mysterious chest. Later when he gave it more thought, he couldn't figure out what it was that had brought forth that distant memo-ry just then, at such a badly chosen moment.

He'd been very interested in athletics as a young man. He'd never tried his own hand at it, even though he had the build of a sportsman, but regularly attended competitions. He was particularly attracted to women's throwing events. Not that there was anything perverse about it. He admired the power and skill of the throwers. In addition, he felt that the spectators wrongfully neglected them as not looking feminine enough.

This was confirmed at the event that had flashed back to him out of the blue on the ladder. The spectators' attention was riveted on the slender, long-legged female high jumpers and hardly anyone was watching the part of the field where shots were being put, even though it was just as exciting.

It was the end of the last series of puts. Only one contestant was left. She was in second place and this was her chance to come in first. The future lighthouse keeper had been rooting for her from the beginning, although he couldn't explain why. Her stature was no different from her opponents'. All that set her apart was her wavy red hair.

She entered the putting circle. In her previous five attempts she had put the shot immediately, but now for some reason she hesitated. She just stood there with her back to the putting circle, looking somewhere to the side. At first he thought she was trying her best to concentrate. He was angry at the spectators cheering for the high jumpers because they were distracting her.

Moments passed and the shot putter didn't move. When the small digital countdown next to the circle indicated she had only seven seconds left for her last put, her sole supporter did something that was quite out of character for someone as reserved as he was.

He jumped up from his seat and shouted, "Put it!" But his cry was drowned out by thunderous applause for the woman who had just bested the highest jump. It was not clear whether the putter heard him or snapped out of her torpor owing to this outburst of joy in the bleachers.

In any case, she began her circular start at once.

When the shot flew out of her left hand, the count-down had reached the number two. The distance she put the shot was not immediately clear. This, however, didn't seem to interest anyone but the other putters and one spectator.

When it was announced that she had put the shot three centimeters farther than the leading contestant, he jumped up again and started to clap, paying no attention to the dubious looks of the spectators around him. After he sat down, he wondered what it was that had inhibited the red-headed young woman to the point of almost failing to put the shot. He pondered a moment, but was unable to detect any reason. In any case, whatever it was, it no longer mattered now that she'd won.

Had he been one of those who knew the shot putter better, he would have concluded that her hesitation was connected to the memory of a dramatic event from the beginning of her career in athletics. At that time she threw the javelin instead of putting the shot, and her first competition almost had a fateful end.

Then as now she had one throw left. She'd gone onto the run-up area and had already started to run, when something on the right caught her eye. She continued with her head turned halfway until she threw the javelin. As soon as it flew out of her hand, she realized the inexorable.

The sharp double-bladed spear had gone too far to the side. She shouted while the javelin was still going up. Her shout reached many ears, but not those of the long jumper who, suspecting nothing, was warming up next to the track at the other end of the stadium.

At first it seemed that he'd been hit in the stomach. The terrified young woman covered her mouth with her hands and collapsed in a heap at the end of the run-up area. When they brought her around, they first cheered her with the news that the worst had been avoided. The javelin had pierced his hip. He wouldn't be able to jump anymore but at least his life was not in danger.

The young woman at first decided to drop athletics too, but the young man she had injured talked her out of it. He told her she had to continue for both of them. She agreed, but changed disciplines. Owing to her build she would still have to be a thrower. She chose the shot because she thought it was the least dangerous for others.

For a while they tried to find out what had made her look to the side while she'd been running with the javelin. Probably owing to the shock she'd experienced, she had absolutely no recollection of those moments. This gave rise to rumors. It was said that she'd caught sight of a handsome sprinter who was lying on the grass limbering up. He was by no means the only good-looking athlete, but the thrower felt that his wavy red hair made him unique.

This time no one asked her why she almost failed to put her last shot. Indeed, except for the one and only supporter, only the other putters were aware of her hesitation. Those who knew about the injured long jumper were convinced she'd been thinking about that. The other women saw the whole thing as a tactical maneuver that they would have to use as well.

∽ 5 ∾

The young woman was glad she didn't have to explain herself. She surely would have disappointed many people if she'd told them what really happened when she entered the shot putting circle. It had not been any sort of tactical subterfuge. Something had crossed her mind, but not the unfortunate javelin throw. She'd remembered another far more innocuous incident in which the long jumper also had a minor role.

When he recovered from his injuries, he invited her out to dinner. She couldn't refuse, of course, although she would have under other circumstances. She had a feeling of guilt about the young man, but nothing else. He wasn't her type. If he decided to try anything, she would have to let him know, in spite of everything.

Luckily, he had no such intentions. They spent the evening making cheerful small talk. Although they spent most of the time talking about athletics, neither one mentioned the unpleasant incident that had brought them together. She soon relaxed and started to enjoy his company, deciding that it would be nice for them to become friends, since anything else was out of the question.

The only small shadow cast that evening came during dessert. An older couple was sitting at the table next to theirs. He was tall and thin, completely gray, but with a thick crop of hair. His comportment was stiff and stern. He was silent most of the time. She was short and round, all in pink. Her matching hat had a wide brim and several brightly colored feathers. She never closed her mouth.

There was no indication that something might go wrong. The liveried waiter went up to take their order. He waited patiently next to the table as the new guests examined the unwieldy menu inside its dark-brown leather cover. Either the abundant selection or their discrimination resulted in a protracted wait.

The lady was the first to speak. She asked for an explanation of several items on the menu. The waiter did not reply. He just looked at her, smiling. She repeated her question, but again there was no answer. Then she turned to her husband who was still engrossed in the menu. He raised his head and addressed the waiter himself. The man continued to stand there without speaking, leaning forward a little, holding a pad in one hand and a pen in the other. The smile never left his face.

After a brief silence, the woman repeated her question in a louder voice. But it seemed to be directed at a statue. Perplexed by the waiter's demeanor, the couple looked around for his colleagues. Right then, however, none of the other staff were in the restaurant's main dining room.

The young woman couldn't imagine what had come over the waiter. When he'd served them, everything had seemed perfectly fine. He'd been very obliging and pleasant. She had no reason to interfere, but as the tension mounted with no relief in sight, she felt more and more uncomfortable, as though personally involved in the problem at the next table.

She looked at the long jumper. He just shrugged his shoulders, clearly at a loss. She felt a knot growing in her stomach, just like before a decisive throw on the athletic field. She had to do something to make it go away. Hesitating just a moment, she reached for her unused wine glass, picked it up and dropped it with a swing.

The explosion of shattering glass echoed in the hush of the restaurant. Every single guest flinched. Some even jumped up. The maître d' and the other waiters swarmed out of the kitchen. Even the head chef made an appearance. But most important of all, the strangely statue-like waiter came back to his senses.

He mumbled a few words of apology and hastened to clean up the broken glass. Realizing what had happened, the maître d' quickly took the waiter's place at the elderly couple's table. His cordiality soon removed their unease and in no time at all nothing in the restaurant indicated that anything unusual had happened.

No one held it against the waiter. On the contrary, they were all reassuring and full of understanding, convinced they knew what had caused the incident. The feathered hat was to blame, of course. It had reminded him of something that happened at that same table. Even though more than five years and three months had passed since then, he still hadn't forgotten the trauma.

The only thing that disrupted the guest's widow's weeds was a yellow hat with ostrich feathers. She was already well along in years and yet had a youthful appearance. She was without an escort and yet not alone. She had brought a cage, holding it by the ring on the domed top.

After she sat down, she took the black cover off the cage. The waiter was on his way to her table and stopped in mid-step. Never before had he seen such a lovely creature. He knew nothing about birds so he didn't know what it was called, but did that matter? Mesmerized, he stared at the magnificent plumage all ablaze, shimmering in every color of the rainbow.

The woman had to clear her throat to bring the waiter to his senses. It took considerable effort for him to tear his eyes away from the cage. He handed her the menu but she waved it away dismissively. She turned towards the bird and addressed it in a low voice full of guttural vowels that sounded like cooing.

The bird replied with a warble that sent shudders down the waiter's spine and filled his ears with the sound of heavenly choirs. When the guest addressed him again, he only half-glanced at her and wrote down the order in a daze. On his way to the kitchen he looked back several times.

It was not until he returned, carrying a roast pigeon in wild strawberry sauce, that he wondered at the woman's unusual choice. Indeed, eating a bird in the company of another bird did not seem quite proper. But of course, it was not for him to judge the guests' preferences.

He set the plate of roast pigeon before the woman, poured her a glass of white wine and wished her a pleasant meal. This time he did not look back as he walked away. When he reached the place he stood while waiting to serve the guests, he turned around again, looked towards the table with the cage—and was horrified.

He had misunderstood. The dish was not intended for the woman but the bird. The plate was inside the cage. The creature with heavenly plumage and a divine song was tearing off pigeon meat with its beak and gobbling it voraciously. The woman watched it with a smile as she sipped her wine.

The waiter felt nauseous. Putting both hands over his mouth, he ran to the men's room and spent a good ten minutes there, first with his head over the toilet and then splashing his face over the sink. It took a little while longer to muster the courage to go back to the restaurant's main dining room.

He looked reluctantly towards the place where the beauty had defiled herself so foully, fearing a new attack of nausea, but there was no cause for concern. The woman with the cage had left. On the table was a plate full of tiny bones and a half-drunk glass of wine.

The waiter decided at first to leave the profession, even though he had talent that promised a successful career. It took the restaurant owner a long time to make him change his mind. It was only when the owner gave him a raise and promised to ban birds from the restaurant that he accepted.

∽ 6 ∾

The waiter had no reason to disillusion his colleagues and the maître d'. Let them think the old trauma was behind the whole thing. They wouldn't have had much understanding for his unseemly conduct if they knew what had really caused it. The memory that resurged as he was waiting for the guests to make up their minds was not stirred by the feathers on the pink hat because they weren't ostrich feathers. He never did figure out what had called forth that event of six years and seven months ago which had lain dormant for so long.

An undertaker friend of his had asked him to the Funeral Association's annual costume ball. He reluctantly agreed to go. He didn't like this type of party and he didn't know how to act in the company of morticians. His friend assured him that it was just a costume ball like any other and he had no reason to worry. He would see, in effect, that undertakers were more inclined to enjoy a bit of fun than people with far cheerier professions.

He vacillated a long time in the costume supply shop until he finally chose a Frosty the Snowman mask. Even though the mask was more of a caricature, it somehow seemed the most appropriate.

The costume ball was in full swing: blaring music, flowing drinks, rafters echoing with laughter. Everyone hid behind their masks and this added to the dissolute, loose atmosphere. Among so many grotesque faces, Frosty the Snowman seemed quite artless, until the highpoint of the party when the time came for the undertakers' reel.

Everyone danced. More than one hundred fifty undertakers and guests surrendered completely to the whirling rhythm. Two turns were made, hands on the hips of one's partner, and then the couples split up and new ones formed. The room seemed filled with a multitude of whirling, volatile circles.

Since the waiter wasn't a good dancer, he would rather have sat it out, but that was impossible. Fortunately, he quickly mastered the simple steps and then the dizzying rapture seized him too. Squealing and whooping masks changed before him without letup.

He had just put his hands on the hips below a fiendish witch mask that certainly didn't match the luxuriant dark wavy hair and slender build, when his new partner stopped dead in her tracks. This caused a chain reaction, such as when one of many interconnected gears suddenly stops. The harmonious atmosphere reigning until then collapsed like a house of cards. The orchestra fell silent because it had lost its purpose.

The waiter stared in confusion at the slits in the witch mask where chestnut eyes stared at him emptily. At the same time, he felt the reproachful glances of the other dancers shoot straight at him in the muffled silence. They clearly believed that his clumsiness had caused the holdup.

Panic was already coursing through his body when he realized what he had to do. He ripped off the Frosty the Snowman mask. Nothing moved for a few moments and then the young woman's hands resting limply on his hips suddenly held him tight.

He hoped he had properly interpreted the sign and

led her into the whirling dance again. Only two circles were needed for all the gears in the room to start working. Even before the music started up again he had a new mask in front of him. He didn't put his own mask back on. The undertakers' reel continued triumphantly and everyone forgot the brief interruption.

In the general tumult at the end when the masks were removed, he was unable to find the face of the young woman with the wavy hair and chestnut eyes. On the way back from the costume party his friend explained what had undoubtedly caused the dance to break off. It was the Frosty the Snowman mask, of course, and an incident that had happened the summer before.

The young woman, whom everyone considered to be the prettiest member of the Funeral Association, had been in a bank when there was an attempted robbery. She was standing in line in front of the counter when a shot rang out behind her. She turned around in alarm to see a heavyset man wearing a Frosty the Snowman mask, holding a gun. Speaking calmly, as though nothing unusual was going on, he ordered the employees to raise their hands and the customers to lie on the floor, then disarmed the guard who hadn't had time to react.

Just as he went up to the counter and handed over a bag to be filled with money, the alarm went off. Metal shutters dropped over the windows the same moment. The robber ordered the employees to continue as though nothing had happened. Then he took the bagful of money, went to an armchair in the corner and sat down.

In less than three minutes the wailing of a police siren came from outside. A telephone line to the robber was soon set up. Still speaking calmly, he ordered the police to send him a helicopter in twenty minutes so he could get away with the loot. He threatened to start killing the hostages he was holding in the bank if they didn't meet his demands.

When the time was up and he was asked to be patient since they were having trouble finding him a helicopter, he simply hung up. His eyes slid over the customers on the floor and then he motioned with his gun for the young female undertaker to get up. An older man lying next to her tried to protest, but stopped as soon as the barrel was pointed at his head.

He took the young woman to a back room. Everyone waited in horror for the ominous shot, but nothing was heard. Ten minutes later the customers started getting up slowly, and the more courageous employees lowered their hands. They looked at each other in bewilderment.

At the sound of the back door opening, they quickly returned to their former positions. The robber came out of the back room. He was no longer wearing the Frosty the Snowman mask and his gun was gone. A few moments later the young woman appeared. One hand held the pistol barrel gingerly with two fingers and the other held the mask.

The telephone rang that same moment. The police announced that the helicopter was on its way. The robber replied that it was no longer necessary. He had decided to surrender. He hung up the phone and returned to the armchair next to the bag of money where he waited quietly for them to arrest him.

The police tried to find out what had happened in the back room. The young woman, however, refused to talk, even when threatened with being accused as an accessory. They couldn't get the robber to loosen his tongue either. Not even the promise of a lighter sentence was any help.

None of the pretty undertaker's colleagues asked why she'd interrupted the last dance. They were all convinced they knew the reason. But even if they'd asked, there would have been no reply. The unusual incident in the circus that had suddenly surfaced was no one else's concern. She couldn't fathom what had summoned that memory in the middle of the whirling, but it certainly hadn't been Frosty the Snowman.

It was just after her thirteenth birthday. Two of her girlfriends had talked her into going to the circus that had just come to town. She didn't like circuses, particularly not the acts with trained animals. She was horrified at the thought of the torture they went through just to entertain the crowd.

Fortunately, this circus did not have many trained animals. The show was already well along and there had only been a little monkey that seemed to be thoroughly enjoying itself. Just when she'd begun to hope that was it, a lion taming act appeared at the very end.

It was immediately clear that the three large beasts, a male and two females, were quite agitated. The tamer had to crack his whip constantly and raise a chair to get them to obey his commands. The lions thrashed their paws menacingly as the tent reverberated with angry roars.

The high point of the act was when the tamer put his head into the male lion's open mouth. He seemed reluctant, then signaled the audience to be quiet. Silence reigned. He put down the chair, laid the whip on it and cautiously headed towards the lion.

As he drew closer, the future undertaker was suddenly struck by the great cat's beauty. Everything about it seemed harmonious and full of raw energy. Even its roar that had made her shudder a moment before now seemed almost melodious.

The tamer stood stock-still for a moment in front of the lion. Then he slowly raised his hands and opened its jaw. He looked the animal straight in the eye for a few moments, then put his head between the pointed teeth.

The admiring audience watched with bated breath as the tension quickly rose. It seemed they could hardly wait for the act to end so they could thunderously applaud. But the seconds drew out and nothing happened. The tamer's head did not come out of the lion's mouth.

When it became clear that something was wrong, the crowd began to fidget. Was the lion preventing the tamer from removing his head? The man made no movement that would indicate he was in trouble, but the animal was clearly struggling to keep its jaws open, as though wanting to close its mouth as soon as possible.

While many in the audience put their hands over their eyes, horrified at what seemed imminent, the girl suddenly felt a thrill such as she had never experienced before. It was as if the tamer's head was inside her own mouth. She started to open and close her jaws.

She didn't snap out of this peculiar trance until the chattering sound caused one of her young woman-friends to look at her strangely. She clenched her jaw firmly shut in embarrassment. That same moment, to everyone's relief, the tamer finally took his head out of the lion's mouth.

While rounds of applause still filled the tent, the young woman stood up and left without a word. She never went to a circus again. When she got home, she firmly resolved to be an undertaker when she grew up. She never told anyone the reason for this decision.

Unlike the audience, the circus staff took the end of the lion tamer's act in stride. It was not unusual for him to keep his head in the lion's mouth for quite some time. That meant that he was thinking of a tragic event from his youth.

He had the adventurous spirit that went hand in hand with becoming a lion tamer and often set out to explore uncharted regions. Once he chanced to meet a young woman with a similar penchant. He didn't hesitate a moment to accept her invitation to join in the search for a mysterious underground city in the heart of the jungle.

With the help of an ancient map, they proceeded through the wilds, overcoming dangerous obstacles along the way. When they finally reached their destination at the close of the ninth day on the road, an amazing sight awaited them. The setting sun illuminated a rocky elevation carved in the shape of a human skull.

In place of the mouth was a gaping semicircular opening into a cave. The only way to enter was to get on one's hands and knees. The young woman was all set to go right in, but he managed to talk her out of it. Night was about to fall and they were quite tired. It would be better to sleep outside and start exploring in the morning.

When he awoke, the young woman was not next to him. He realized at once what had happened. He rushed to the entrance, but had a surprise in store. Inexplicably, the opening had shrunk. He could no longer go all the way inside; only his head would fit.

Filled with dark foreboding, he stuck his head through the opening. He assumed he wouldn't see anything, but never guessed the reason: not because of the darkness but just the opposite—because of the dazzling light. It was as if the sun itself had moved into the cave. He had to squint to prevent himself being blinded.

He heard the young woman's terrified voice from down in the depths. She begged him to leave at once. He, of course, would never have left her, but that's when he felt the stone mouth start to close around his head. Terror-stricken, he pulled it out at the last moment before the opening in the skull disappeared for good.

The only way to get inside was with dynamite, but he hadn't brought any with him. Driven by despair, he reached civilization in only six days. He got the equipment he needed and rushed back, but when he got there the skull-shaped elevation was nowhere to be seen.

He wandered frantically through the nearby jungle for days, hoping he'd gone astray without the map that had stayed with the young woman. But there wasn't a trace of the entrance into the underground world of light. Finally, totally crushed, he had to give up.

〜 8 〜

The lion tamer was glad that no explanation was due to the circus staff as to why he'd hesitated from taking his head out of the lion's mouth. As an honest man he didn't want to lie, which is what he would have had to do to avoid even greater trouble. It was better this way. Let them believe that he'd remembered the incident in the jungle. They'd all shown consideration for that trauma, but it would certainly be lacking if they knew what thought had imperiled the act and put his own life in danger.

He had suddenly remembered a distant auction he'd attended more out of curiosity than to buy anything. The small town where he'd settled for a while after retiring from his life as an adventurer held auctions every Saturday morning in the only movie theater in town.

The locals usually brought small household items to sell: vases, candlesticks, inkpots, bookends, old medals and coins, porcelain figurines, picture frames, sets of silverware, wall clocks and watches. Nice little things could be bought for a trifle.

Nothing indicated that anything unusual would happen at the auction. A pipe-cleaning set from the last century, two gramophone records of operatic arias and a teapot that could only be used as a decoration had all been sold. Their brisk sale was certainly facilitated by the smooth tongue of the experienced auctioneer, a retired lady doctor with salt-and-pepper hair and a large mole on her left cheek.

Her assistant lifted the next item on the list for that Saturday. It was a harmonica in a little, worn-out cardboard box. He handed it to the closest person in the front row. The custom was to give the auction attendees a chance to see the offered items up close. As it went from hand to hand, the auctioneer would sing its praises.

The harmonica had just reached the future lion tamer when he realized that something was wrong. He looked around in confusion and noted that everyone's eyes were turned toward the auctioneer. Instead of a stream of words bubbling out of her mouth, she was as silent as a stone. Her eyes were staring blankly somewhere above the attendees' heads.

The former adventurer was in a bind. He didn't know what to do with the little box. The man on his left didn't seem interested in taking it and there was no sense in handing it back to the woman on his right who had given it to him. In the tense silence that settled over the movie theater, he wavered briefly over what to do. Then, without knowing what brought him to it, he took out the little instrument and started to play.

Had the circumstances been normal, everyone would have considered this quite uncouth. But now the aversion was missing. Heads slowly turned towards him. Faces were smiling. A few moments later there was spontaneous applause. The lion tamer stopped playing and bowed in bewilderment.

The auctioneer's voice came to life that same moment. As though waking from a dream, she started animatedly to highlight the qualities of the harmonica. The lion tamer's neighbor took it impatiently, but kept it only briefly since the other auction-goers could barely wait to see it up close.

The excited bidding that soon followed led to a dizzying price for the little instrument. It was bought by the fat owner of the butcher shop who doubled the pharmacist's last bid. The former adventurer only took part in the bidding briefly and then withdrew. He realized that something unusual was going on, but he didn't have a clue what it was.

Later that day in the bar that was the center of the small town's social life, he heard the story of what had struck the auctioneer dumb when the harmonica went on sale. It was the memory of an incident from her youth.

Just like every other Sunday morning during the summer, she had been walking with a girlfriend in the nearby rolling hills. They always went the same way, covering eleven-and-a-half kilometers through the picturesque countryside. When they reached about halfway, they would stop to rest for a quarter of an hour on a bench made of roughly hewn wood on the edge of the forest.

That morning they could already see from a distance that someone was sitting there. At first they thought it was one of the locals, but when they got a bit closer it turned out to be a stranger. Her girlfriend proposed that they head back, but the future auctioneer, who was studying medicine at the time, convinced her that they had no reason to worry. What could happen to them?

As they drew closer, the features of the man on the bench became more distinguishable. Although neither one of them spoke, they both thought the same thing. Never before had they seen such a handsome young man. They had a terrible time keeping their eyes off him in spite of the rudeness of such staring.

When they were some fifteen paces from the bench, the young man reached for the inside pocket of his jacket and took out a harmonica. As though oblivious to their arrival, gazing somewhere off in the distance, he put the little instrument to his lips and started to play. The young women stopped and looked at each other in amazement.

The melody was simple, but seemed to have something intoxicating about it. It didn't have the same effect on both young women. Her girlfriend became nervous and wanted to leave again immediately, while the future auctioneer was enchanted.

Not long after the young man started to play, he got up from the bench, turned around and headed into the forest. The dense underbrush and foliage soon swallowed him up. He didn't seem too far away, though, since the pleasing music reached them clearly on the other side of the opaque curtain of vegetation.

The young women looked at each other again and then, without a word of explanation, the medical student headed into the forest. The auctioneer's girlfriend watched in disbelief as she disappeared at the same place as the young man and shouted in alarm for her to return, but all that came back from the forest was the sound of the harmonica.

She turned this way and that in confusion for a while, not knowing what to do. She didn't have the courage to go into the forest too. Finally she headed back to the small town, almost at a run. Two hours and ten minutes later she was back at the bench, this time with two policemen.

When no one replied to her calls, the policemen headed into the forest. They came back fifteen minutes later empty-handed. An extensive search was launched that same afternoon. Much of the countryside was explored, but there was no trace of the young woman and the young man.

The search was suspended because of the dark and then continued the next day with specially trained dogs, again with no results. When the search party returned at the end of the next day with the job undone, it was clear that they would have to give up. The earth seemed to have swallowed up the people they were looking for.

The young woman had already been given up for lost, when she suddenly appeared in town four days after her disappearance in the forest. There was no sign that anything was wrong with her. She seemed serene, as though just returning from her customary walk.

They showered her with questions, wanting to find out what had happened. But she stubbornly refused to divulge anything, even to the police who called her in for an interview. Since she hadn't broken any law by disappearing, they had to reconcile themselves to her silence.

This, however, gave rise to various rumors. They even reached her ears, but she just laughed everything off. The gossip gained momentum when she continued to take her Sunday walk, no longer accompanied by her girlfriend.

Those who were most inquisitive started to follow her at a distance. They watched her enter the thicket behind the bench, but no one had the courage to go in after her. Some who went up closer swore that they heard the sound of a harmonica coming from the underbrush.

The young woman would stay in the forest for two or three hours, and then return to town beaming with joy. This went on until the beginning of fall when she went back to the city and her medical studies. The next summer she went home again for vacation. She continued taking walks, but no longer towards the bench on the edge of the forest.

9

When it came time for the harmonica, the auctioneer had indeed remembered that long-past summer, but this is not why she'd been lost in thought; rather it was because of another more innocent memory that flashed out of the blue right afterwards.

As a young intern, she'd gained experience assisting at operations. She was on duty when they started bringing in people who had been injured in the collision of two subway trains. All the surgeons who were not on duty were quickly summoned. The operating rooms were in a state of emergency.

On the table in front of her was a patient with serious internal injuries. He had already bled quite a bit and had to be operated on at once. The surgeon, however, had yet to arrive and she, who was insufficiently skilled, did not have the courage to undertake anything attended just by an anesthetist and a nurse.

When she looked through the double glass door and saw the surgeon rush into the scrubbing-up room, she was relieved. He went straight to the sink, then dried his hands in the hot air from the hand dryer on the wall. He pulled on his gloves and headed for the operating theater. But instead of going in, he suddenly stopped in front of the door.

She stared at him in disbelief, not realizing why he was taking so long. And then it dawned on her what could be the reason. She hadn't worked with him yet, but she knew about the incident of the tweezers left inside a patient. Although he was reputed to be an excellent surgeon, this oversight had almost cost him his job.

The operation had taken place in this very room. He certainly must remember it in embarrassment whenever he went in. But now was not the time to let that memory get in his way. How could he fail to save the injured man whose life was hanging by a thread because of an incident that, however unpleasant, had nevertheless ended happily?

But the surgeon just stood there, staring straight ahead blankly, and she realized she had to break through the paralysis that bound him. The anesthetist and the nurse were clearly too disconcerted to do anything.

She waved at him to come in, but he didn't move. She called to him, but it was like talking to a deaf person. She finally went up to the door and called him in a louder voice. This didn't snap him out of it either.

She felt herself giving way to panic. Briskly opening the double door, she stretched out her hands towards his shoulders, wanting to shake him, but this wasn't necessary. He snapped out of it the moment she touched him.

She didn't remove her hands right away. They stayed there joined together for a few moments, gazing fixedly into each other's eyes. Had the circumstances been otherwise, one of them might have said something, but there was no time for idle chatter. They had to get straight to work.

Three hours and fourteen minutes later the patient was moved to the intensive care room. He had a long recovery ahead of him, but what counted was that he'd been brought back from the brink of death. The intern and surgeon never worked together again, so there was no chance to continue the conversation that they had never even started.

The Second Loop

The lawyer darted into the elevator after the door had already started to close. He sighed deeply. On a morning plagued with mishaps this was the first time that lady luck had smiled on him.

First he'd carelessly cut his left thumb with a grapefruit knife during breakfast. It was a tiny wound, but it took him a long time to stop the blood gushing from his fingertip. He'd bloodied all of three towels and had to put on a rather large Band-Aid that detracted from his polished look.

Then he spilled coffee on himself. He had a white napkin tucked into his shirt collar, but several brown drops were nonetheless sprinkled on his light jacket and shirt. He wasn't normally clumsy and certainly wouldn't have spilled the coffee if he'd waited for it to cool off a little. It was so hot that he'd pulled the cup away from his mouth in reflex. He tried to get out of the way but wasn't fast enough and almost fell off his chair. Ten minutes were lost changing clothes.

As usual when he was in a hurry in the morning, he took a taxi. He would have gotten there on time even with the rush hour if traffic hadn't come to a complete standstill three intersections from his destination. A bus and a truck full of chickens had collided. No one was injured and the damage wasn't serious, but a multitude of small yellow creatures was scattering all over the street and sidewalk. He waited impatiently in the stopped taxi for the commotion to pass, but it only got worse. Finally, he got out and ran the rest of the way, watching carefully where he stepped until he was far enough away not to crush any chickens.

The elevator had already started when he pushed the button for the seventeenth floor. He glanced at his watch. It was one minute and thirty-five seconds to nine. Great. In spite of all his troubles, he wouldn't be late. This was a very important business meeting. He took out his handkerchief and wiped his beaded forehead and the back of his head and neck. He was completely flushed. Hopefully it wouldn't be too conspicuous. In any case, he would quickly catch his breath.

He seemed to be sharing the elevator with Frosty the Snowman. Everything the short, older gentleman wore was white: his suit, hat, bowtie and shoes. Even his shoelaces. In addition, he had silver hair under his hat brim and a silver mustache.

When their eyes met, the old man nodded. Even though the lawyer was not accustomed to engaging in conversation with strangers, especially those with an eccentric look to them, he returned the nod, making an exception owing to his highly excited state.

But his good mood was not destined to last. Just as he looked at the little floor display where the number eleven was replacing the number ten, two terrible things happened at the same time. The elevator stopped with a gentle shudder in between the floors and they were plunged into pitch darkness.

He barely refrained from swearing.

"What's this?" he growled.

The question was not directed at the only other passenger in the elevator, but the old man answered nonetheless.

"It looks like a power cut."

He said it in the voice of a man who was not in a hurry. This lack of alarm only heightened the lawyer's anger.

"How can there be a power cut?"

"It happens."

"It can't happen! We live in a civilized world, don't we?"

"Accidents happen there too."

"So what should I do now?"

"Be patient."

"But I can't be patient! My meeting starts in less than . . ."

He raised his left arm automatically to look at his watch. He stared in the darkness for two or three seconds, then pushed a button on the right-hand edge of the watch that lit the dial.

"I'm already late!"

"No you're not."

"What do you mean? It's already half a minute after nine."

"There isn't any power where they're waiting for you at the meeting, either. They'll know what held you up."

The lawyer was glad the old man couldn't see his face. It showed the same expression he had in court when the prosecutor outsmarted him with some simple witticism.

"I'll give them a call anyway."

He felt for his cell phone in the inside pocket of his jacket. A little island of shiny blue appeared but everything was soon plunged into darkness again.

"There's no signal." The lawyer's voice was now more dejected than angry. "What does that mean?"

"That means the power is out not only in this building but in this part of the city as well. Or maybe the whole city is blacked out."

"That's not possible. I've never seen such a blackout." He was silent for a moment. "Could it be a terrorist attack?" he asked almost in a whisper.

The old man chuckled. "People always think the worst. It doesn't take terrorists for the power to be cut."

"All right, so how long will we have to wait until the power comes back?"

"Who knows? It depends on the breakdown. It might be short or it might be hours."

"Hours?" shouted the lawyer. "That's out of the question. There are three trials I can't afford to miss."

"Force majeure will justify your absence. In any case, there won't be any trials without electricity."

Silence reigned for a few moments.

"I can't stay here for hours," announced the lawyer despondently. "I already feel claustrophobic. They have to get us out of here as soon as possible."

"Do you know how many elevators are stuck in the city? It would take days for them to free us all. The power will certainly come back first. Maybe very soon."

"But if it takes a while, I won't be able to stay on my feet that long. I have varicose veins."

"There's a remedy for that," replied the old man. "If it lasts a long time we can sit on the floor."

"Sit on the floor in this suit? Do you know how much it cost? I already ruined one this morning."

"I'm going to sit down."

"You'll be even the worse for wear in white."

"No, I won't. The floor is clean."

There was a rustle of cloth as the old man sat down.

"You might be interested to hear of a similar incident," came his voice from down below. "A bit of entertainment. What else can we do while we're waiting?"

The lawyer had already opened his mouth to refuse in scorn, when the thought of hours of silence in the darkness seemed even less appealing. In any case, he could always interrupt the old man if the story was boring. He placed his briefcase on the floor, leaned against the back wall of the elevator and shifted his weight onto his left foot.

"Go ahead," he said in the voice of a man about to have his tooth pulled.

⌒ 2 ⌒

"I have a friend who's a retired priest, a wonderful man. He's a real pro at pinball in spite of his advanced years."

"A priest who plays pinball?"

"Yes. Don't be surprised. Priests have even stranger hobbies. For example, the young priest who took over from my friend plays pool before every wedding. All by himself."

"How can you play pool like that?"

"It seems you can. But that's nothing. What would you say to a priest who is obsessed with counting birds?"

"What do you mean—counting birds?"

"As soon as he sees a flock flying over the church, he rushes for his camera and takes a picture. Then he carefully counts the birds on the photo."

"Why?"

"Who knows? He certainly must find some meaning in it. Maybe he's searching for God."

"Among the birds?"

"People search for God in the most unexpected plac-es. Wait until you hear what happened to my friend when he was fishing. He was still young at the time and was in the company of an old monk who shared his affinity for chess."

"Your friend has no lack of hobbies."

"All you can do is envy his fulfilling life. So, they were sitting on a riverbank on a beautiful summer's day. Their fishing poles were stuck in the ground and had little bells at the top that would ring if a fish started to bite. Between them was a chessboard on a blanket."

"Idyllic."

"Yes. But not for long. They were engrossed in a game that had already lasted more than two-and-a-half hours. No outcome was in sight. It was the monk's turn. He mulled it over for a long time. When he final-ly made his move, suddenly, without rhyme or reason, he got up and walked into the river."

"Fully dressed?"

"That's right. In the heavy habit he was wearing in spite of the hot weather. He walked in between the two poles up to his thighs and stood there like that for a few moments, staring somewhere up high, then bent over and plunged his head in the water."

"Was he trying to cool off? Could it have been sun-stroke?"

"He'd always tolerated the heat stoically before. My friend got up and stared at the monk in amazement. He didn't know what to do."

"Why didn't he join him? He probably could have used some cooling off too."

"He didn't feel like cooling off. It soon became clear

that something serious was happening. The monk's head was still underwater."

"Some people can hold their breath a long time underwater. Even longer than five minutes, I've been told."

"Probably. But eleven minutes passed before the young priest realized that he had to do something."

"Eleven minutes? That's impossible. Anyone would have drowned in that time. It must have just felt that long. Fear has magnifying eyes, you know. Besides, how could he know how much time had passed?"

"By the chess clock next to the board. He had eleven minutes less to use when he finally ran to the river to pull the monk out of the water."

"And? Did he pull him out?"

"No, he didn't."

"Why?"

"Just as he grabbed him around the waist, the bells rang out, even though the poles hadn't moved. The sound was as loud as though enormous fish that you'd never find in an ordinary stream were caught on both hooks at the same time. The terrified priest let go of the monk and scurried out of the water. The bells went silent that same moment."

"It seems they weren't whales after all. So, what happened in the end? Did the monk drown?"

"No. Two-and-a-half minutes later he finally raised his head."

"Thirteen-and-a-half minutes? That is by far a world record. Did he ask to have it recognized? He had a witness. Indeed, not a very courageous one. . . ."

"He didn't ask for anything. He even stopped fishing. And playing chess."

"It looks like he cooled off a bit too much. Did he tell his friend why he'd kept his head underwater so long?"

"Yes. He said he was talking."

"Underwater?"

"Yes."

"How can you talk under the water? Who in the world was he talking to?"

"He didn't say."

"Did your friend ask him?"

"No, he didn't."

"He wasn't interested in finding out?"

"He didn't have to ask. He knew the answer."

"Really? Well, I don't. Would you mind enlightening me?"

"Isn't it obvious? With God, of course."

"God resides in a river?"

"In rivers too, so it seems."

"Oh, I get it. All right. But there's something I don't understand. You said you were going to tell me about a similar incident. I don't see any similarity between the story of an underwater God and a power cut in an elevator."

"There isn't any. I mentioned this just in passing. The conversation led us to it. Now I'll get to the point. Unless I'm boring you, of course."

"Certainly not. I'm having a great time."

"The priest often had pinball contests with his dentist who was an even better player and took part in official competitions. Once while he was taking the train to a tournament, something strange happened."

"The train fell into a river and he talked to God too?"

"No, but they did meet with misfortune. An earthquake occurred while they were going through a long tunnel."

"That's what you call bad luck. Were they crushed under the crumbling rocks?"

"We wouldn't have heard his story if that had happened. It was a blessing in disguise. If they'd been out in the open they could've easily jumped the rails. The line was interrupted in several places but the tunnel, however, was solidly built so the tremors didn't damage it. The train cars weren't damaged in the least."

"Too bad. If they'd been hit, the insurance would have paid big time. So what was the misfortune?"

"The rocks tumbling down the mountain slope buried both ends of the tunnel. They were trapped inside for a day-and-a-half until the exit was finally cleared."

"That's more of an unpleasant situation than a misfortune. They were certainly more comfortable than we are in this elevator."

"No, they weren't. They didn't have any electricity either."

"Did the earthquake knock out the grid?"

"That's right."

"Don't trains have reserve sources?"

"They do. But they turned off the lights after seven-and-a-half hours to save the generator for more urgent needs."

"At least they could sit down while they were waiting in the dark."

"Yes, they were sitting and talking, like we are now."

"I hope we won't have to wait a day-and-a-half. Particularly since not all of us are sitting."

"I hope so too, but it might be some time. Come on and join me. Like I said, the floor's clean."

"I'll hold out a little longer. The power might come back any minute. Is that the end of the story?"

"Oh, no, this is just the beginning."

~ 3 ~

Before the lights went out, the dentist had barely exchanged a few words with the only other passenger in the compartment. He was sitting next to the window when the dentist entered just a few moments before the train's departure. The man was plump with graying hair, watery eyes and ruddy cheeks. He was wearing a three-piece gray pinstriped suit.

They said hello to each other and then the man went back to the book he was reading. The dentist sat on the opposite side next to the door and became likewise engrossed in a magazine about pinball machines. They would have traveled in silence were it not for the soft music from the p.a. system.

When the car started rocking in the tunnel, the dentist jumped up from his seat and grabbed hold of the door to the compartment. He didn't open it all the way because the train suddenly stopped. A new shock soon followed, accompanied by a roar that seemed to come from all directions. It was even more palpable because now it wasn't competing with the clattering wheels.

The dentist rushed into the corridor and exchanged looks of alarm with several other passengers who had also panicked. He stood there briefly, then returned to his compartment when the shaking stopped.

"An earthquake," he said to the other man anxiously.

The man, who had not raised his eyes from his book, as though none of this had anything to do with him, finally looked out of the window, even though nothing could be seen outside.

"Yes, looks like an earthquake," he replied as though confirming that it had started to rain. The mild music that continued to pour out of the loudspeaker above the door matched his equanimity.

"We might've been hurt," said the dentist with a touch of reproach at the man's lack of concern.

The man glanced into the pitch dark once again, then shook his head.

"I doubt it," he said briefly, then went back to his book.

When it was soon announced over the p.a. system that they would be kept in the tunnel for some time owing to rockslides, the dentist's companion was equally unperturbed. He glanced at the loudspeaker, barely shrugged his shoulders, then continued reading.

He only became agitated hours later when it was announced that the lights were about to be turned off.

"What a pity," he said in frustration, then closed the book and put it in the briefcase on the seat next to him.

For a time only the sound of a soothing piano filled the darkness that soon engulfed them.

"If you don't mind," said the man unexpectedly out of the darkness, "this reminds me of a story about an actor friend of mine. You might have seen him in the theater. First he was a hit playing a ladies' man and then later became a great comedian."

"I don't make it to the theater very often."

The dentist said this in a voice that was intended to tell his companion that he didn't feel like talking. Indeed, saying so little in such dramatic circumstances and now being long-winded in the dark! But the man paid no attention to this obvious hint.

"Such a waste. We must try to fill every moment with art. There is so little time."

"Not everyone's inclined towards the arts."

"Yes, that's true. More's the pity. Even my friend who

47

is an artist often wastes time on things that don't have much to do with the arts. For example, he's completely crazy about his hobby and never passes up a chance to go hot-air ballooning."

"What's wrong with that? I'm wild about my hobby too. I play pinball."

"It's all a waste of time, of course, but at least you stand firmly on the ground and nothing unusual can happen to you."

"So what could happen in a balloon?"

"It's not all as harmless as it might seem up there. You'll see when I tell you about a recent adventure of his."

He didn't start the story right away because the music was suddenly interrupted by a message saying that the p.a. system was about to be turned off to save electricity. They spent a few moments in silence.

"He invited a young woman from the theater, a prompter, to go with him. She had never flown in a balloon before and was frightened before they took off, which is understandable. But as soon as they were aloft her fear was replaced by delight. Did you know that riding in a hot-air balloon often causes such a feeling?"

"No, I didn't."

"At least in the beginning. But after a while boredom inevitably sets in. Looking at the dreary landscape tires you out. That would be the perfect time to do some reading, but hot-air balloonists rarely care about that. What do you suppose my friend and the prompter preferred to do?"

"I don't know."

"They sat on the bottom of the basket and started playing cards. Just imagine."

"I play cards a lot too."

A deep sigh came from the darkness by the window.

"But it wasn't fated to be an ordinary game. They'd been playing less than ten minutes when the young woman suddenly dropped her cards and without so much as a word climbed onto the edge of the basket."

"Did she jump?"

"No. She headed in the opposite direction. Before the bewildered actor knew what was happening, she started to climb up the balloon."

"How can you climb up a balloon?"

"Some balloons are covered with netting. If you're a skilled enough climber, it can give you a foothold."

"You'd have to be awfully skillful to do that. One false move and you've had it."

"The prompter turned out to be quite agile. But not my friend who didn't have the courage to go after her. He just waited helplessly in the basket, fearing that the worst might happen any moment."

"What in the world induced her to pull such a stunt?"

"She wanted to reach the top of the balloon."

"Why?"

There was no immediate reply from the end of the compartment.

"Do you believe in God?" he finally asked in a soft voice.

"No."

"Then you'll have a hard time understanding why."

"What does God have to do with scrambling crazily all over a balloon?"

"The young woman climbed up the balloon to talk to God. At least that's what she told my friend when she came back down some twenty minutes later, all aglow."

"How did he take it?"

"He wanted to know a bit more, but she gave him only silence in return. All she asked was that they land immediately."

"I hope he packed her off to a madhouse as soon as they hit the ground."

"He didn't have a chance. Just before they got all the way down, the prompter jumped out of the basket and ran away. She was never seen again."

Silence reigned again for a few moments.

"That's all quite interesting," said the dentist at last, "but I don't understand how our predicament reminded you of this peculiar story."

"It didn't remind me of this one but another one."

"So why did you tell me this one?"

"No special reason. It just crossed my mind. Now I'll tell you the other story. Unless you have something against it, of course."

This time the sigh came from the seat next to the door.

"What could I have against it? How better to pass the time than telling stories? We can't exactly read in the dark."

"No, we can't, unfortunately. Well now, my friend the actor had the same mailman for years. Over time they became friends and he often invited him in for coffee when he brought the mail."

"An actor and a mailman don't seem much like soul mates."

"They were both cat lovers, that's what they had in common. The actor had three and the mailman all of seven."

"I would never join their company. I'm allergic to cat hair."

"I'm allergic to goose feathers. I break out in spots as soon as I see a goose. Even on a picture."

"Isn't that going a bit far? How can the picture of a goose make you break out in spots?"

"You don't believe me? You don't happen to have a picture of a goose on you, do you?"

"Where would I get one? And even if I had one, what good would it do? You wouldn't be able to see it in the dark."

"I'd break out just the same. They even affect me in the dark, word of honor."

The seat by the door was silent for a moment.

"All right, I believe you. But let's get back to the actor and the mailman."

"Yes. Once while they were having coffee, the mailman told the actor about a strange incident during the war."

"The mailman must have been getting on a bit."

"Yes, he was just about to retire at the time and the incident happened in his youth. He hadn't rushed to the basement when the air raid siren went off because he couldn't find his cat anywhere. He only had one at the time."

"What would have happened if he'd had seven?"

"I can't even imagine. Bombs were already starting to fall when he finally found her cowering under the kitchen cupboard. A new problem arose as he was running down the stairs. The power went off."

"How awful."

"It wouldn't have been so awful if he'd taken a flashlight like every other time. But he'd forgotten it in his hurry and there was no time to go back. He groped his way down to the basement in the dark as explosions shook all around him."

"He could have lost his life because of a cat."

"He probably would have considered it a gallant

death. Luckily, no bombs fell on his building. He finally reached the basement, but another surprise was waiting for him there. It was pitch black inside."

"Hadn't any of the other residents taken a flashlight or candle?"

"There were no other residents."

"Why not?"

"It turned out that some had stubbornly stayed in their apartments and others had looked for a safer shelter."

"So the mailman was all alone in the basement with a cat?"

"He wasn't alone."

"Didn't you say there were no other residents?"

"The man who said good evening from the other end of the basement was not a resident. The air raid siren had caught him in the street so he'd sought refuge in the nearest building."

"I hope he wasn't allergic to cat hair. Then it would have been better to stay outside."

"It seems he wasn't bothered by it. He stayed in the basement until the all-clear siren sounded."

"Then it's a story with a happy ending."

"Yes. In the end they happily went their separate ways. Would you like to hear what happened before that?"

"I like stories with a happy ending."

 4

The mailman felt for a wooden trunk to the left of the door and sat on it. He held the cat close to this chest and petted her. Every explosion that came from above, now somewhat muffled, made her jump.

"It's really fierce tonight," said the invisible stranger from the other end of the basement.

"Fierce."

"I thought I'd make it home on time, but I was wrong."

"It's best not to go out at all in the evening."

"I wouldn't have gone out if my dog hadn't escaped. I looked for him everywhere. I live four blocks away. You might think it unreasonable to expose myself to mortal danger because of a dog."

"Not at all. I reached the basement at the last moment because my cat went into hiding as soon as the siren sounded. I wouldn't have left the apartment without her. How about you? Did you find your dog?"

"No, I didn't. Poor thing, who knows where he is now. I hope he found cover someplace. The explosions drive him crazy. I'll continue my search as soon as the bombing stops."

"If you'd found him we'd be in a pickle now."

"Why?"

"Well, the cat's with me. They would have smelled each other and you know what happens when dogs and cats are near each other."

"You're wrong. Nothing would have happened. Natural hostilities are suspended when animals face a common danger. During a flood, for example, you'll find both a wolf and a fawn on the same log."

"I suppose so."

"In any case, I didn't find Rex."

"I can help you look for him afterwards."

"That's kind of you, but it wouldn't be any use. He's certainly hiding somewhere. He won't come out until he hears my voice."

"I hope you find him."

"Thanks."

A violent thud shook the building's foundations, causing a shower of plaster and bits of brick to rain down from the ceiling.

"That one was close," said Rex's owner when the sound died down.

"In the neighborhood," agreed the mailman, holding the distraught cat more firmly in his arms.

"Animals are strange, you know."

"What do you mean?"

"Otherwise incompatible species sometimes go together. An old friend of mine has a parakeet. Indeed, she almost lost it recently in a fire but a brave firefighter saved the bird at the last moment. He went back into the attic room for the cage even though flames were closing in."

"He must have been an animal lover too."

"Undoubtedly. They are the noblest of people. But wait until you hear the story about the parakeet. Ever since she bought it, she's taken it to the zoo every Saturday morning, weather permitting."

"Why?"

"So it can mix with the other birds."

"I didn't know the zoo's management allowed that."

"They don't. She sneaks it in."

"How does she go about it?"

"You won't believe it. She puts it in the cage with birds of prey. Mostly with eagles and hawks."

"And what happens?"

"The parakeet flies straight to a bird of prey, spends some time chirping with it, like chatting, then goes back to its owner."

"And nothing happens to it?"

"Not a thing. Like it's come to visit friends. Real camaraderie."

"That's a hard one to believe."

The conversation was briefly interrupted by a new explosion nearby, somewhat weaker than the previous one. This time there was less debris from the ceiling.

"And what would you say about an even stranger incident in the zoo?"

"With the parakeet again?"

"No, but with the same old friend. One Saturday she took a young relative who had come to visit her to the zoo. He was studying veterinary science, so a trip to the zoo was just up his alley."

"Did he have a chance to see the parakeet number?"

"Yes, and he was astounded. But that's nothing compared to what happened when they reached the bear cage."

"Did the parakeet go in there too?"

"No, but the young man did."

"What's that you're saying?"

"Just that. All of a sudden, without a word of explanation, he went up to the cage door, opened it and stepped inside."

"The door to the bear cage was unlocked?"

"My friend swears it was not only locked but had additional security with a chain and padlock. But the young man went in nevertheless, like nothing was standing in his way."

"But how? Well, all right, that's irrelevant right now. What happened to him is more important. Did he come to harm? Bears are extremely dangerous animals."

"The bears didn't pay him the slightest attention. They continued to doze in a corner of the cage."

"What did the young man do?"

"He headed straight for the stone habitat where they spend the night and take shelter from bad weather."

"What was he after in there?"

A sigh came from the other end of the basement.

"He went to have a talk with God."

"Come again?"

"That's what he told my lady friend when he came out of the cage some ten minutes later. Once again he had no trouble opening the locked and chained door."

"Was he some kind of religious fanatic?"

"Just the opposite. He took pride in his atheism."

"Then where did he get the idea of talking to God in a bear's den?"

"That remains a mystery. He soon dropped out of veterinary school and withdrew to an isolated life on a remote farm. Animals are his sole companions and he refuses to have anything to do with humans."

"I never imagined all the things that take place in a zoo."

The cat on the mailman's chest let out a protracted meow.

"Don't be afraid, it will soon be over," he said gently, petting her. "She's as afraid of the dark as she is of explosions."

"It's no fun being stuck in the dark. Just imagine how my old friend's hairdresser felt. She spent a full sixteen-and-a-half hours in darkness as impenetrable as this."

"How awful. Was she in a basement or bomb shelter too?"

"No. On a choppy sea."

"That would be worse than bombing for me. I couldn't put up with rough water even for a short time. How did she get into such a fix?"

"She saved up a long time for a tropical sea cruise. It was almost over when the crew received word that a tidal wave was headed their way. It was caused by an underwater earthquake. Even though the boat was built to withstand heavy storms, it would never make it through. The passengers and crew had to be urgently evacuated."

"Would they be safer in lifeboats?"

"Not in ordinary lifeboats. But the ship was supplied with a sufficient number of special little unsinkable vessels. They were hermetically sealed and each one had room for two people. The hairdresser was put in with a woman she didn't know."

"Weren't there any lights inside?"

"There were. But they went out after the tidal wave hit. And so did their radio beacon. That's why it took so long to find them."

"How dreadful. I'd go crazy under such stress, in the dark, tossed around by the waves."

"Oh, no, after the tidal wave passed the sea was calm. Their ventilation worked and they had food and various beverages so it wasn't all that bad. After a while, when the excitement wore off, they relaxed and started to talk. They even enjoyed themselves. The rescuers found them in a good mood."

"Even so, talking for sixteen hours . . ."

"It seems as though women have greater stamina than we do in that regard."

"I'd really like to know what they found to talk about for so long."

"I don't know all of it, of course, but I can tell you the small part I heard from my old friend. I find it interesting."

"Go ahead. What else can we do anyway until the all-clear siren?"

⌒ 5 ⌒

"This is what I call a luxury cruise," said the hairdresser. "They even put champagne in the lifeboats."

"What luck that you found it in the dark," replied her fellow passenger. "How ironic if all you had found was water."

They didn't introduce themselves. It seemed somehow inappropriate since they couldn't see each other.

"I've got a nose for good liquor. There's no way I could have missed it. The first thing I grabbed was a bottle of champagne."

"What a shame we have to drink it out of plastic glasses. It seems like a sacrilege."

"It would be even worse to drink it right out of the bottle."

"Yes. That would be blasphemy."

"They could have put in real glasses. Maybe even crystal, to match everything else."

"When you think about it, they equipped this little vessel like a love nest. So why didn't they assign us to the boats differently?"

"Male-female?"

"Yes." The other woman started to giggle. "Maybe they thought we made a good couple."

The hairdresser's giggle sounded strained.

"If that's the way it is, they reached the wrong conclusion about me. I enjoy your company, of course, but I wouldn't have had anything against being put in with one of the crew members. I noticed several really handsome sailors."

"So did I. They have to take care of their looks on all inclusive cruises."

This time both of them laughed merrily.

"What kind of men do you like?" asked the hairdresser, taking another sip of champagne in the dark.

"Athletically built. Actually, athletes. They're the best."

"Really? I haven't tried any athletes yet."

"If you get a chance to choose, I suggest long jumpers. They're unbeatable."

"Don't marathon runners have the greatest stamina?"

"Only while they're running. Otherwise they lose momentum after the first round. Even during the first round."

Laughter filled the little cabin again.

"I'll keep your advice in mind."

"But to tell you the truth, long jumpers can fall short too."

"Really?"

"I dated one for a while. Everything was fine until some tomboy javelin thrower hit him by accident. He changed after that."

"It's no wonder if the javelin hit him in . . . a sensitive spot."

"It didn't. His sensitive spot was untouched. He changed in his head."

"How so?"

"When he was recuperating in the hospital, something strange happened. Shall I tell you about it?"

The hairdresser nodded in the dark.

"I'm all ears."

"A lady friend came to visit him. She was a long jumper too and I think she was in love with him. Not that it did her any good because she was really ugly in that way only sportswomen can be."

"Yes, they're usually not very good-looking, although some are quite striking."

"But not very often. And they're too mannish for my taste."

"Some men like that."

"Men come in all shapes and sizes. In any case, I didn't have to worry about the long jumper. She sat at his bedside for a while and was just about to leave when she suddenly headed for the bathroom without saying a word."

"If we open another bottle, we'll have to go there soon too."

"I don't know how they worked that one out. There must be instructions somewhere, but how can we see them in the dark?"

"No way. We have a choice. Stay away from the champagne or do it without a bathroom."

"You mean . . ."

"What else?"

The other woman started to giggle again.

"I never stay away."

"I always regret it when I do."

"The long jumper, however, didn't go to the bathroom for that reason. I doubt that she ever filled up her bladder. Athletes usually do that by sweating."

"Number two can't get out by sweating."

"No, it can't, but she didn't need the bathroom for that either."

"So what was she after in there?"

"My long jumper was rather surprised when he heard the shower go on in the bathroom."

"That's really going too far. Athletes love to hit the shower, that's fine, but couldn't she have bided her time? I've never heard of someone taking a shower during a hospital visit."

"Wait for the end. You haven't heard anything yet."

"Did she come out of there naked? Maybe she wanted to take advantage of the situation while he was still weak."

"She didn't. She was fully dressed and sopping wet when she came out several minutes later. But that's not the main point either."

"So what is?"

"The conversation."

"What conversation?"

"My long jumper claimed he heard her talking to someone through the sound of the water. He couldn't make out the words, but he's convinced that she was talking."

"Was he the only one using the bathroom?"

"Only him."

"Did he get up to see what was going on?"

"He still couldn't move on his own."

"Who else could she have been talking to but herself? People often make noises when they're in the shower. Sing, whistle. Maybe athletes talk. I wouldn't be surprised. Did he ask her when she came out?"

"Yes."

"What did she say? She must have been embarrassed."

"She said she was talking to God."

The cabin suddenly went silent.

"I know that women who go in for sports are peculiar, but this is a really special case. They should have kept her in the hospital for observation."

"They didn't have the chance. She left right away."

"All wet like that?"

"Yes."

"What hogwash. The world is full of crackpots."

"She had another fit that day. She headed for the track.

She didn't even get out of her street clothes and suit up. Instead she took a running start and jumped. Only once. Then she left and no one ever saw her again."

"That's the best part. If only all the other weirdos would disappear like that too."

"She disappeared as the world record holder. Unacknowledged, though."

"How's that?"

"Only one jump and in wet clothes. The people who were there measured it later. They swear that no one has ever jumped that far."

"How can that be? People really exaggerate. I don't believe it."

"My long jumper believed it. That's why we split up."

"You did the right thing. Hats off to his other virtues, but you should stay away from men who get one thing stuck in their head. The men I prefer don't really have very much in their heads. At least they don't give you a headache."

"I might get a headache if I overdo the champagne. I don't think I'll have any of the second bottle. What fun it would be if the sea got rough and I was lying here glassy-eyed from too much champagne. If I throw up in this little cabin we're in for a horrible time."

"Someone will probably find us soon. The captain said we shouldn't worry, all the vessels are equipped with radio beacons and help is already on the way."

"You never know when it will get here. We're on the high seas, a tidal wave swept by not long ago, it's reasonable to expect we'll have to wait a while to get out of here. But what would you say about what happened to the long jumper's coach in the middle of town? The man spent the whole night with a stranger in a ghost train. And it was just as pitch black as it is in here."

"A ghost train?"

"Yes. He got into one of the little cars just before closing time. The other man was in the car behind him. When they were about halfway through, suddenly all the lights went out and everything stopped. They waited some time for the lights to come back on and the ride to continue, but that didn't happen."

"So what did happen?"

"Slipshod organization. One guy didn't tell the other one that people were still inside. They just turned everything off and left, convinced that the ghost train was empty. When they came back in the morning, they had a surprise in store."

"Didn't the two men try to get out?"

"That is still unclear. They claim they tried, but couldn't find the exit in the dark. It seems, however, that it was fear that kept them in their cars."

"Men. They could have called someone on their cell phones."

"One didn't have a cell phone and the battery was dead in the other one's."

"What did they do all night long, scared shitless?"

"Well, that's an interesting story. Do you want to hear it?"

"Sure. I love tales of male heroism."

∽ 6 ∽

"Did you hear?"

"What?"

"Listen."

The two forgotten ghost train visitors spent a few moments listening hard.

"I don't hear anything."

"There was something like rustling."

"Where?"

"I'm not sure anymore."

"Maybe it just seemed like it."

"Maybe."

"Even so, alert me right away if it seems like it again. We have to be on our guard."

"Yes, we do," agreed the coach, his head turned half-way. "We're really in a jam here. When I just think that I didn't even want to go into the ghost train. I don't know what came over me."

"People often do things they don't want to," replied the passenger in the rear car. "I don't like this sort of excitement either, but here I am anyway. Of course, if I'd thought something like this was possible. . . ."

There were seven or eight meters between them, so they had to speak up.

"Would you like to come into my car? Then we wouldn't have to shout to each other."

"I lose my bearings in the dark. I might not find you."

"Follow my voice. You can't get lost."

"There might be obstacles."

"What kind of obstacles?"

"Just before the lights went out, some sort of hunch-backed freak popped up in front of me waving an enormous axe."

"I know. It scared me to death when it came at me first. But it probably doesn't work without electricity."

"Probably. Nevertheless, I'd rather not wander around in the dark while there's an axe nearby, even if it's lowered."

"Hey, nothing will happen to you. Just stick to the track."

"I'd rather not. Why don't you come to me?"

"I get dizzy when I don't see. I would start to sway as soon as I stood up. I've slept with the light on ever since I was little."

"A friend of mine who's a judge can't stand the dark either. He's already twice divorced because his wives couldn't sleep with the light on and listen to the endless rain, night after night."

"But it doesn't rain every night."

"No, it doesn't. He has a recording of falling rain. Not just ordinary rain but a real downpour. With thunder now and again. He plays it all night long, that's the only way he can sleep."

"It's no wonder his wives left him. The slightest sound disturbs my sleep. Who could put up with a storm in the bedroom every night?"

"He finally found a wife whom it didn't bother."

"Do such women exist?"

"She puts on a sleeping mask, stuffs her ears with cotton wool and sleeps like a log."

"It wouldn't work for me even if I poured wax in my ears."

"The judge feels like doing that during the day."

"Why?"

"Because his wife never shuts her mouth. She's the exact opposite of him. He's very reserved and a man of few words."

"He's got to pay some way or another for what he gets at night."

"There are other differences between them. They don't go together at all: he's tall and thin and she's short and round. The way they dress is worlds apart. He, as befits a judge, is always in a discreet dark suit, and she loves bright colors in spite of the fact that she's getting on. Pink is her favorite color. Just imagine. Then when she adds a large hat with multicolored feathers, it's enough to boggle the mind. What a fright!"

The coach chuckled.

"She could put in a performance here."

"You said it. Once when they were in a restaurant, the waiter serving them was stunned into silence. They barely brought him round."

"I don't envy your friend the judge."

"But you ought to see his wife's younger half-brother. Until recently he, and not she, was the judge's main nightmare."

"Really?"

"The young man was a talented poet until something happened to him. One morning he suddenly decided not to open his eyes anymore."

"I never liked artists. Each one is weirder than the next."

"Yes, some are really touched in the head. They finally had to put the poet in a mental institution. Since that was his only oddity, they considered him a mild case. They let him out on the weekend to visit his half-sister."

"The judge must have really loved that. Did he try to cure him with that recorded thunder of his?"

"Do you think it would have worked?"

"You never know what might have a therapeutic effect on the mentally ill. So what did they do over the weekend with a man who refused to see?"

"They took him for walks, holding him by the arm as though he were blind."

"Well, he really was blind for all practical purposes. If he didn't open his eyes it was like he didn't have any."

"One day when they were taking one of those walks something unexpected happened. They were in a park when he suddenly stopped and raised his head towards the top of a nearby chestnut tree."

"How could he see it if he wasn't looking? Was he squinting?"

"I don't know. In any case, a swarm of butterflies flitted out of the leaves that same moment."

"What were butterflies doing in the top of a chestnut tree?"

"Somehow they materialized there. They didn't fly away but stayed above the tree like some sort of downy yellow cloud."

"What about the poet?"

"The poet stood there, eyes closed, face turned upwards. Then his mouth started to open."

"Was he asthmatic?"

"No, he wasn't, his breathing was fine. He looked like he was talking to someone."

"Did they hear anything?"

"Not a word. It was a completely soundless conversation, like he was deaf and dumb."

"What did the judge and his wife do? They must have felt awkward if there were other people around."

"They just watched in bewilderment. What else could they do? It only lasted a few minutes. He stopped opening his mouth as suddenly as he'd started."

"Did they ask him what he was doing?"

"Yes. He told them that he was talking to God."

The ghost train suddenly sank into silence.

"What was God doing in the top of a chestnut tree with butterflies fluttering above it?"

"I have no idea. I'm not an expert in theological matters."

"Did they take the poet right back to the mental institution?"

"They escorted him there. He led the way."

"Did he open his eyes?"

"No. They were still firmly shut."

"So how could he lead them there?"

"He told them he'd got back his sight."

"And they believed him?"

"He acted in all ways like a man who could see perfectly well."

"How strange."

"When they got to the institution, he asked them not to take him home for the weekend anymore. He no longer wanted to go out. Nevertheless, they went back seven days later, hoping he'd changed his mind, but he hadn't. The poet's half-sister was quite distraught at their parting and the judge considerately tried to leave the impression that it was hard for him too."

"Although he was relieved, of course."

"Of course. Who wouldn't be? Just like we will be relieved when we finally get out of here. When do you think they'll let us out?"

"Tomorrow morning for sure, if not before."

"What shall we do until tomorrow morning?"

"Should we try to sleep?"

"In a ghost train? I wouldn't get a wink of sleep."

The coach chuckled.

"Maybe the storm recording the judge uses to fall asleep would help?"

"That's all I need. But if you feel like sleeping, be my guest."

"I don't feel like sleeping either."

"Then we can talk."

"We don't have much choice."

"A situation similar to this just occurred to me. Would you like to hear about it?"

"I hope it doesn't have God in the leaves."

"It doesn't."

"Wonderful."

"My friend the judge has a permanent court recorder. She's a meticulous and reliable person, and good-looking too, although no longer in her prime."

"That's not a drawback as far as I'm concerned. Quite the contrary. I prefer mature women."

"Me too. In addition, the court recorder keeps her figure by going in for sports."

"One more recommendation. I'm a professional coach."

"What's your sport?"

"Track and field."

"Then I doubt you could be her coach. As far as I know, weightlifting isn't a track and field sport."

"No, but that wouldn't stand in the way of a nice friendship. There aren't many women who lift weights."

"She only lifts weights in the summer. In the winter she skis."

"Wonderful. I love to ski too."

"Once when she was skiing, the incident that I want to tell you about happened."

"Skiing incidents can be quite exciting."

"This was not only exciting but dangerous too."

"Skiing's not a harmless sport."

"Certainly not. Here, just listen to what happened. She was taking a cable car up the mountain when an avalanche came crashing down the slope."

"That's really dangerous. What happened to the cable car? I've heard of cases where an avalanche cut down all the poles like they were saplings."

"These held up. But the cabins were buried under a layer of snow."

"Lucky she wasn't on a chairlift."

"Yes, she would have suffocated at the very least. As it was, she was imprisoned until just before morning when the rescuers finally managed to dig them out. It certainly wasn't pleasant spending the night in the impenetrable dark and the mountain chill."

"The snow was a help there. It protected her at least a little from the cold. Was she alone?"

"No. There was a younger skier in the cabin with her."

"Then that was a real blessing in disguise." The coach started to chuckle again. "They could keep each other warm."

"They did indeed spend the night with their bodies pressed together."

"She must have liked that. Young skiers have hot blood."

"Have you ever tried to make love in minus eighteen degrees, in a snowsuit? Not even the hottest blood does any good."

"Something just crossed my mind. The two of us are lucky too. Imagine if this had happened in winter. We'd have had to keep each other warm and neither of us has hot blood anymore."

"I never had any to keep another man warm."

"Me neither. But circumstances change a person. Well, anyway. So how did they spend the night with their bodies pressed together like that? Were they able to get any sleep?"

"They didn't sleep a wink."

"So what did they do?"

"The same thing we are. They talked."

"What did they talk about until daybreak?"

"Wait and I'll tell you."

༄ 7 ༄

"Actually, I don't like winter," said the young man.

"What kind of skier are you if you don't like winter?" asked the court recorder.

They were sitting pressed together at the corner where the wooden benches met. Even though they couldn't discern the noses on their own faces in the pitch black, it still seemed they could see the invisible snow pressing against the small cabin on all sides. The young man put his arms around the court recorder and periodically rubbed her shoulders and firm biceps.

"You can be a skier in summer too."

"Do you mean when it's summer here? Only the rich can go skiing in that part of the world where it's winter. A court recorder can't even dream about it."

"I didn't mean traveling to another hemisphere."

"Then on an artificial substrate? That's always seemed like a poor substitute to me. It only counts as skiing when the substrate is natural."

"I agree. But snow isn't the only natural substrate."

"What else is there?"

"Sand."

"Oh, yes. I've heard of skiing on sand. But it seems somehow unnatural to me."

"You're wrong. Try it just once and you'll see for yourself that sand is just as much fun as snow."

"What's there to like about skiing in a swimsuit?"

"Tons of stuff. If nothing else, a swimsuit's a lot more practical and cheaper than a snowsuit. Plus, your whole body tans and not just your face."

"But falling on sand that enters every bodily orifice . . . Just thinking of it gives me goose bumps. I only swim on pebble beaches."

"It doesn't enter exactly everywhere, and falling on sand is much more pleasant and safer than falling on snow. There aren't any rocks lying in wait underneath to tear you up."

"Even if I wanted to ski on sand, that's impossible here. As far as I know we don't have any slopes like that."

"We have a few that aren't much to speak of. For real fun you'd have to go abroad. They've made real mountains out of sand in the desert."

"There, you see. How could I afford that with a court recorder's salary?"

"It's not at all as expensive as traveling to the other side of the planet. If an undertaker can afford it, I'm sure you can too."

"Undertaker?"

"Yes. I have a friend who's an undertaker. For years he's been going to a desert country in the summer to ski."

"I didn't know that undertakers were fond of skiing."

"There are lots of false impressions about them. They are usually considered to be gloomy guys, just like the job they do. But they're just the opposite, really cheerful people."

"Is that so?"

"Yes. Once he invited me to the annual undertakers' costume ball. You should have seen them let down their hair. I've never had a better time."

"Who would have thought?"

"And the last dance! I get dizzy every time I think about it. At one moment, though, there was a brief holdup caused by one of the dancers. But nothing can stop undertakers from having a good time. They just kept on going like nothing had happened."

"Amazing." The court recorder was quiet for a moment. "How crazy can you get?"

"What's that?"

"Here we are talking about skiing in a swimsuit in a hot desert while our teeth are chattering."

"It might warm us up a bit."

"I doubt it," she replied, with a bitter laugh.

The young man rubbed her upper arms again.

"It's possible to freeze in the desert too."

"Yes, the nights are cold."

"They are out in the open. But not in a hotel room."

"They can be cold if you overdo the air conditioning."

"You might catch cold from that but not freeze."

"So how can you freeze in a hotel room?"

"By spending the night in the refrigerator. They are big enough in desert hotels for someone to fit inside if you take out all the shelves."

"Who would be crazy enough to spend the night in a refrigerator?"

"A saxophonist. My friend took him along to pay him back for the exceptional way he played at the undertakers' costume ball."

"I've always thought musicians have a screw loose. Did he have heat stroke? That's another thing that can happen when you ski in the desert."

"He didn't. He spent almost the whole day inside. He wasn't very attracted to skiing on sand."

"So what happened to him?"

"That's never been explained."

"Because they found him dead?"

"No. When the maid opened the refrigerator in the morning, she found him both hale and hearty. He didn't even get the sniffles."

"How can that be? Maybe he was lying about spending the whole night in the refrigerator. He might have gone in just before the maid arrived."

"He didn't. The things he'd taken out to make room for himself were room temperature."

"Was the refrigerator plugged in?"

"It was turned all the way up. And the maid thought the saxophonist looked really chilled."

"You can't spend the whole night in a refrigerator turned all the way up without even getting the sniffles."

"I agree, you can't."

"So what's the explanation?"

"There isn't any."

"Wasn't there an investigation?"

"There was no need. The saxophonist hadn't broken any law by spending the night in the refrigerator instead of the bed."

"They didn't suspect suicide?"

"He seemed too content for a suicide."

"Did he at least say what he was doing in there?"

"He did. The undertaker found out as they were flying home."

"And?"

"He closed himself in the refrigerator so he could talk to God."

"Come again?" asked the court recorder after a few moments of dead silence in the dark cabin.

"I asked to have the saxophonist's words repeated too."

"I don't think I'll go skiing in the desert after all. It's true that mountains have their bad side, but at least no one goes off the deep end like that. I hope your friend stopped inviting that musician to the undertakers' costume ball."

"He couldn't have even if he wanted to. The saxophonist stopped playing and withdrew completely from the world."

The court recorder started to giggle.

"When you think about it, maybe after talking to God he became the perfect musician to play before the undertakers."

A muffled creak came from somewhere above.

"Is that the rescuers?" she asked hopefully, looking up.

"It's more likely the pole creaking from the load," replied the young man. "The rescuers couldn't reach us so quickly. We're almost on the top and they'll start at the bottom."

"How much longer will we have to wait?"

"Who knows? Probably until morning."

"That long? We'll freeze to death by then."

The young man rubbed both her arms and then her legs.

"No we won't. The snow is our ally now. It's a lot colder above the snowdrift."

"Just thinking of that makes me warmer."

"This isn't all that bad. Worse things could happen."

"We can always console ourselves with that."

"We just have to be patient and everything will be all right. What would you say, though, if you'd been the undertaker's car mechanic? He was closed in a cramped space and total darkness just like us, but was in no danger of freezing or any natural disaster. Even so, he would have readily changed places with us, even if it meant staying here a lot longer."

"What didn't he like about where he was?"

"He was with a young woman in a bank vault. They were being held hostage by a robber. He threatened to kill them if his demands weren't met."

"How awful. How did it end?"

"They were released after thirteen-and-a-half hours of tense anxiety. The robber got away with the money."

"A happy ending for everyone but the bank. But we shouldn't feel sorry for the bank, they must have had insurance."

"Happy endings don't last long."

"What does?"

"Yes, what does. The robber was caught in one of the next holdups. Actually, he turned himself in after talking in private with one of the female hostages he was going to kill."

"Why?"

"It was never cleared up. But at least we know what happened to him, he ended up in prison. The young woman's fate, however, remains unknown. It seems she had an adventurous spirit. She went into the jungle and never returned."

"How awful. What about the car mechanic? What became of him?"

"He alone came out unscathed. At least for now. But he found it pretty tough getting over the time in the safe."

"Who wouldn't? They must have felt like they were on death row waiting for the executioner. What did they do in such circumstances?"

"What could they do in a pitch dark safe? They sat there and talked, just like us."

"I doubt it was just small talk. What do people talk about when they might be about to die?"

"It just so happens I know that. The undertaker told me what the car mechanic confided in him. Would you like to hear?"

"I'm all ears."

"We'll suffocate," said the auto mechanic in a panic-stricken voice.

"No, we won't," replied the young woman. "You'll have an easier time breathing if you sit down like me instead of walking around. There's always more oxygen near the floor."

"How do you know I'm walking around? You can't see me."

"I can hear you."

"Then you've got good ears."

"That's useful even when you can see."

Rustling filled the dark vault as the car mechanic sat down on the floor.

"How can you be so calm?" he asked her.

"Why should I get upset?"

"Why? He's going to kill us."

"No, he won't."

"Why do you think he won't?"

"Did you see his eyes?"

"I didn't see a thing. I was frightened to death when he fired like that at the ceiling. What do the robber's eyes have to do with it?"

"The eyes are portals to the soul. He doesn't have the eyes of a murderer."

"What kind of eyes does a murderer have?"

"Murderous."

"That's informative."

"It's hard to describe. But if you come up against one you'll have no trouble recognizing it."

"I hope I never look into the eyes of a murderer. Do you mean to say that's happened to you?"

"Several times."

"You must lead a very unusual life for a young woman."

"Exhilarating."

"So what happened when you met those murderers?"

"I'm still alive."

"I can see that. Or rather hear. Were you ever held hostage before?"

"Several times."

"You certainly are experienced for your age. In a bank, like now?"

"This is the first time I've been put in a vault. But it wasn't always people who imprisoned me."

"How's that?"

"Once a gorilla held me and a gardener girlfriend of mine captive."

"What? A real gorilla?"

"Have you ever seen a fake one in the jungle?"

"How did it hold you captive?"

"It forced us to jump into a hole and then stood over it."

"What did it want? To eat you?"

"Gorillas don't eat people."

"Then what was it all about?"

"I couldn't tell from his eyes. It's harder to read an animal's eyes."

"What happened?"

"It started to feed us. It threw fruit into the hole, mostly bananas and mangos."

"I bet it did want to eat you. You just looked too thin so it wanted to fatten you up."

"Who ever got fat on fruit?"

"Maybe it . . . fancied you?"

"Would you fancy a female gorilla?"

"All right, how did it all end? Were you rescued?"

"Would I be here now if we weren't?"

"I mean, how did you pull it off?"

"Four-and-a-half hours later the gorilla suddenly turned and left. We thought it had gone for more fruit, but it didn't come back. Dusk was already falling when I decided to climb out of the hole. It wasn't easy and I fell back twice before I reached the top. I was black and blue all over."

"Was the gorilla nearby?"

"There wasn't a trace of him."

"What about your girlfriend? Did she climb out after you?"

"No. She wasn't agile enough. I had to go look for a liana to pull her out."

"The gorilla would have been a big help there. Even thin people aren't light. You must have had a hard time."

"Actually, I didn't. She refused to come out when I threw her the liana."

"Was she afraid?"

"She wasn't afraid. She wanted to stay in the hole."

"Smart young woman. I'd rather spend a night in the jungle in a hole than out in the open. You should have stayed there too until morning. I can't even imagine what you were doing in such a wild place."

"She decided not to come out after a conversation she had while I was gone."

"The gorilla didn't go into the hole while you were out looking for a liana, did he?"

"In what language would my girlfriend talk to the gorilla?"

"How do I know? Maybe they used sign language?"

"In the dark? And what would be the attraction of staying in the hole with a gorilla?"

"All right then, who was she talking to?"

"God."

The silence that descended on the impenetrable darkness of the vault was almost palpable.

"You didn't buy such nonsense, did you?" said the auto mechanic at last in a low voice.

"I didn't buy anything. I stayed next to the hole and fell asleep just before dawn. When I woke up the hole was empty."

"Did she manage to climb out by herself?"

"I don't know. I never saw her again."

"That just goes to show what happens to people who wander around the jungle."

"It's obviously safer in civilization."

"A bank robbery is just a rare exception."

"Do you think the only way that people in the civilized world end up enclosed in the dark like us is when someone forces them at gunpoint?"

"Either that or when there's a situation like a power outage. Why would someone stay in the dark of their own accord?"

"To win a bet."

"I've heard of all kinds of weirdos, but never one like that."

"I have. Not one but two."

"Really?"

"Yes. In the small town where the gardener lived for a while, the pharmacist and butcher made a bet about who could stay the longest in an enormous wine barrel."

"Empty?"

"Have you ever tried to get into a full barrel?"

"How did they ever come up with such an idea?"

"They were constantly competing with each other.

At the monthly auctions they would always bid up the price of some trinket just to get the better of the other. They made the bet in a bar after drinking several more glasses than they could hold."

"Didn't they come to their senses when they sobered up?"

"They probably did, but they were already in the barrel by then. And their vanity wouldn't let them back out."

"So how did the clash of two vanities end?"

"A tie. At the end of the fifth day they were taken out of the barrel, even though they wanted to stay inside some more."

"They weren't bored sitting in the dark for so long?"

"Apparently not."

"So what did they do all that time?"

"They mostly talked. What else could they do?"

"I doubt they were just chewing the fat."

"They had a very interesting conversation."

"How do you know?"

"You can't hide anything in a small town. Shall I tell you about it?"

"Why not? We don't have anything better to do either."

⌒ 9 ⌒

"Why don't you just give up?" asked the pharmacist after a long silence. "You're just torturing both of us for no reason."

"You give up," replied the butcher.

"You know perfectly well I won't."

"I won't either."

"You're as stubborn as a mule. Don't you think it's

stupid for us to sit here like fools? Everyone's probably laughing at us out there."

"They are laughing at us."

"So how can you let them?"

"They'll laugh even more at the one who goes out first."

"They'll laugh for a split second and then forget it."

"Let them laugh at you for a split second."

"You're so hard-headed. Why on earth did you propose this? But why am I even asking? You were roaring drunk."

"You weren't in any better shape when you took me on."

"Even so, you're more to blame."

"No I'm not."

"Yes you are."

"No I'm not"

"Yes you are."

"No I'm not."

They sank into silence again.

"There's no sense in trying to convince you. So why did you choose a barrel?"

"What's wrong with a barrel?"

"Aren't you the least bit aware of what could happen in here?"

"What could happen?"

"You haven't heard any stories about barrels?"

"What stories?"

"Of course you haven't. How could a butcher hear, for example, about a philosopher who lived in a barrel?"

"Was he drunk too?"

"What are you talking about?"

"So why did you move into a barrel?"

"He was tired of running into guys like you."

"How long did he stay in the barrel?"

"A long time."

"There, you see. We have nothing to be ashamed of. If some philosopher could stay in a barrel a long time, we can too. Why should we be worse than him?"

"You're impossible."

"Maybe it's not right for a pharmacist to take after a philosopher? If that's the way it is, you're free to go. No one's keeping you."

"I won't go. But you could, after you hear another story about a barrel."

"With another philosopher?"

"No. Two philosophers would be too much for a butcher. Your head might start spinning."

"Then with a drunk?"

"I don't know any stories about drunks."

"All right then, who else but a philosopher and a drunk would spend time in a barrel?"

"Weirdos."

"What kind of weirdos?"

"Just listen. One of my old colleagues had an assistant in his pharmacy. The young man was very talented at preparing medicines and in addition he was quiet and reserved."

"The exact opposite of my assistant. He's not only clumsy but blabbers nonstop."

"He's trying to fit into his surroundings. One day something strange happened. When my colleague came to take over the afternoon shift, he found the door locked."

"The assistant left without saying goodbye? Did he rob him too? Guys like that are capable of just about anything."

"In the butchers' trade to be sure, but not in ours. The pharmacist thought that for some reason the young man had to go out urgently and didn't have the time to let him know. But when he tried to unlock the door with his key, he couldn't. The assistant's key was in the lock on the inside."

"Had the guy sneaked into a corner to take a nap? My guy is always on the lookout for a chance to goof off."

"The old man forced his way into the pharmacy and checked all the rooms, even the storage room in the basement, but there was no trace of his assistant."

"Had he climbed out the window?"

"None of them was open."

"Pharmacists may be the devil's minions, but even so they can't disappear from a completely closed pharmacy."

"They can't."

"So what happened?"

"The assistant finally appeared when the pharmacist was getting ready to go home in the evening."

"He'd been inside the whole time?"

"Yes."

"He must've had a hiding place that the old pharmacist didn't know about. My assistant's a real pro at finding holes to crawl into just to get out of working."

"The old pharmacist heard a noise in the basement storage room. He rushed down there and at first didn't recognize his assistant at all. How could he since the young man was covered from head to foot in cough syrup?"

"Unbelievable. Where did all the syrup come from?"

"The assistant made it himself and kept it in a barrel. They filled the bottles from it."

"Why did he pour it all over himself?"

"He didn't. He'd spent several hours in a barrel filled with thick syrup."

"You don't expect me to believe that, do you?"

"Believe it or not, that's what happened."

"Come on, now. No one would last five minutes in syrup. How would he breathe?"

"I don't know. Maybe through a straw."

"All right, let's say that it was somehow possible. But what on earth was he doing in a barrel of syrup? We all know that pharmacists are a bit touched, but I've never heard of any going off their rockers."

"I can tell you why he went into the barrel. He told his boss."

"I'm all ears."

"To talk to God."

Silence reigned in the large barrel for a few moments.

"He talked submerged in syrup with a straw in his mouth?"

"That's what he claimed."

"Did his boss give him a thrashing? I'd beat the living daylights out of my assistant if he appeared like that and then tried to sell me such a ridiculous story."

"Pharmacists don't solve their problems with beatings."

"You don't say. So how do you solve them? What did the old pharmacist do?"

"He didn't have to do anything. His assistant left as soon as he cleaned himself up. He stopped being a pharmacist."

"Good going. It seems like spending time in a barrel brought him to his senses."

"The same can't be said for you, unfortunately. Maybe a butcher has to stay longer in a barrel to come to his senses? But let me warn you. Staying too long in the dark is not all that harmless."

"Hey, now you've scared me. If only you could see me—I'm trembling with fear."

"You'll lose some of that swagger when you hear another story."

"About a barrel again?"

"No. A barrel's not the only place where it's totally dark. Other places are too, an elevator for example."

"The elevators I take are well-lit."

"As long as there's power. And sometimes the power is cut."

"Sometimes, but not for long."

"Sometimes it can last a while. Just listen to what happened to the old pharmacist's lawyer."

"I'm all ears. I love to hear horror stories in the dark."

"You might not like this one. The lawyer was rushing to an important meeting. A pharmaceutical company had offered to buy the pharmacist's right to manufacture the cough syrup that had become very popular."

"Wasn't it the assistant who made the syrup?"

"Yes, but his employer had the patent rights. That's the contract they signed."

"So now someone tell me that pharmacists aren't crafty."

"No more than butchers. But let's get back to the lawyer. His whole morning had been filled with bad luck. First he cut himself with a grapefruit knife, then he spilled coffee on himself and finally he had to get out of his taxi because the traffic had been completely stopped by chickens scattering in all directions from a truck that hit a bus."

"Bad luck always goes in threes."

"This was the fourth and worst. It happened just after he got in the elevator, convinced that in spite of all the obstacles he would still make it on time."

"The power was cut?"

"Yes."

"How long did he stay in the elevator?"

"Be patient. It's a long story."

The Third Loop

The truck driver wanted to kill himself.

He stared blankly through the windshield at the impossible sight before him. Traffic lights changed in vain. Angry honking from all four sides was just as vain. The vehicles at the intersection were stopped as though anchored there. Most of the pedestrians didn't dare walk either. Scuttling chicks were all that moved.

They were everywhere. The yellow invasion was scattering in all directions from the freight section of the truck that had been hit by a bus. It made no difference where the blame for the accident lay. There were no injuries and the damage to the vehicles was small. Even so, this was truly the end of the world.

All the driver could do was get back into his cab and wait, although he didn't know what for. The police still hadn't managed to make their way through the morning traffic. Even when they got there, they wouldn't be able to do anything. No one could do anything.

A special effect from the movies crossed his mind. Pieces of a porcelain vase rise off the floor, come back together and produce a whole vase on a low table. Only magic could put the chicks back in the truck. But who could pull it off?

He reached for the glove box in front of the passenger seat next to him. Among other things, he kept a bottle of sleeping pills there that he took occasionally on long trips because he had a hard time falling asleep in a strange bed. He had recently put a gun in the glove box too. The roads weren't as safe as they used to be.

Before he could open it, someone knocked on the passenger door of the truck. He raised his head and saw the face of an elderly woman at the window. She had bright cheeks, a pronounced double chin, and was wearing a green coat and matching pillbox hat.

He thought at first that she was from one of the nearby cars and probably expected him to undo the mess he'd got them into. But she didn't look in the least angry. She smiled at him and waved her hand.

The driver glanced at her dubiously before opening the window a crack.

"Good day," she said cordially.

"It's anything but good," he replied in a glum tone.

"Believe me, there have been worse."

"I believe you, but that's little consolation right now."

The woman raised her other hand. A tiny fluffy yellow creature was in her palm, its head cocking this way and that.

"I caught one of your chicks."

The driver sighed.

"That's great. All we have to do is catch the other three thousand and everything will be fine."

"Would you mind if I got in?"

The driver scrutinized her skeptically.

"Just to talk," she hastened to add. "It won't do any harm and it might be of some help."

The driver hesitated briefly before opening the door.

There was clearly no threat of danger from the elderly woman. And even if there were, it made no difference.

"I'm afraid I'm beyond help."

The woman settled into the seat and closed the door. She placed the hand holding the chick in her lap and started petting it with the tip of her middle finger.

"Don't be like that. It's not so bad."

The driver made a sweeping gesture before the windshield.

"I don't see anything cheerful about this."

"Things will sort themselves out somehow."

"How?"

"Bigger problems than this have been sorted out. Often all by themselves."

"You're quite an optimist."

"Optimists live longer."

"Then I will be short-lived."

"That's something you can never know."

The driver opened his mouth to say something, but noticed just then that a change had taken place in the almost static scene at the intersection. It took a moment for him to realize that the stoplights were out.

"Hey, that's all we needed. The power's been cut. Now there will be complete chaos."

"Yes, it is unfortunate."

"Unfortunate? If this isn't grounds for suicide, then I don't know what is."

His eyes slid to the glove box in front of the woman.

"It's strange about suicide," she said. "There are all kinds of motives. Some you'd never think of."

"Is that so?" replied the driver, glancing sideways at the guest in his cab.

"Yes, it is. What would you say, for example, about

a nobleman who took his own life when he discovered that his shirt was missing a button?"

"Couldn't he have taken someone else's life?"

"First he killed his servant, but it seems that wasn't enough."

"He must have been devastated about the button. Unimportant details infuriate me too sometimes. But not as much as that."

"There's got to be self-restraint. Where would killing ourselves for trifles get us? It's another thing if the reason is serious. Like what happened to the poet who retired to a village so he could write in peace. While he was out for a walk, a goat entered his house and ate half the manuscript of his new collection."

"He didn't kill himself for that, did he?"

"He felt the loss was his ruination. Not to mention the highly undignified end to half the manuscript."

"But he had the other half,"

"Have you ever written poetry?"

"No."

"Then you can't imagine what it means to lose even one verse, let alone half a collection."

"I'm glad I'm not a poet."

"The poet's calling is not without drawbacks. Nor is any other calling, for that matter. But as far as suicide is concerned, those that seemingly have no motive are the strangest."

"Do they exist?"

"Oh, yes. They're by no means uncommon."

"You know a lot about suicides."

"They've always intrigued me. Would you like me to tell you about an interesting case?"

The driver took a good look at the smiling old woman still petting the chick. Then he glanced at the glove box.

"Why not?" he said at last, shrugging his shoulders. "What else do we have to occupy ourselves while we wait for things to sort themselves out?"

∽ 2 ∾

Whenever the conductor was on tour somewhere, he spent most of his free time in museums. He went there not only as an art lover, but also because visiting museums brought him the peace of mind he needed before a concert.

Nothing indicated that anything unusual would happen this time. There weren't many visitors on a Sunday. He'd spent as much as fifteen minutes alone in rooms with high ceilings and tall windows. It was a chance to enjoy the museum's lauded art collections without being disturbed.

He almost missed the small landscape painting on the way out of room number four. It was completely stifled by the size and bright colors of the painting next to it. To give it the attention it deserved, he had to go right up close to the canvas.

A stream was flowing through idyllic countryside. The grassy bank rose gradually to a leafy oak on the crest of a knoll. Its green crown seemed to quiver against the blue sky. Two fishing poles were stuck into the bank at an angle with little bells at the top, indicating the presence of people who could not be seen.

As the conductor stood there, eyes fixed on the small painting, he was struck by the feeling that he'd seen it somewhere before. This was not unusual. All landscapes resemble one another. It must have been another painting in another museum. In his younger days he would have had no trouble remembering the exact painting, but now it seemed beyond his reach.

That's when his underrated memory surprised him. A picture almost identical to the one before him suddenly surfaced from the buried depths. It was not, as he had assumed, another painting. The scene he'd seen beside the stream was real.

He'd still been a student at the time and had spent his free time bird-watching. He'd spend hours roaming the gentle terrain around the town where he was studying, binoculars frequently raised in hopes of catching sight of a rare species.

One day as his binoculars skimmed the rolling terrain, his attention was drawn to two monks beside a stream. They were fishing, although their attention was not on the fishing poles but a chessboard on the grass. Watching people secretly was bad manners, but who could resist the temptation at that young age?

Just as he was about to stop, concluding that chess players immersed in the game weren't all that interesting, the older monk stood up and walked thigh-deep into the stream without taking off his habit. Then he did something even stranger: he bent over and plunged his head into the water.

As the minutes passed and the monk didn't raise his head, the future conductor grew nervous. Was this some sort of outlandish bet between the chess players? The older one had lost the game and now his punishment was to keep his head underwater for a long time. The young man didn't know how long a person could hold their breath, but he certainly couldn't hold his that long.

He thought he should do something, even if it meant giving himself away. He couldn't just stand there and watch a man drown. But before he could take any action, the younger monk beat him to it. He rushed into the stream, grabbed the old monk around the waist and tried to pull him out.

He struggled for a few moments without success. Then he suddenly let go of the old man, stared at the fishing poles and hastened to the bank. Even though he was watching fixedly, the student couldn't figure out what had made the young monk give up. He'd jumped as though there'd been a noise, but no sound reached the place where the student was hiding.

The student had already started running towards the distant stream when the old man finally pulled his head out of the water. From the looks of it, the man didn't seem at all like someone who'd almost drowned. He had a little chat with the young monk, then walked away. The student watched him until he disappeared into a nearby clump of trees. Then he lowered his binoculars. He had never spied on anybody since.

Bewildered by this memory, the conductor examined the landscape carefully once again. It was just a coincidence, but the similarity was truly amazing. It was as though what he'd seen long ago through the binoculars was now hanging before him. Only the two monks were missing, but they could easily be imagined on the bank of the stream.

He remained in front of the canvas a while longer, then finally shrugged his shoulders. He'd already headed towards the door to room five, when a new reminiscence stopped him mid-step. Even though it had nothing to do with the small painting, the conductor looked at it again.

He'd taken the train to a town where a new concert awaited him. As they were going through a tunnel, an earthquake struck. They ended up trapped for a day-and-a-half because landslides blocked the openings. After the first temblor, he'd rushed out of the compartment.

Among the other passengers who'd gone into the corridor, he caught sight of his dentist at the other end. He nodded, but the man took no notice in the commotion. After everything had calmed down, the conductor hesitated briefly as to whether to go and join him, but decided that he didn't feel like talking. He would be more comfortable staying alone in his compartment.

He wasn't bothered too much when the power was turned off hours later. He liked being in the darkness. He spent some ten minutes in total darkness in his dressing room before every concert. This was the best way to relax and drive away needless thoughts.

He was also relieved when the p.a. system went off. The sickly sweet piano compositions didn't agree with him. In the silence he would be able to hear real music in his head. It was easy to imagine that instead of being in the heart of a mountain, he was on the podium before an orchestra that was smoothly following his guiding hands.

Although the transition was imperceptible, he suddenly realized that the music wasn't coming from his head. He stood up, but not to get closer to the loudspeaker. What he heard couldn't possibly have come from there. It would have been simply blasphemous to stay in his seat.

He couldn't tell how long he stood there, immobile, head thrown back and eyes wide open to the darkness, even after everything around him sank into silence. It had been hard to regain his composure after experiencing such unparalleled rapture.

While it was still playing, he was struck by the painful certainty that he would never hear this divine music again. When the rapture passed, he collapsed onto the seat, filled with the emptiness of despair. His thoughts turned darker than the gloom surrounding him. That was the first time he felt the urge to commit suicide.

But the urge had no chance to gain momentum. He couldn't figure out a way to take his life in a tunnel. The long hours that followed, while he waited with the other passengers to be freed, dulled his initial resolution. When they finally got out, all that he felt was rancor. No one found this unusual. What was to be expected after the predicament they'd been in?

Now, as he looked at the small landscape, wondering why it had made him think of the incident in the train that he'd done his best to forget, the urge suddenly returned with all its initial force. There was no lack of opportunity at present. He chose the way that seemed the shortest and fastest. And he didn't even have to leave the building.

The roof-top garden of the four-story museum held an exhibit of sculptures that had been brought there temporarily from various parks, so they could stay out in the open. He went up, ready to wait a little if there were any visitors, but impassive marble statues were all there was to see.

He headed straight for the wrought iron railing. He'd feared it would be much higher and with spikes at the top. But they clearly had not counted on suicides here. The low barrier was easy to get over.

He took hold of the upper part of the railing with two hands, but before he had time to raise his foot, a voice came from behind him.

"Do you know how far it is to the ground?"

He turned around and looked at the elderly woman approaching him. Everything she wore was green: coat, pillbox hat, shoes. She must have been standing behind one of the statues. He should have checked more carefully whether he was alone.

"No, I don't. I'm not very good at judging heights."

"You don't have to judge. Just do the math. The building has four floors and a ground floor. Let's say each of the five levels is four meters high. You noted the high ceilings, didn't you? Five times four is twenty."

"Only twenty meters? It seems much higher to me."

The woman stopped at the railing and placed her hands on it too.

"Don't underestimate twenty meters. If you were, say, intending to kill yourself, that would be quite high enough."

She looked down for a moment, then smiled. The conductor did not smile back.

"Actually, the height isn't at all important," she continued. "What do you suppose was the lowest height for a suicide?"

The conductor hesitated slightly before answering.

"I don't know."

"The height of a dresser. Not even one meter."

"How can you commit suicide off a dresser?"

"Easily, if you fall the right way, upon the right object."

"I don't follow you."

"There was an expensive vase on the dresser. The owner found it smashed on the floor in the morning. It seems that the cat knocked it over during the night."

"And that's why he decided to kill himself?"

"People kill themselves for even less valuable things."

"Why didn't he kill the cat instead?"

"He thought of it at first, but couldn't do it. He was very attached to the cat. He didn't even scold it."

"So how did he kill himself?"

"He climbed onto the dresser, then just leaned forward, hands behind his back."

"But he'd just get bruised that way or in the worst case break a bone. But not die."

"He fell head first onto the fragments of the vase. A sharp splinter pierced his temple."

"What a stroke of bad luck."

"That's not what he would have thought. But there are opposite cases. One suicide kept increasing the height from which he jumped, but never managed to carry out his intention. His injuries got worse and worse, but he was still alive. He finally gave up after surviving a fall off a six-floor building."

"Six-floor building? That's impossible."

"Believe it or not. Jumping from a height is the least reliable way for someone to shorten their life."

The conductor examined the elderly woman in silence.

"You know a lot about suicides."

"I find them very interesting. Particularly those with unusual reasons. What would you say, for example, about one like this?"

She indicated the sculptures.

"A sculptor committed suicide?"

"A stonecutter. He decided that suicide was all he had left after he made a mistake carving a tombstone. It had been ordered by a diva while she was still alive so she could see the stone she'd be lying under."

"I'm not at all surprised. I'm quite familiar with the vanity of opera singers."

"Yes, they are renowned for that. The stonecutter, however, put not only the date of birth but the date of death."

"How could he know what year it would be?"

"That wasn't clear to him either. He wasn't aware of what he'd done until he finished the carving."

"Why didn't he simply destroy the tombstone and make a new one? That would be less drastic than suicide."

"Superstition. Stonecutters are a rather superstitious lot."

"What superstition?"

"He was convinced that he'd prophesied the singer's death. He felt like a murderer."

"Nonsense. Surely she didn't die that year."

"Yes, she did."

"That's just a coincidence. He shouldn't have been superstitious. Then everything would have been all right."

"Perhaps. But at least he had a reason, even if it was senseless. The most unusual suicides, however, are those whose cause you can't find."

"I didn't know there were any like that."

"More than one would expect. Some cases are real mysteries. Would you like to hear one such story?"

Before answering, the conductor looked down the side of the museum. Then he sighed and shrugged his shoulders.

"Why not?"

∽ 3 ∾

The postcard came in the morning mail. The astronomer easily recognized the handwriting. The only person who wrote so illegibly was his colleague who had recently traveled to the other side of the world. He would stay there half a year taking part in a project that gathered together experts in the field of x-ray astronomy. The astronomer didn't envy him since the observatory was on a remote mountain and autumn had just started in that hemisphere.

He tried to decipher the scribble for a while, but without much success. The words were not only hard to read but often written in shortened form. In any case it didn't matter. The postcard certainly didn't contain any important message, just a greeting and probably an attempt to be witty. His colleague was famous for telling jokes that only he found funny.

Why on earth had he sent a postcard? It was so old-fashioned in the era of electronic mail. But when you thought about it, his colleague was old-fashioned in many ways. Except for his profession, where he was a trailblazer of modernity. That's why they'd invited him to join this illustrious project.

The astronomer was in for a surprise when he turned the postcard over. He'd expected a picture of the mountain observatory, perhaps from some unusual angle. But instead, he saw one more confirmation of his colleague's odd sense of humor: a multitude of large, colorful balloons parading against a dark-blue background.

The astronomer smiled, wondering why his colleague had chosen this particular postcard. The answer would remain as unfathomable as the greeting. Just as he was about to put it with the junk mail, his eyes fixed on a detail that he'd missed the first time.

One of the most distant balloons, and thus tiniest, was covered with a net. He brought the picture up close to get a better look. He needed but a moment to realize what had attracted his attention, and then his excellent memory effortlessly brought back the incident of many years ago.

At the time he'd been a trainee at the observatory.

One of his duties was to maintain the telescope during the day when it wasn't in use. Dust was constantly settling on the large lens. After having removed it, he double checked his work, training the telescope on the distant mountain range that would suddenly seem within his reach.

That day he'd chosen a somewhat closer target. As he was cleaning the lens, he noticed with his naked eye a small circle that was the only thing marring the blue background. Balloons were a rarity there. He cleaned the lens and then looked through the eyepiece. His field of vision was almost filled with a colorful pear shape that seemed to be glued to the firmament.

He felt awkward at the sight of a young woman and an older man. They were just getting up from the bottom of the basket, certainly not suspecting that curious eyes had found them all the way up there. He'd never understood the inclination to voyeurism. He raised his hand to the control knob to turn the telescope away from the airborne tryst, but did not complete the action.

He stared in disbelief at the young woman who suddenly climbed onto the edge of the basket, holding onto the rope. What was she up to? Could it be that she hadn't gone up in the balloon for amorous reasons? It hadn't crossed her mind that the older man might try to take advantage of the basket's cramped quarters for his lustful intentions. Certainly she was only threatening him. She wouldn't really jump, would she? Killing herself because of someone's advances made no sense.

And what if she'd made up her mind? He had to do something. He couldn't just stand there and watch. But what could he do? If he called the police, it would take them some time to arrive.

Should he film the incident? It wouldn't help the

young woman, but at least he would have evidence against the man who'd driven her to her death. But there wasn't time for that either. It would take him at least a quarter of an hour to prepare the device for photographing heavenly bodies. All he could do was stay by the telescope and watch closely as the sole eyewitness.

That's when he received another surprise. Instead of jumping, the young woman started to climb up the pear shape. The astronomer watched with bated breath as she deftly grabbed hold of the net covering the balloon. She pulled off this reckless stunt bravely, as though an abyss of at least two kilometers wasn't gaping below her.

The older man shouted something inaudible to her but she paid no attention. When she came to the hemisphere, she disappeared from his sight. Now only the astronomer's distant eyes were watching her. She kept on climbing until she reached the top.

Then she simply sat down, legs crossed, as though resting at the top of a hill. Nothing seemed to be happening. It wasn't until the astronomer increased the magnitude so only the young woman's head was in the eyepiece that he noticed she was opening her mouth as though talking to someone. Her eyes were closed.

The inaudible conversation lasted about twenty minutes and then her head suddenly disappeared. The astronomer hastened to widen the field of vision and caught sight of the young woman going back down the balloon as deftly as she'd climbed up it. Soon she joined the man in the basket.

The astronomer felt a guilty pang. He'd been wrong about the older man. But how could he have known that the young woman would turn out to be so odd?

The man seemed upset as he was talking to her. Then he took hold of the balloon controls and the colorful pear started to descend.

He didn't follow them any further. He raised the large tube towards the distant crags wrapped in mist, firmly resolving to use only them in future to check how well he'd cleaned the lens.

The astronomer held the postcard a little longer, smiling at this distant memory. As he placed it among the rest of the mail, another old memory surfaced unexpectedly from the past. He wondered at this, since it was not connected in any way to the crowd of balloons. Quite the contrary, the darkness that accompanied it was exactly the opposite of the sunny day on the picture.

He was eleven years old when war broke out. His father had been mobilized, so he was left with only his mother. That day she'd gone to the food distribution center as she did every afternoon, but failed to return before the air raid siren went off. He was terrified of the bombing, so he headed straight for the basement, overcoming his somewhat lesser fear of the dark.

He'd hoped to find his neighbors there, but no one called out from the gloom. He hesitated briefly whether to stay there alone or go back, and then the first explosion resolved the dilemma. He was crouching in the deepest corner, covering his ears with his hands, when there was another explosion.

When he lowered his hands, he could tell by the rustling that someone else had entered the basement, but he didn't dare call out because he didn't know who it was. He thought of making his presence known when they were soon joined by the mailman from the third floor, who'd brought along his cat, as usual. But he decided to remain hidden when it turned out that the first newcomer was not one of the neighbors. His mother had given him strict orders to stay away from strangers.

He listened for a while to their small talk about cats and dogs, interrupted by close or distant explosions. And then, right when the stranger started to talk about an unusual event in the zoo, the boy could suddenly see.

He didn't see what was still wrapped in the basement's gloom. At first he didn't even recognize what was manifested so clearly before his eyes. Looking straight ahead in confusion for a few moments, he finally realized that they were stars.

There were many more of them than on the clearest summer night. Even though the vision seemed unreal, he wasn't afraid. He gazed, enthralled, at the countless little steadily shining points. And then the stars began to move.

Those closest to the edge of the boy's field of vision slid outside of it, while new ones emerged in the center, seemingly out of nowhere. This enchanted him even more. He wanted to clap, but had enough presence of mind not to give himself away. He no longer heard the two men, although he was still aware that they were in the basement with him.

The change that came was sudden. As though the source in the middle had suddenly dried up, no new stars poured out of it. When the last ones had scattered outside his field of vision, darkness reigned.

Just when the boy thought that the amazing show was over, the source came back to life. This time, instead of stars, something like gossamer started emerging slowly. Before it had completely taken shape, he realized that before him was a giant eye watching him fixedly.

Part of his consciousness told him he should be afraid of such scrutiny but, quite to the contrary, he was filled with something he'd never felt before. The rapture urged him to rush toward the eye, to plunge into it.

A strong explosion, accompanied by showering bits of ceiling, instantly demolished the shining apparition. He had to bite his lip to stop himself from groaning in frustration. There was nothing but darkness around him. He wanted to bring back the eye with all his heart, but didn't know how. The thrill suddenly sank into despair.

And then he was struck by an impulse totally uncharacteristic for his age. If he only knew how to do it, he would kill himself without a moment's hesitation. He thought of running out and letting the bombs have him, but the two adults would certainly stop him. All he could do was sit there in hiding and somehow struggle with his despair.

When the bombing finally ceased more than two hours later, his disappointment had worn down to numbness. He waited for the two men, whose conversation he hadn't followed, to leave the basement before he departed as well. He was almost at his apartment when something rather consoling crossed his mind. When he grew up he would study the stars. That was the only way he dared hope to see the great eye again.

Roused by the old memory, the suicidal instinct suddenly stirred inside him. He still hadn't been able to find what he was looking for, even though he'd become an astronomer, and realized that very moment that this would never happen. He'd hoped in vain for another glimpse of the apparition from the dark basement of long ago. And how can a man live without hope?

This time he didn't have to dither over how to carry

out his intention. Was there anything more fitting than to hang himself on the telescope's huge tube? It might not have helped him reach the great eye, but it could certainly serve this purpose.

He put the postcard on the pile of letters, then went to the tool room. He took some rope and made a noose at one end. This time there was no one to stop him. It would be a full three-and-a-half hours before his colleagues from the next shift arrived at the observatory.

But he had a surprise in store when he returned to the telescope room. An elderly woman in a green coat and matching pillbox hat and shoes was standing next to the entrance.

"Hello," she said with a smile.

The astronomer swore to himself. He'd completely forgotten that the observatory was open to visitors on Thursdays. It was no wonder he'd forgotten, though, since no one had come by in ages. People weren't very interested in astronomy. Oh well, there was nothing to be done. A quarter of an hour, which was how long they usually stayed, wouldn't make any difference.

"Hello," replied the astronomer. He hesitated briefly over what to do with the rope, then put it next to the telescope mount, trying to make the noose inconspicuous.

The woman nodded in that direction.

"Did you know that suicides most often resort to hanging?"

The astronomer looked at her suspiciously for a few moments.

"No, I didn't," he said at last, shaking his head.

"Yes. Statistics have shown that as many as forty-three-and-a-half percent take their lives like that. Strange, isn't it?"

"Why is it strange?"

"You'd expect those who take their own lives to spare themselves unnecessary suffering. That's the least they can do for themselves, unless they're masochists. Suicide by hanging is among the most painful methods."

The astronomer was silent for a moment before he replied.

"I didn't know."

"It's been scientifically proven. Plus, hanging isn't always reliable."

"You don't say."

"There is the well-known case of a middle-aged hog farmer who decided to kill himself because of unrequited love. He tried to hang himself all of seventeen times, without success."

"What can go wrong with hanging?"

"Most often the rope. People underestimate their weight, so instead of their neck vertebrae breaking, the rope breaks. And the hog farmer was quite heavyset."

"But there must be a rope thick enough for even the largest people."

"That's what he thought. He used thicker and thicker ropes, but every one of them broke."

The astronomer glanced at the telescope mount.

"Unbelievable."

"Yes, unbelievable. You can just imagine how much these failures frustrated him. In any case he had weak nerves and a short temper."

"Even someone with nerves of steel and a mild temper would have to explode after so many failures. How did he make it through seventeen attempts?"

"He was pigheaded. The initial reason soon stopped being important. Suicide became a matter of pride."

"How did it end?"

"He finally gave up. He had to admit defeat when he was unable to kill himself even after he replaced the rope with a chain."

"The chain broke too?"

"No. The hook he'd attached the chain to was pulled out of the roof-beam. And it had held up under the fattest hogs."

"That's real bad luck."

"Soon he had even worse luck. Just after he'd gotten over his obsession with suicide, he was hit on the head by a stray golf ball as he strolled with his new sweetheart quite far from the golf course. He was killed on the spot."

"Fate. Things don't happen the way we plan, but how they're fated to happen."

"Sometimes we decide our own fate. Take, for example, the case of a scientist who used an optical device like you."

He indicated the large tube.

"A telescope?"

"A microscope. He was a biologist. They'd just received a new electronic microscope. It could magnify two orders of magnitude better than the previous one. He was overjoyed at the chance to see what he'd been unable to see before. He never suspected what awaited him."

"What could await him there?"

"A message."

"What kind of message?"

"No one ever found out. The very first time he looked through the microscope, he jumped out of his seat. He started talking confusedly about the letters he'd seen."

"Letters?"

"Yes. He said that tiny creatures had formed them with their bodies."

"Nonsense. Did anyone else have a look?"

"Yes. No one else made out any letters."

"Of course not. Who ever heard of literate viruses?"

"The biologist, however, stood by his statement. He even claimed the letters formed words."

"Now viruses will turn out to be writers. And what was allegedly written?"

"He wouldn't say. He just stammered that the message was horrific."

"They should have sent him on vacation. Scientists lose their way when they're overly tired."

"If they had, he might still be alive. The next morning they found him dead on the floor of the laboratory. He'd gone back during the night without being noticed."

"How did he die?"

"He killed himself in a terrible way. He ate the slide with the sample he'd looked at under the microscope."

"How awful. Couldn't he have chosen something less drastic?"

"He explained in his farewell note that it was the only way he could save the world."

The astronomer shook his head.

"People take their lives for the strangest reasons."

"That's nothing. Perhaps you'd be interested in hearing about another unusual case."

Silence reigned for a few moments.

"You know a lot of stories about suicides."

"Yes, a lot. I like interesting stories. How about you?"

The astronomer looked at the rope on the floor, then at his watch.

"Me too."

∽ 4 ∾

Ever since the hunter had stopped hunting, he had gone to the zoo every Saturday. He'd hunted until the age of sixty-eight when gout forced him to stop. He missed the proximity of wild animals and this was the only place in town where he could be close to them.

He always chose the same bench at the top of a small rise in the middle of the zoo. From there he had a view of almost all the cages, but he kept his eyes closed most of the time. He wasn't bothered by the visitors' dubious looks.

By depriving himself of his eyes, he gave his nose free rein. He was proud of his acute sense of smell. When he'd hunted, he'd relied on it above all, since he would catch the smell of his quarry long before he saw it. He was able to sniff out almost all the game in a broad circle around him.

Sitting on the bench, he had no trouble detecting each of the many animals surrounding him. Each had a special smell that singled them out as much as their appearance. His nose even made out the animals that couldn't be seen from that spot.

He frowned when he got to the zoo on the first Saturday of summer. The weather was nice so he'd expected a crowd, but never had he seen so many visitors before. It wasn't that people bothered him. Long ago he'd learned how to ignore their smell and concentrate on the ones that interested him. But what if his bench on the rise were taken?

He was relieved to see that no one was on it. Visitors were wandering around but no one, it seems, felt like sitting down. When he got up close, however, he noticed that it wasn't quite empty. There was a little plush bear at one end.

It didn't catch the eye because it was the same brown color as the bench. It must have been left behind by a child taking a rest with their parents. They might still be in the vicinity. The hunter picked up the bear and raised it in the air, but even though many people were looking his way, no one claimed it.

He settled on the bench and put the bear next to him. He'd keep an eye on it. If the parents noticed that the toy was missing while they were still in the zoo, they might realize where they could find it. He was just about to close his eyes and surrender to the smells, when one more look at the bear suddenly brought back a distant memory. His eyes stayed open.

He was forty-two-and-a-half at the time. He still hadn't started to hunt and didn't go to the zoo very often. That day he'd gone out of boredom. The boredom had continued even as he wandered among the cages. The smell of animals was repulsive to him then and his acute sense of smell only made it worse.

This boredom was disrupted by something that happened next to the bear cage. Just before he reached it, the odd behavior of a slender young man caught his eye. If it weren't for the elderly woman with him, he would have thought the young man was a vandal because he was fumbling with the lock on the cage door.

Then he opened it and stepped inside. The guy's lost his mind, concluded the future hunter, watching in disbelief as the young man walked calmly towards the stone habitat. He paid no attention to the three bears in the opposite corner. The large, brown animals were dozing peacefully as though they hadn't heard the intruder, even though his shoes crunched on the gravelly ground.

The young man went into the habitat. The minutes

passed slowly and nothing happened. What's he up to, wondered the bewildered observer in front of the cage. The older woman also seemed puzzled. She tried to remove the lock and chain herself, without success. Luckily, the bears were still undisturbed.

Finally, the young man came out of the habitat. He headed for the door with slow steps, opened it without any trouble, then closed it behind him. He spoke to the woman briefly. When they left, they looked like ordinary visitors at the zoo.

The future hunter waited for them to move off a bit before going up to the door and checking the lock and thick chain. There was no sign that they had been forced. Maybe the young man had got hold of the key? That was not impossible, but what would explain the bears' disinterest? And what had he done in the habitat?

He wondered whether to tell the zoo authorities about it. They would have a hard time believing him. What evidence did he have, anyway, to back up his story? He was suddenly tempted to try to go in too, but gave up on the idea immediately for numerous reasons. In the first place, because he didn't know how to open a locked door.

He stood for a while in front of the cage. Nothing was happening. The bears were asleep, oblivious to the rare visitors. When he finally moved off, he reached a firm decision, even though he couldn't explain what led him to it. He would become a hunter.

Now he patted the plush bear on the bench next to him and closed his eyes, but another memory forced them open. How strange, he thought. Where did that come from? It had nothing to do with bears or hunting.

He'd been a sailor in his younger days. His striking good looks got him work on luxury liners. The lonely passengers who'd paid handsomely for all inclusive packages had to be provided with the satisfaction they expected.

The cruise had proceeded as usual until the signal was given for immediate evacuation. They were in the path of an enormous tidal wave caused by an underwater earthquake and would be safer in the two-seater lifeboats than on the huge ship. The captain hesitated briefly as to how to assign the passengers and crew. Finally he decided not to mix them. There was no more time for pleasure.

As he waited to get into the vessel with one of the ship's cooks, the young sailor exchanged glances with two female passengers just before the hatch on their boat was lowered and hermetically sealed. Both of them had already given him the eye.

If he'd been given the chance, he would have chosen the somewhat younger hairdresser. Although she was no beauty, it certainly would be nicer with her in a first-class boat, including champagne, than in a no-frills vessel intended for the crew with a fat travel mate who seemed to have brought all the kitchen smells with him.

The tidal wave left them without any lights. The cook, who was claustrophobic, panicked even more. He spent a full two-and-a-half hours babbling in terror before he finally fell asleep. Even the sailor's loud snoring was an improvement over his wailing.

He was starting to fall asleep too, when something jolted him awake. He opened his eyes wide, but they were of no use. His nose, however, wasn't bothered at all by the darkness or even the cook's kitchen odors and bodily fumes that saturated the cramped space.

The fragrance that suddenly arose overpowered the

bad smells much as beauty eclipses ugliness. Never before had he smelled anything quite as captivating. He began flaring his nostrils rapidly in order to absorb as much of it as possible. Every breath thrust him deeper and deeper into an intoxication that seemed to have done away with natural limitations. The sensation of floating was entirely convincing.

The floating ended with an abrupt fall, as though the sailor's invisible support had been removed. The fragrance was suddenly gone. How was that possible? He knew that smells never disappear all of a sudden. He started sniffing everywhere feverishly, but only got a whiff of the cook's odor; its increased repulsiveness now filled him with nausea. He barely held back from vomiting.

The despair that overcame him was as deep as his fervor of a moment before. It wasn't just that he'd lost the fragrance, but the painful suspicion swept over him that he would never find it again. The pinnacle had passed, never to return. Suicide had never crossed his mind before, but now it seemed the only way out of his plummeting despair.

Yes, but how could he do it? He had no experience in this regard. The vessel only opened from the outside, so he couldn't go out and drown. If it were a first-class boat, he could break a bottle of champagne and cut his veins. But a plastic water bottle wouldn't do the job. He couldn't think of any other way.

When the rescuers appeared hours later, they found the cook rested and cheerful after a good sleep, and the sailor in deep depression. His dejection was ascribed to the stuffiness that the ventilation system had been unable to fix. Why he soon decided to abandon the sailor's profession remained a mystery.

The old man's despair of long ago flared up unexpectedly on the bench in the zoo. His forebodings had turned out to be right, for he had never again smelled that unique fragrance. Now it would quite certainly remain inaccessible in the short time he had left. What had been the purpose of living all those empty days?

This time he didn't have to think twice about how to put an end to his suffering. A simple and painless means was in his pocket. On his way to the zoo, he'd stopped by the pharmacy. Just to be on the safe side, he would swallow a whole bottle of gout pills.

He wasn't afraid that someone would see him. It could all be done unnoticed. No one pays attention to old folks lazing in the sun. He took out the bottle, opened it and shook out a handful of white pills. He put the bottle back in his pocket and was just about to pop the pills in his mouth, when someone addressed him.

"What a lovely bear you have."

He quickly lowered his hand to his lap, then raised his eyes. Before him stood an elderly lady in a green coat. Her pillbox hat and shoes were of a matching color.

"Lovely, yes," replied the hunter. "But it isn't mine, I found it here. Someone forgot it. It's not yours, by any chance?"

The elderly woman shook her head, then pointed to the empty part of the bench.

"Is it free?"

The hunter hesitated but a moment, then stood up and bowed.

"Of course. Please sit down."

"People are quite negligent," said the woman once she had sat down. "Not only do they forget things but they pay no attention to what's happening around them. Someone could kill themselves in such a busy place as this and it's questionable whether anyone would even notice."

"Kill themselves?" repeated the hunter falteringly.

"Yes. Not with a gun, of course. That wouldn't go unnoticed. But in some inconspicuous way, like swallowing a fistful of pills."

The hunter stared at the woman, unconsciously clenching the hand in his lap.

"Suicides often resort to taking an overdose of medicine," she continued. "Although that's the least reliable method."

"Is that so?" asked the hunter.

Trying to move as casually as possible, he raised his hand and put it in his jacket pocket, opened his fingers and let the pills slip out. He wiped his hand a little on the pocket lining, then took out his hand and laid it in his lap again.

"Yes. Maybe you've heard about the short-sighted suicide's failed attempt?"

The hunter shook his head.

"I don't know much about suicides."

"He wasn't wearing his glasses when he looked in the medicine cabinet for the medicine he wanted to take to kill himself. He was convinced he'd found the right bottle."

"But he hadn't?"

"He hadn't, which soon became evident. Dramatically so. He spent a day-and-a-half on the toilet seat."

"Laxative?"

"A full bottle."

"How humiliating. But isn't a full bottle of any medicine lethal?"

"Not at all. Another ill-fated suicide is the best proof of that. He got hold of lots of medicines, just in case, but then couldn't decide which one to take."

"Why didn't he take them all?"

"It seemed too uncouth for him. He wanted to leave this world in style."

"So what style did he choose?"

"A mixture. He decided to make a cocktail."

"What kind of cocktail?"

"He filled a coffee cup with different pills. But not at random, mind you. He was careful to make sure that the colors matched."

"Why, he was some sort of aesthete."

"Quite discriminating. Aesthetics, however, gave him considerable trouble."

"Did he end up on the toilet seat too?"

"No, what happened to him was more illustrious. He had a vision."

"Vision?"

"Yes. When the cocktail started working, instead of dying in peace, as he'd hoped, something appeared to him."

"What?"

"He never told anyone. But it must have been important because it banished the thought of suicide completely."

"So everything had a happy ending?"

"Not all that happy. When the effect of the medicine mixture wore off after a while, the vision disappeared too. He worked feverishly to make another cocktail to bring it back, but couldn't hit on the right combination of colors."

"I thought aesthetes had a good memory."

"He thought so too. Unfortunately, he was mistaken."

"So what happened?"

"He swallowed cocktail after cocktail, but instead of bringing back the vision, all he did was ruin organ after organ. In the end he would certainly have died if they hadn't put him in a hospital and then an asylum for the mentally ill."

"It just shows what an excessive affinity for aesthetics can do to a suicide."

"Suicides come to even more unusual ends, even when they're not aesthetes. I know of a very interesting case."

"You're a real expert on suicides."

"They are quite edifying, aren't they?"

"I suppose."

"Shall I tell it to you?"

The hunter patted his jacket pocket lightly.

"Please do."

⟳ 5 ⟲

The plumber was sitting next to the window, staring at the rain. The glass was streaked with shifting whorls as drops bounced off the bare metal tables and chairs in front of the bistro. Puddles on the sidewalk had joined to form a uniform surface of water.

Elbows on the table, head in his hands, a half-drunk glass of red wine on the table in front of him, he'd tried to read the newspaper someone had left there, but the headlines alone seemed darker than the weather, so he pushed it to the end of the table. He was sleepy even though dusk had only just started to fall.

His tool bag was under his chair and his cell phone was in the upper pocket of his overalls. That was his whole workshop. Customers called him on the phone and he would rush to take care of a plumbing problem.

When he wasn't working, he sat there and waited. The nice bistro owner didn't mind if he spent even the whole day there and drank only one glass of cheap wine. He could have waited for the calls at home, but then he'd have felt too lonely.

Once he'd had a real workshop with three employees, but he'd gambled it away, as he had everything else. Now he didn't own anything he could lose at roulette. The worn-out tools in his bag and the outdated cell phone were almost worthless, and the little that he earned was barely enough to cover food and rent for his basement room.

Pedestrians hurried by every so often under their umbrellas. He saw them in a blur, as moving outlines without much detail. They seemed faceless, blending into the grayness that street lighting had yet to soften.

A young woman without an umbrella came running from the left. Her yellow raincoat had a hood, but it wasn't raised. Her hair hung in long wet locks. She stopped in front of the window, her back turned to the bistro. She seemed to be waiting for someone.

Staring at the dark strands clinging to her neck and shoulders, he remembered something that had happened long ago. He'd been working for a service that maintained the water and heat installations in the city hospital. It was a poorly paid job that didn't provide him with the wherewithal to go to the casino. It wasn't until later, when he had his own company, that he became a regular customer.

He was checking the fittings on the central heating pipes stretching along an enclosed terrace that was common to all the rooms on the floor. At first he paid no attention to the woman's voice coming over the sound of the shower from the little bathroom window at the top of the wall. It wasn't until he'd taken a few steps away from it that he realized something was wrong.

The male ward was on the fifth floor. He stepped back to the railing and counted the rooms from the left. That athlete who'd been hit by a javelin at a contest was in the fourth room. Had he already recovered to the point of receiving guests who needed to take a shower at the end of their visit?

He went up to the bathroom window and grabbed hold of a nearby pipe. If anyone appeared on the terrace, he would pretend to be fixing something on it. He listened intently, but couldn't make out the words because the shower spray drowned them out.

Something else seemed strange. The visitor had to be talking to someone. If she were talking to herself, she wouldn't pause as though listening to someone's reply. But the athlete's voice couldn't be heard. There was no other voice.

He was suddenly tempted to fetch a ladder and peer through the open window, but that would too dangerous. If he were caught, he'd lose his job. Who would believe him to be motivated not by voyeurism but by mere curiosity?

And then it dawned on him that this was unnecessary, because there was a simple explanation for what was going on in the bathroom. Advanced technology really did lead to some odd behavior. It must have been a waterproof cell phone for people who couldn't live without one even in the shower.

He had to see the wounded athlete's guest. Indeed, what did a woman look like who takes a shower while visiting the hospital and keeps her cell phone with her? He left the terrace and went into the corridor. It wasn't hard to pretend that he was doing something near room number four.

The door opened just a few minutes later. The guest came out and rushed towards the elevator. He looked at her in disbelief. She was sopping wet, as though she'd taken a shower with her clothes on. Her short brown hair was pressed flat against her head. The water pouring off her left a wide wet trail.

He continued to gaze after the visitor even when she had disappeared inside the elevator. He thought of going in to see the athlete and ask for an explanation, but concluded it would be a waste of time. The guy must be just as strange if he was attracted to a woman like that.

Instead, he went to the personnel department and quit his job. The hospital was no place for him, not only because of the low salary but also because of the people he ran into there. For a long time he'd been thinking of starting up his own company. This was the right time to do it.

Now the bareheaded young woman raised her left wrist and looked at her watch. She shrugged her shoulders, turned and ran in the direction she'd come from. Her lagging image lingered a few moments after she had left: a bright yellow spot against a gray background. Before it vanished, an even more distant event surfaced from the plumber's memory, although nothing obvious had led to its resurgence.

He'd just moved to the big city and started learning the plumber's trade. He still didn't know anyone and was lonely, particularly on Sundays. He could barely wait for the amusement park to open at noon and often stayed there until evening. Once he stayed there until the next morning.

He'd got on the ghost train just before it closed.

When the little car stopped and total darkness reigned, he thought at first that it was part of the show and waited anxiously for something scary to burst out of the gloom and pounce on him, but nothing happened.

Some ten minutes later, he understood what had happened from the conversation of two invisible men in the cars in front of his. The ghost train employees had accidentally closed the ride while visitors were still inside. They had to choose between trying to get out or waiting until morning.

When he realized that the older men lacked the courage to do anything, he decided he'd offer to go and look for the exit. But then he found their fear amusing. What if he played a little joke on them first? The scaredy-cats deserved it.

He took a coin out of his pocket and started scraping it on the metal part of the car. Whenever he did it, the two heroes would stop talking and listen intently. Who knows how long the apprentice's pranks would have lasted if his turn hadn't come to be frightened too.

A large circular object suddenly popped up in front of him. He was so frightened that he overlooked the fact that the other visitors were still talking calmly, as though he was the only one to see the apparition. In his confusion, it took him a few moments to realize what was standing before his eyes.

It looked like an upright roulette wheel. He'd never been in a casino, of course, but he knew what a roulette wheel looked like. The alternating red and black fields on the edge of the circle were only interrupted in one place by a green interloper.

The wheel started turning and the numbers began to play. Fields on different parts of the wheel would light up briefly. He watched this random play for a while, spellbound, until he suddenly realized it might not be all that chaotic. There seemed to be some sort of pattern.

Although uneducated, he had a talent for mathematics. He started connecting the points that lit up on the wheel with imaginary lines. The pattern formed by the lines would mean nothing to someone unskilled with numbers, but his eyes managed to find the hidden meaning of the picture that was slowly emerging.

Every lighted number added a new fragment to the mosaic. Many were still missing to complete it, but luckily the young man had more than enough time. The ghost train employees would not appear before morning and by then the secret of the roulette wheel would be revealed to him completely.

But he had less time than expected. The employees weren't the only threat to the construction of the mosaic. In the exaltation that came over him, he'd completely forgotten the long-winded men up ahead. Suddenly they burst out laughing.

The sound was like an earthquake. The wheel shook, then the shaking seemed to subside, but finally the wheel began to crumble as numbers fell off and vanished the moment they left the circle's perimeter.

As soon as the deconstruction began, the apprentice plumber jumped off the seat of his car and stretched out his hands in a futile attempt to stop the roulette wheel from falling apart. But where the large wheel had appeared nothing palpable remained. When the last field vanished, all his hand held was solid darkness.

He crumpled onto the seat. At first he was seething with anger at the men who had recklessly destroyed the depiction of the roulette wheel, and toyed briefly with the idea of organizing an unforgettable night on the ghost train for them. But this would only give vent to his feelings and would not bring back the mosaic. Nothing could summon it from the void.

This was a painful realization. The despair that filled him was reminiscent of the only time he'd had to face the loss of someone dear. The thought of death suddenly seemed like a deliverance. It was the only refuge from his sinking desolation.

It was easier to make this decision, however, than to carry it out. He might have figured out a way to take his life if he could have seen what was around him, but how could he in the pitch black? All that crossed his mind was to look for the ax that had been mentioned at the beginning of the conversation still ongoing in front of him, but even if he found it, what then? A man can't chop off his own head.

This suicidal impulse had dwindled by morning. The surprised ghost train employees ascribed his somber mood to the tight spot he and the other visitors had been in. The two men were even more surprised to see him, but were considerate enough not to reproach him for the scraping that had frequently disturbed them, lest any mention be made of their courageous response.

The unexpected memory of this event summoned the thought of death yet again. It appeared once more as a deliverance, this time from a much deeper abyss. Back then life was in front of him, he'd had the right to hope, but now it lay ruined behind him, without a glimmer of that hope. Particularly not on such a gloomy day as this.

He'd squandered everything he'd earned in the false expectation that the casinos would let him continue putting together the mosaic whose contours had appeared to him so long ago. The ill-fated plumber, waiting in a bistro for infrequent customers to call, now couldn't even pay the entrance fee.

He looked at the glass on the table in front of him. The color of the wine was a clear signal. What had been inaccessible on the ghost train was now within reach. Broken glass was as effective as the executioner's ax. He would go to the men's room so that no one would stop him.

He took the glass and had started to get up when a female voice stopped him. Immersed in gloomy thoughts, he hadn't noticed that an elderly woman in a green coat and matching pillbox hat and shoes had approached.

"Is it free?" she asked, indicating the other chair at the small round table.

The plumber looked around the bistro. Several tables were empty.

"If it's company you're wanting, I'm not the right choice," he said, still halfway up. "And I'm just leaving."

She nodded towards the glass in his hand.

"Looks like blood, doesn't it?"

He sank back into his chair and put the glass down.

"Like blood?" he asked softly.

The woman sat down across from him.

"Yes. Did you know that some people avoid red wine because of the similarity? It makes them nauseous."

"I'm glad I'm not one of them. That would take away one of the few pleasures I have left."

"How do you feel about real blood?"

"Who can stand it except doctors and butchers?"

"It's not easy for them either. Particularly when they see their own blood."

"That's not easy for anyone."

"Particularly not for suicides."

The plumber gazed at the wrinkled face for a few minutes without responding. Her lips were curled into the shadow of a smile.

"Is that so?" he said at last.

"Yes. Perhaps you've heard about the librarian who decided to kill himself by cutting his veins?"

He shook his head. "No, I haven't."

"He didn't even know he was hypersensitive to blood until his first attempt. It failed the moment he cut himself because he fainted at the first sight of blood."

"Why didn't he try another way, one without any blood?"

"Because he was stubborn. Suicides are usually like that. It was cutting his veins or bust."

"Did he succeed in the end?"

"Yes and no."

"What do you mean?"

"He's no longer among the living, so you might say he succeeded. But not the way he wanted."

"So how did he go?"

"Blood was the death of him, but not his own."

"Whose, then?"

"He was in a traffic accident after another failed attempt. They took him to the hospital where he got a transfusion, but they accidentally gave him the wrong blood type."

"All things considered, he had no reason to be disappointed."

"I'm sure he would agree. But not all transfusions have a favorable outcome."

"Really?"

"A retired jockey was injured in the same accident. He was headed for the cemetery to visit the grave of his recently deceased wife. He received the right transfusion, but that's when all his troubles began."

"What can be bad about good blood?"

"As soon as it flowed through his veins, he heard his late wife's voice in his head."

"How could that happen? It must have been just an illusion."

"Probably, but the illusion was very convincing."

"Well, all right, even if that's true, I don't see anything bad about it. Some people would be happy to have a chance to talk to the dead."

"He was happy, too, but not for long. After a while his old blood canceled the effect of the new blood and the voice went silent."

"At least he got rid of the illusion."

"That was the problem. He didn't want to get rid of it, he wanted to bring it back. He felt as though his wife had died a second time. He asked to be given another transfusion."

"They didn't believe him, did they?"

"Of course not. They refused to give him another transfusion."

"And it ended at that?"

"No. During the night he sneaked into the storeroom where they kept the blood supplies. He gave himself a transfusion, but nothing happened."

"Of course nothing happened. The first time had nothing to do with the transfusion but with the shock he'd experienced. That happens sometimes. Did he come to his senses after that?"

"On the contrary. He kept on injecting blood into himself until he completely overloaded his bloodstream. They found him dead in the morning of a cerebral hemorrhage."

"Some people really go too far."

"That's nothing. I know of an even stranger case."

"You seem to be a fan of suicide stories."

"You might say that. So, shall I tell it to you?"

The plumber stroked the thin stem of the wine glass.

"Sure."

~ 6 ~

The photographer was sitting in a train station wait-ing room. He wasn't going anywhere and wasn't wait-ing for anyone. He was there just for the train. The composition could not have been smaller: a locomotive and one car. When it arrived in about twenty minutes, it would depart for its last trip: to the railroad museum. He was there to immortalize it.

He'd arrived at the station half an hour previously. He always made thorough preparations for his photo shoots. He'd chosen a good spot on the fourth plat-form and wasn't afraid that someone would take it. Everyone would crowd onto the fifth platform to be as close as possible, and the train would look best from a little distance.

He spent a short time in the station bar, but it was too smoky and noisy. In addition, the waiter behind the counter looked at him askance when he ordered a glass of buttermilk. He took just two sips, paid and left.

It was quiet in the waiting room and smoking was not allowed. He took the latest issue of the magazine he worked for out of his camera bag and started to leaf through it. Suddenly the silence was broken by an up-roar.

Young boys aged nine or ten in scout uniforms came

bursting into the waiting room and filled up all the seats. Some were left standing. The young man who was their leader had thin legs that looked even thinner in the wide legs of his short pants.

The photographer sighed and put the magazine back in his bag. In his younger days he'd have paid no attention to the crowd around him, but with age such things bothered him more and more. And so did a lot of other things. He looked forward to retiring in two years and nine months, but was also afraid of it. Even now, while he was still working, he felt more and more lonely. When it was his time for the museum, he would have nothing but his two pet hamsters. And they weren't much company, if they even lived until then.

He put the strap of the bag over his shoulder and was just getting up when his eye fell on one of the boys who hadn't found a seat. He was smaller than the others and seemed more withdrawn. He was standing in a corner holding a butterfly net in front of his face like a shield against the wicked world.

The photographer sank back into his seat. It had been a long while since he'd thought of the incident this net pulled from his memory. He'd been much younger at the time and still enthralled by the desire to be an artistic photographer. In his spare time he wandered around town and took pictures of anything that seemed exceptional.

He was just getting ready to leave the park one day after spending about forty minutes there without catching sight of anything interesting, when something told him to stay a little longer. Three walkers detached themselves from the others on the main path.

A middle-aged couple had taken a side path. They were the exact opposite of each other: she was short and round, dressed in a bright suit, and he was tall and lean, in a dark suit that clashed with the cheerful colors of the park. The young man between them could have been their son or a close relative. He looked a little like the woman in pink.

There was something wrong with his sight. Since he wasn't wearing dark glasses, he might not have been blind, but for some reason his eyes were closed. The older couple guided him by holding his arms. The photographer headed after them inconspicuously, keeping his distance.

They stopped in front of a large chestnut tree. The young man raised his head towards the treetop and the man and woman looked at each other, puzzled. The next moment, a multitude of yellow butterflies flitted out of the leaves.

The photograph raised his camera without delay and started taking pictures. The sight was truly unique. Nothing had indicated that so many butterflies were hiding in the treetop. In addition, they didn't fly away but fluttered just above the tree, resembling a quivering cloud.

The strange phenomenon lasted only a few minutes. When the young man lowered his head and turned around, the butterflies dropped back among the leaves. There was no sign that anything had happened. Except in the camera, of course.

The photographer was overcome with excitement. Lady luck had finally smiled on him. He'd been in the right place at the right time. All great photographs are taken like that. And only great photographers take such pictures.

He hid the camera behind his back when the three unusual walkers passed by. He hadn't broken any law by taking their picture, but if they had something against it, he preferred to avoid any discussion. He was in a hurry to go home and develop the film.

Just before he rushed towards one of the park exits, he noticed an unexpected change. Although the young man's eyes were still closed, he was now walking on his own as though he could see. The older couple was two or three steps behind him, no longer holding his arms.

The photographer stared for a long time at the film in the darkroom. The feeling of loss was mixed with puzzlement. This was impossible. He vividly remembered the yellow cloud above the treetop. All the walkers in the vicinity had stopped, enthralled at the sight. Even so, all the many pictures he'd taken showed nothing but blue sky above the chestnut tree.

He destroyed the negative before he left the darkroom. Photographs of an ordinary tree in a park were worthless. Any amateur could have taken them. Regardless of the explanation for the disappearing butterflies, one thing was certain. He was not fated to become a great photographer. He lost all his illusions.

A new commotion brought him out of his reverie. Another little scout came in, spoke to the thin leader briefly and he then called out loudly for the boys to go out onto the platform. They rushed towards the door in disorder.

The photographer looked at his watch. The train he was waiting for would arrive in ten minutes. He should get moving too. He had started to get up again when his eye fell once more on the little boy with the butterfly net who was among the last to leave.

Just as on the first occasion, the suddenly revived memory forced him to sit back down on his seat. Even though it too had been summoned by looking at the net, it had nothing to do with butterflies but with an incident from his youth when he still skied regularly.

He'd been alone in a funicular when an avalanche came swooping down the mountain. He watched in terror as the enormous white wave rushed towards him. When it got very close, he raised his hands and shut his eyes instinctively, but the little cabin held up under the blow. When he opened his eyes, all he could see through the window was packed snow.

The relief at having survived was diminished by the worry of what lay ahead. Hours would pass before the rescuers could dig him out. They might not reach him until morning. Night would bring a drop in temperature in spite of the fact that the snow above him would provide a little protection from the cold on the surface.

If he'd gone into the cabin in front of his, he could have counted on the middle-aged woman and young man to keep him warm. But he avoided the company of others whenever possible. Plus, he didn't have the patience for empty conversations, particularly with people he didn't know.

It was still afternoon when the cabin went completely dark. He pushed the light switch, but nothing happened. The power must have been cut off. Not only would he freeze, but he would have to sit in the dark.

The cold made him sleepy before nine o'clock. He couldn't let himself fall asleep. Then he would surely freeze to death. Whenever he felt his eyes start to close, he would stand up and do a few jumping jacks in the cabin's cramped quarters. This also warmed him up a bit.

And then when it was already past midnight, he started losing the will to resist. Taking a rest was so tempting. A weak voice inside him fought against it, but a much stronger voice convinced him that nothing would happen if he took a nap. Besides, he wasn't that cold anymore.

Just as he was about to fall into soft, warm sleep, he was shaken out of it. Something seemed to be rocking the cabin. He opened his eyes, but what he saw was not the darkness he expected. It was the exact opposite of darkness.

The previously invisible windows were now shining. He got up slowly and looked around in confusion. Never had he seen such perfect colors before. Their shapes were fluctuating and seemed to undulate like flames.

He'd seen the northern lights once, but that was just a paltry intimation of the show before him now. Without even trying to come up with an explanation for the impossible phenomenon, he simply stared like a spellbound child at the soundless play of colors surrounding him.

He couldn't judge how long it lasted; it might have been just a few minutes or maybe much longer. It ended just as it had begun, with a creaking sound from the nearby funicular pole announcing another quake. He took hold of the grip in the middle of the cabin to keep his balance.

At first he thought that someone had drawn opaque curtains over the windows. He went up to them and started wiping his hands feverishly across the glass to remove the blinds that cut him off from the light. But all he found was a smooth, cold surface with a mass of black snow pressing ominously on the other side.

Frustration surged through him when he sat down on the seat. He wanted the show to continue with all his heart; his eyes were still filled with the afterglow of the inimitable fireworks. But he suspected there would be no continuation. Everything he saw from then on would be only a pale shadow of the pure colors that had just appeared to him by some miracle.

Once again two voices appeared in his head. The weak one asserted that it was just great that he'd come fully awake, while the other one tried to get him to go back to sleep so he could drive away the despair that filled him and forget everything. The persuasiveness of the stronger voice easily prevailed.

In the morning, rescuers found him huddled on the seat, completely frozen. He didn't tell anyone what had happened. While he was recovering, he decided to turn his hobby into a profession. Even though he knew the chances were slim, only as a photographer could he dare to hope of reaching the colors that remained under the avalanche. And he had his whole life before him.

Now, in the hushed station waiting room, the realization suddenly came crashing down on him that all trace of that hope was gone. And not much was left of his life. He felt sick at the thought of the days he would spend in the company of his gray hamsters. Even ordinary colors would be lacking.

This was a chance to finish what should have happened in the mountains. Some sort of balance would be struck by becoming a news item himself after so many years recording them with his camera. The best thing would be to take a picture of himself as he jumped in front of the train, but unfortunately, that was impossible. One of his colleagues would be sure to take a good picture.

He started to get up, but was stopped a third time.

"It simply can't be done."

He was so absorbed in his memories that he hadn't noticed the elderly woman in a green coat and matching pillbox hat and shoes who'd taken the seat next to him. She was holding an open book.

"Excuse me?"

She raised the book a little, cloth-bound in the same dark-green.

"In the end the heroine jumps in front of a train, but that's not at all easy."

The photographer remained halfway up briefly, then sat down again.

"What's so hard about it?"

"Have you ever tried to jump in front of a train?"

"Would I still be alive if I had?"

"It's certainly not out of the question. You'd probably injure yourself but not die."

"I thought trains were lethal."

"They are, when going full throttle. There'd be no way to save you if you got in their way. Even the occupants of a tank which once stopped on the rails paid for it with their lives. But it's quite a different story when a train is entering a station."

"Aren't the wheels just as dangerous at lesser speeds?"

"To be sure. But how do you get under them?"

"You just jump, I assume."

"One ill-fated suicide tried to do it eleven times in a row. Without success. He suffered various injuries, of course, but nothing worked."

"He must not have been very agile."

"On the contrary. He was a gymnast in his younger days."

"Why didn't he go out onto the open rails? He wouldn't have had any trouble there."

"It had to be at a train station. For sentimental reasons."

"Maybe he should've been more persistent. Why did he give up in the end?"

"He was banned from entering the station."

"That must have been a heavy blow."

"Very. He tried in vain to convince them that he'd given up the idea of killing himself. All he wanted was to keep going to the station."

"They might have accommodated him."

"They didn't dare take the risk. Who ever believes a suicide? But he got the better of them."

"How?"

"He became a railroad engineer."

"How could they let him after all that?"

"No one ever asked him about it. Railroad engineers are in great demand."

"That's just wonderful. We don't have the slightest idea about who's driving when we travel by train. The person might get it into their head to enter the station going full throttle. They'd take a lot of innocent people with them to their death."

"He had no intention of doing anything like that, but even so he died on his very first trip. They brought him fish for lunch from the dining car. A bone got caught in his windpipe. Luckily, he managed to stop the train before he choked to death."

"He didn't have to go to all that trouble."

"Who knows what lies ahead? If a retired investigator had known, he never would have ordered blackberry pudding in the dining car on the same trip."

"Did a bone get into the pudding too?"

"No, it was perfect. The investigator loved sweets."

"So what went wrong?"

"When he fell asleep that night, he dreamed about the people he'd questioned."

"Did the inspector's conscience prick him? He must've been cruel at his job."

"He was known for his resourcefulness in forcing confessions out of people. Nothing that left any trace, but quite effective nonetheless. His favorite was a tub full of honey. After spending about twenty minutes in it, everyone confessed to crimes they hadn't even been charged with."

"What does that have to do with the pudding?"

"The people he'd questioned were holding large bowls full of blackberry pudding."

"It's amazing how mixed up things get in dreams. Did they love it too?"

"No, they didn't even try it. They were pouring it over the inspector who was lying in a tub on a table in the dining car."

"I suppose he couldn't get up and run away, as often happens in dreams."

"That's right. He just watched helplessly as the suspects' grinning faces appeared above the tub and they poured pudding over him. When it got over his head, he woke up with a scream."

"I bet he never ate pudding again, did he?"

"That's right. And more than that. He drowned in it."

"Drowned?"

"Yes. He discovered where food was prepared for the dining car. He got in there at night and plunged into a large tub full of pudding. First he wrote a suicide note."

"What an awful way to commit suicide."

"It depends on how you look at it. That would be a sweet death to an optimist."

"There's no accounting for taste."

"In any case, meeting your death in pudding is a lot less painful than ending up under train wheels. Besides, that isn't a very original suicide. I know some that are much more peculiar."

The photographer motioned to the book the woman was holding.

"Have you read a lot about suicides?"

"Yes, a lot. Shall I tell you about one that's beyond compare?"

The drawn out whistle of the locomotive could be heard outside. The photographer raised his head and saw commotion on the fifth platform.

"I'm all ears," he said with a sigh.

∽ 7 ∾

Weather permitting, the bank clerk spent the late afternoon on the quay. He sat on a bench and gazed at the forest on the other side of the river with the enormous sky rising above it.

After spending his workday in the safe-deposit room, this time out in the open was precious to him. The safe-deposit boxes were below street level so there weren't any windows. This hadn't bothered him at first, but as the years passed he became increasingly apprehensive.

The metal that surrounded him and the cold neon lighting increased the feeling of imprisonment. He tried to soften it with potted plants, but they soon faded without the sun. He put a poster of a snow-covered mountain on the wall, but had to take it down because the bank management didn't like it. And there had been no understanding for the quiet background music he played to chase away the painful silence.

Visiting the quay was like being set free. On fine days he'd stay by the river for a long time. He wasn't in any hurry. No one was waiting for him at home. He would just sit there, staring spellbound at the wide open space in front of him.

He loved the play of colors most of all. The forest changed its guise slowly, following the seasons, but the sky gave it a different look almost every day. The prevailing hue depended on the amount of cloud coverage.

For a long time, it was pure colors which gave him the greatest pleasure. The deep blue of the summer sky was in perfect harmony with the dense, fluttering green of the vegetation. But over time he came to like less pure combinations. On some autumn days, the overcast sky seemed to hug the almost bare treetops. The sight wasn't very beautiful, but he felt a kinship with it, as though sitting in front of a gigantic mirror.

River gulls and vessels were all that disturbed the static panorama. He rarely saw any passenger liners, but not a day went by without a barge or two. Then their drawn-out whistles would join the screeching of the birds.

As a barge was making its way before him, slowly advancing upstream, something on it caught his eye. He'd seen barges loaded with sand before, but this one made him think of a long-past incident.

The sand was an unusual yellowish color, similar to the sand he'd seen the only time he'd been in the desert. The package tour hadn't been cheap nor had he been interested in skiing on the dunes, which was what attracted most of the tourists. He'd saved up for a long time for the chance to change his monotonous life, even if only briefly. And the desert had seemed as different as he could get from his daily surroundings.

As soon as he got there, however, harsh reality dispelled his idealized notions. During the day, it was too insufferably hot to stay outside very long. He'd never been able to stand the heat, and the sun there was really scorching. It wasn't much better after the sun went down. The temperature would drop all of a sudden and he had carelessly forgotten to bring any warm clothes.

So, once again he was in prison. This time, however, it was an opulent one, so spending the whole day there was bearable. In the beginning he'd tried to find a kindred spirit among the hotel guests who didn't go out much either, but he'd never been good at connecting with people.

As though suspecting he wouldn't find the hoped-for company, he'd brought more than enough books for two weeks. He read in the foyer the first few days and then withdrew to his room after accidentally discovering a feature that was not mentioned in the hotel brochures.

He'd opened the large refrigerator in his room out of curiosity, not in order to take something. The tour guide had warned them of the high price of everything inside. He was curious to see what could be so expensive. He didn't see anything special, but he did hear something exceptional.

He had no idea there were refrigerators that played music. As soon as he opened the door, the sound of a saxophone rang out. His eyes swept over the brightly lit interior, but couldn't make out the speakers. The music seemed to come from all around him.

The saxophone was his favorite instrument. He'd even tried to play it, but turned out to be untalented. He had a lot of saxophone music in his collection. His time in the safe-deposit room would have been much more bearable if the bank's management had let him listen to it, even through earphones. But they wouldn't let him do that either.

He realized after the first notes that the saxophonist was a true maestro. But he couldn't quite recognize him or the composition he was playing. How strange. The bank clerk had been convinced that saxophone music held no secrets from him.

He surrendered to the music, enthralled. A full ten minutes passed before he closed the door, feeling guilty. He couldn't keep the refrigerator door open just to listen to the saxophone. The things inside that were supposed to be kept at a low temperature would warm up. They might present him with a huge bill for the spoiled food.

Then it occurred to him that he might be able to listen to the refrigerator music on one of the music channels available to the guests. He went to the console next to the bed and checked it out, but none of the channels had any saxophone. He went back to the refrigerator and opened it. The same instrument was still playing.

He closed the door again, then went to the armchair by the window and tried to read, but couldn't concentrate on the book. Knowing he was just a few steps from enchanting saxophone music that he couldn't listen to filled him with frustration.

He finally got up, went to the refrigerator and turned the cooling knob all the way up, then left the door ajar. The room had air conditioning, so the food and beverages inside wouldn't warm up. And it was enough to hear the divine sound.

His sojourn in the desert hotel turned out to be pleasanter than he'd expected after realizing he'd be without company. He took great pleasure in reading to the accompaniment of the splendid refrigerator music. Whoever had selected it must have been a saxophone fan too. Not a single other instrument was to be heard. Could he have wished for anything better?

He thought for a moment of inquiring about it at the reception desk. He wanted to add the compositions he'd heard to his collection. But he held back. What if the whole idea was for the refrigerator to play only when the door was opened to take something out? He hadn't caused any harm by keeping the door constantly ajar, but they might reproach him for it. There'd be no trouble tracking down what he had heard when he got home. He had a good memory for music.

But when he got back, he made absolutely no effort to track down the music and practically halved his collection. He sold all the records with even a hint of saxophone music.

None of this would have happened if the tour guide hadn't gone from passenger to passenger in the airplane on the way home and asked for their impressions. The unsuspecting bank clerk highly praised the refrigerator music. After a quick verification, it turned out that the refrigerators of all the other guests had been silent.

Then the tour guide remembered something that might have been connected to the mysterious phenomenon, although it wasn't clear how. There had been a saxophone player among the last group of tourists. He'd stayed in the same room as the bank clerk. Nothing set him apart in any way until just before they went back. For some unexplained reason, he'd spent the whole night in the refrigerator. The strangest thing about it was that he hadn't caught cold, even though the temperature was only four degrees.

The sand-filled barge had already gone around the bend in the river when the bank clerk remembered something else. This time he couldn't figure out what had brought that even more distant event to mind. It had nothing to do with what was before his eyes or with the previous recollection. But who can say what kindles our memory?

He'd just been hired by the bank. Spending his days in the safe-deposit room was still bearable. He'd been in the small men's room when the red light suddenly went on that signaled a robbery was taking place. He hurried to pull up his pants and leave, but the lights went out before he managed to do so. He was terrified when a burst of gunfire echoed from above, only slightly dampened by the thick walls.

He decided to stay in the men's room. If the robbers were to break into the safe-deposit room, he'd be better off out of their way. They might not check whether anyone was in the small side room.

His knees turned to jelly when he soon heard voices through the door. He crouched next to the toilet bowl, paying no attention to the fact that he looked ridiculous even to himself in that position. Stock-still, he listened intently, expecting to hear the sound of forced entry, perhaps even an explosion. But silence was all that came from the main safe-deposit room.

Had the robbers gotten hold of the keys? No, it would have been impossible to open the boxes and take out the valuables without a sound. He finally got up and carefully put his ear to the door, then jumped when he soon heard two voices: a young woman's and an older man's.

He was quickly relieved when he grasped from what they were saying that they were hostages, not robbers. Just as he was opening the door, he realized that it was better not to give himself away. If he joined them, he'd become a hostage too and wouldn't be able to help them. He pulled the door to but didn't close it, so he would have no trouble listening.

Although the circumstances didn't warrant it, the conversation started to amuse him. The young woman seemed more level-headed than the middle-aged man who didn't even try to hide his fear. She calmed him down and comforted him, mocking him gently. The bank clerk barely restrained his laughter on two or three occasions, mindful at the same time that he could be a candidate for mockery as well.

The young woman had just started a story about a strange bet, when he suddenly had a vision. At first he thought the lights had gone back on, but if that were the case he would have seen the slightly opened door in front of him and not the sandy beach of a tropical sea with the sound of slow, rolling waves.

The sight was so convincing that it seemed as though all he had to do was take a step to reach the beach. As he stared ahead in confusion, someone got there first. Like an actress entering a shot, a young woman in a yellow bathing suit with long brown hair appeared from outside his field of vision and headed for the water. Her bare feet left footprints in the soft sand.

He wasn't at all surprised when he recognized her immediately. It could only be the young woman whose voice, now muffled and unintelligible, could still be heard from the room next door. He didn't agonize over the pointless issue of how he could recognize someone he'd never seen. Worrying about something so inconsequential seemed absurd just then.

Captivated, he watched her go up to the water. She stopped a moment at the drift line on the sand. Although he couldn't see her face, he suspected that she was smiling as she watched the play of the sea as it advanced and withdrew. He reached for her, but didn't have the strength to touch her.

Then she came towards him of her own accord. She entered the water slowly, stopping every so often, as though still uncertain whether to surrender to it completely. She stopped when the water reached the top part of her swimsuit, arms outstretched just above the surface. She seemed to be having second thoughts as to whether she should turn and go back.

She didn't do so, but she also didn't do what seemed like the only other possibility. Instead of swimming, she continued to walk along the bottom until she went all the way under. Brown locks undulated briefly on the surface and then nothing disturbed the water but the waves.

The bank clerk wasn't worried at first. He liked to swim underwater a bit too before he broke to the surface. But time passed and the young woman didn't surface. When he finally understood that she never would, he went completely numb. Several long moments passed before he realized that he couldn't just stand there and watch.

Instead of rushing after her without further ado, he first had to struggle with the predilection for neatness that urged him to take his suit off first. He would ruin it if he went into the water. But there was no more time for such considerations. It would be too late if he hesitated even in the slightest.

Only a short stretch of sand separated him from the sea, but as soon as he walked towards it, the vision vanished, leaving him alone in the dark again. Instead of his foot finding the sand, it hit the door. The female voice fell silent in the safe-deposit room. Dead quiet reigned for a while, full of intent listening.

The bank clerk finally sighed with relief when the talking resumed. He closed the door as quietly as possible and sat on the lowered toilet seat. A horde of questions swarmed through his head, but none was important compared to his one desire. He had to see the young woman.

No opportunity arose. It took another hour-and-a-half for the police finally to enter the safe-deposit room and free the hostages. He didn't come out of the men's room right away because he wasn't sure what was happening. When he finally came out, they'd already taken away the young woman and middle-aged man.

He couldn't risk asking the police or bank management about her. He wouldn't be able to give a convincing explanation as to why he was interested. If he'd mentioned the vision he had seen in the darkness, he certainly would have lost his job. How could the bank entrust the care of the safe-deposit boxes to an employee in a dubious mental state?

Although he'd always preferred vacations in the mountains, now he started spending them at the seaside. He looked like a man who could never settle down on a beach. He'd spend a little while among the bathers, looking around keenly, and when he didn't see the brown-haired young woman in a yellow bathing suit, he'd head for the next beach.

The futility of this search had long been clear to him. If he hadn't been so dedicated to it, he might have found a partner and spent his life differently, but what use was it since he couldn't stop? He coped somehow with his fate, although his blood pressure had risen with the passing years. Now, however, as he stared dully at the river empty of barges, for the first time he felt himself collapsing under the weight of the past. Even if he were to find the young woman now, would it make any sense?

What stretched before him in the short time he had left was completely devoid of hope: tedious days in the safe-deposit prison and lonely nights in the prison of an empty home. The moments of freedom by the river would be less and less sufficient to mitigate his agony. Why sink into that abyss when the path to deliverance stood open before him? The young woman had shown him this long ago. It was only a few steps to the shore.

But before he managed to stand up, an elderly woman in a green coat, pillbox hat and shoes stopped in front of the bench. Lost in his memories, he paid no attention to the rare strollers on the quay. Why didn't she walk on? He didn't want any eyewitnesses.

"Do you know the temperature of the water, by any chance?" she asked with a little smile, motioning her head towards the water.

"No, I don't. Probably low."

"It shouldn't be more than seven degrees. With the onset of winter, it will go even lower."

"It's cold everywhere in winter, even in the water."

"That's right. Although that's usually not borne in mind."

"Who would care about it? No one swims in the river in winter."

"Some oddballs even break the ice so they can go swimming. But they know what's in store for them, so they prepare properly. The problem is with those who go into the river totally unawares."

"Are there people like that?"

"Oh, yes. Suicides, for example."

The bank clerk looked at the woman again for a few moments in silence.

"Suicides?" he repeated softly. "Why would it make any difference to them?"

"They don't think it makes any difference either until they step into the water. A lot of them hesitate, though, as soon as the icy water touches their skin."

"That means they aren't determined enough."

"Yes, they are, but they're sensitive to the cold. Here, take the case of the man who owned a flower shop who simply couldn't get over the loss of his library in a flood."

"And that's why he decided to kill himself? Couldn't he just buy the books he'd lost?"

"Booklovers often become attached to one specific copy. They wouldn't accept even a copy of the same edition as a replacement."

"I wasn't aware of that."

"The florist decided to drown himself in a river so he'd die just like his books. Unfortunately, it was late fall like now."

"He could have postponed the whole thing until warmer weather came."

"Suicides are renowned for their impatience. And their persistence. The florist made all of sixteen attempts."

"Why did he need so many?"

"He was getting used to the cold water. He would go in deeper each time. On the sixteenth time, the water finally reached his head."

"And he drowned?"

"No. He was so proud of overcoming his sensitivity to the cold that he started to swim instead of drowning. He even swam across the river twice. When he got out, he was filled with a passion to live. The thought of suicide was the farthest thing from his mind. To assuage his grumbling conscience, he placed a commemorative plaque to the drowned books in his flower shop."

"Icy water doesn't have to be lethal, it seems."

"It doesn't. But water in a glass might be."

"If it's dirty?"

"Not only in that way. Even the cleanest is dangerous if drunk to excess."

"I didn't know that either. How much would you have to drink to do yourself in?"

"It depends on your build. A former wrestler, a really large man, didn't die until the eleventh glass."

"Why on earth did he drink them? Was he mourning a book collection too?"

"No, he was playing cards with friends, but not for money. The one with the worst hand would drink a glass of water."

"How peculiar."

"Wrestlers have always lived in a world of their own."

"Lady luck must've turned her back on the poor guy if he had the worst hand eleven times in a row."

"No, she didn't. He only had bad cards the first three times. After that he had the strongest hand."

"So why did he keep on drinking water?"

"Because of his new sight."

"New sight?"

"Yes. After the third glass he suddenly seemed to be able to see his friends' thoughts. They appeared before him clearly."

"Unbelievable. Maybe they put something in his water to daze him."

"No, they didn't. There were unopened bottles of mineral water at the beginning of the card game. Others drank the same water later on without any consequences."

"Even so, why didn't he stop? He certainly must have felt distressed before the eleventh glass."

"Even the third one was a problem. Instead, he kept pretending he had the worst cards so he could drink. He was so thrilled to be able to read others' thoughts. Before he died he quarreled with all his friends. It seems they didn't have a very high opinion of him."

"He didn't have to kill himself to find that out. Most friends are two-faced."

"That's right. But you're mistaken if you think the reason for that suicide is unusual. Some are a lot more bizarre."

"You're a real anthology of suicide stories."

"You might say so. I'll tell you about one exceptional case, if you like."

The bank clerk glanced at the water with a flock of cawing crows circling above it, against the leaden sky.

"Please sit down," he said, indicating the free part of the bench and rising slightly. "It's just the right time for cheerful stories."

∽ 8 ∾

The retired botanist would have tolerated old age better if his movement hadn't been restricted. Because of a weak heart, no longer could he spend hours every day wandering through the countryside, as he had most of his life. For him, being confined to the house was like undeserved punishment.

He did have a little garden, but in it he felt like a reader who has only one small book left from an enormous library and it's one he's read over and over. But then he remembered that the town had its own small library made up of plants.

The botanical garden hadn't occurred to him right away because he didn't like visiting it. His aversion dated back to when he was a student. Even though it was a useful place for educational purposes, he found it artificial. Such orderliness went against the essential chaos of the plant world.

But now he could no longer choose. He dropped by the botanical garden from time to time, leaning on the cane he'd made for himself before he stopped going into the forest. He tried to ignore the benches and low lights along the asphalted paths so he wouldn't feel he was in a park.

He couldn't figure out what an orange plastic fence was doing in the middle of a side path until he got right up next to it. It was placed around a square hole resembling a shaft that was at least a meter-and-a-half deep.

He stood there a few moments, staring down, wondering why it had been dug right here. He looked around, but there was no one nearby to ask. He shrugged his shoulders and was just about to continue his walk, when he suddenly remembered something. His eyes returned to the pit, as though looking into the abyss of time past.

It was his only trip to the jungle. Everything he'd previously learned about the plant kingdom could not compare with the profusion he found there. He set to work without hesitation, having only three weeks at his disposal, while not even an entire lifetime would have been enough to research this lushness in detail.

Filled with enthusiasm, he'd just waved his hand dismissively when warned about the danger lurking in the wild. Besides, he was supposed to spend most of his time in the tops of the huge trees where it would much safer than on the ground. And indeed, until just before the end of his stay he only spotted large game twice, but they paid no attention to him.

And then, on the afternoon of his penultimate day, a noise suddenly echoed from the tangled undergrowth beneath him. Two young women were running from something that was chasing them. A huge gorilla appeared a moment later. The botanist was totally confounded. He had to find some way to help the young women, but didn't know how. If he'd listened to the advice and carried a gun, he could have fired a shot in the air.

But then came an unexpected turn. The young women disappeared before his eyes, as though swallowed up by the earth. It took him a few moments to realize that this was exactly what had happened. They'd fallen into a hole that couldn't be seen from above because it was covered by fallen branches.

Under other circumstances, this would have been very bad luck, since the hole was deep and hard to get out of. Now, however, it saved them from the gorilla that couldn't reach them. And the botanist didn't have to get involved anymore. At least not for the moment.

Without giving himself away, he observed what was happening under the treetop. He feared that the gorilla would think of a way to get down into the hole. Primates are clever. But instead, it did something quite unexpected. It started picking fruit and threw it at the young women.

The gorilla spent hours next to the pit. Then, for no reason, it got up and disappeared into the underbrush. Fearing that it was still somewhere nearby, the botanist didn't dare risk calling out to the young women.

After a while, one of them mustered the courage to try and get out. It wasn't an easy matter and she was quite bruised when she finally reached the surface. She took a quick look around, clearly searching for something to use to help her girlfriend out, but when she found nothing suitable in the surroundings, she left too.

Reassured, the botanist had just opened his mouth to address the young woman in the hole, when he heard her talking to someone. Since there was no other voice, he thought at first that she had called someone by radio. Then he wondered why she hadn't done that a lot sooner. And a radio most likely wouldn't work underground.

Was she talking to herself? She was frightened of being alone, and this was a way to raise her spirits. He couldn't make out the muffled words. He would only alarm her even more if he came forward now. Better to wait for her girlfriend to come back.

She soon arrived, dragging a long liana. She lowered it into the hole, but the young woman refused to come out. It soon transpired that what was keeping her down there wasn't her fear of the gorilla but the conversation she'd just had. So she hadn't been talking to herself or someone on the radio.

The botanist mechanically withdrew deeper into the leaves when he heard the young woman in the hole tell her friend that she had been talking to God. He'd been wise not to give himself away. Seeing the huge primate had frightened him, but it hadn't caused a shudder to run down his spine, as now.

The young woman standing above the hole said nothing in return, as though hearing something commonplace. She put the liana aside and started gathering dry twigs. Soon a little fire was burning next to the opening. This cheered the botanist since dusk was starting to fall. The flames would ward off the predators that were now on the hunt.

The young woman soon lay down next to the fire on a bed of leaves. Watching her fall asleep, the botanist was in two minds. He would rather wait for her to fall deeply asleep, then quietly descend and get away from there, but it was neither easy nor safe to move through the jungle at night. He was a good two-and-a-half kilometers from the camp. It might be smarter to wait for them to come after him. They were probably already on the way. He hadn't ever stayed in the jungle this long.

Then something happened that made him change his mind. The other young woman started to come up out of the hole. There had been no sound to herald this. At first it seemed like a silent apparition. She emerged without the slightest effort, as though standing on a platform that was elevating her.

When she was all the way out, the botanist felt another shudder. There was no support under the young woman's feet. She stood there a few moments without moving, standing on air, and then walked onto the ground and left the small illuminated circle around the fire.

Disregarding the noise he made by breaking branches, the botanist rushed down the tree and ran in the other direction. Had he turned around, he would have had his final surprise. The young woman next to the fire was sleeping soundly as though surrounded by the silence of the grave.

His colleagues who had gone in search of him found him about a kilometer-and-a-half from the camp, all distraught and scratched by the underbrush he'd gone through. Once he had regained command of himself, he told them that he'd been treed by a gorilla that wouldn't leave until dark.

He made no mention of the young women. The next day he left the jungle and never returned.

Now he glanced up at the spruce tree not far from the hole on the garden's path. He tapped the plastic fence lightly and was just about to go around it and continue his walk, when another memory stopped him. What made me think of that long-ago event, he wondered. It had nothing to do with the incident in the jungle.

He'd had an adventurous spirit as a boy and liked to investigate places that were hard to reach or forbidden. Rarely did his friends have enough courage to go along with him. He hadn't been able to convince a single one to join him on a visit to the winery being renovated on the edge of town.

In the evening after the workers had gone, he'd had no trouble entering the building without being noticed by the sleepy guard. He wandered around the wine-making machinery on the ground floor for a while. Large tarpaulins covered everything as protection from the renovation work.

As soon as he entered the cellar, a huge barrel at the end of a long corridor caught his eye. It rose from floor to ceiling and was completely new, unlike most of the other barrels. The scattered carpentry tools at the base indicated that they had put it together there because it couldn't be brought in whole.

A tall ladder was leaning against the front. He climbed up to the square opening on the top. All he could see when he looked inside was the top of another ladder that led into the pitch dark. He hesitated a minute, then went down.

A few minutes later he decided to go back because he couldn't see the nose on his face down there. But just as he put his foot on the first rung, voices came from outside. Someone else was in the cellar. He moved away from the ladder quietly and started to listen intently.

He hoped they were just workers who'd come back for something they'd forgotten. When he heard someone climbing up the outside ladder, he stretched his hands out in front of him and quickly retreated as far as possible from the opening. He didn't want to trip over some invisible obstacle and give himself away. As it was, he still had a chance to escape their notice even if they came down with flashlights. When he reached the back wall of the barrel he squatted down.

Two men started climbing down, but without any kind of light. When they hit the bottom, someone closed the top up above. That's when he grew frightened. What were these two intending to do in the total darkness? He listened intently, but all he could make out was that they'd sat down on the bottom of the barrel.

Protracted silence caused the fear inside him to grow. He couldn't think of a single way to get out of the barrel, and didn't dare make his presence known. All he could do was wait for something to happen.

He sighed with relief when the men finally began to talk. He recognized the voices of the town's pharmacist and butcher. From their angry conversation he soon understood that some sort of crazy drunken bet had brought them to the barrel. Both of them regretted it, but neither one wanted to concede and be the first to leave.

If he didn't want to stay with them in the barrel indefinitely, he would have to speak up. He smiled maliciously at the thought of their alarm when he called out to them. Too bad he wouldn't be able to see their faces in the dark.

The darkness, however, didn't stop him from seeing something else. At first he thought that one of the two adults had turned on a weak purple light. But the bright circle was some distance from where their voices could be heard. It was also strange that they kept on talking, as though not noticing anything.

The little circle started to expand, changing shape. He didn't realize it was a bud until it began to open. He'd seen such accelerated growth in a documentary film on television where a blossom had transformed into an orchid in just a few moments. He didn't recognize the flower that was now before him, but marveled at its beauty.

He stared spellbound at the round purplish petals opening up in the gloom. They were as airy as lace, so his eyes could pierce all the way to the heart of the flower. Something was pulsating gently there, causing the light to brighten and soften. It seemed as though the slightest puff of air could harm that fragile structure.

There weren't any air currents in the barrel, but there were loud guffaws. The butcher laughed derisively at one of the pharmacist's remarks, making the flower tremble at the sound. For a moment it looked as though it would regain its balance, but then it lost it completely.

Petals began to fall off and fade. As the flickering heart went out, it was increasingly laid bare. When it was completely exposed, the radiance suddenly brightened, as though a tiny sun were glowing in the middle of the barrel. It went out the very next moment, leaving behind an ever-weakening apparition.

Watching in disbelief as the purple spots retreated into the oncoming darkness, the first thing he felt was anger coursing through him. He clenched his fists, determined to pounce on the butcher. No, on both of them. They were equally to blame for the flower's disappearance.

But he held back. It was hard to carry out an attack in the dark, and what use would it be anyway? Nothing would return. He was suddenly aware of the painful void left behind by the flower. Uncharacteristically for his age, he longed to join it in nothingness.

The darkness thwarted this as well. He kept squatting dully against the back wall and put his hands firmly over his ears so he didn't have to listen to their stupid conversation. A long time passed before he put down his benumbed hands. Now he heard snoring instead of words. Moving carefully, he felt for the ladder and crept out of the barrel.

Even before he left the winery he knew what he would do when he grew up. Only as a botanist could he dare hope to see the purple flower again.

The futility of that hope now came crashing down on him. His whole life suddenly seemed meaningless. It had certainly had its good sides, but what difference did it make when his greatest aspiration had never been fulfilled? His time still had not run out, but how could he find in this tiny library what he hadn't been able to find in the great world treasury of botanical books?

The urge he'd felt only once before in the great barrel now came over him again. Darkness did not stand in his way this time. And there was no dilemma as to how to carry it out. As an experienced botanist, he knew which plants and berries to choose.

"Perfect, isn't it?"

A voice snapped him out of his reverie. As he stared at the hole, he hadn't noticed the elderly lady in a green coat and matching shoes and pillbox hat who'd come up to him and stopped on the other side of the plastic fence.

"Excuse me?"

She gestured broadly at the surrounding vegetation.

"If someone needed poison, this would be the right place."

"Poison?" he asked, squinting.

"Yes. A botanical garden is like an herb pharmacy with no one in charge. Anyone can come in and take the poison they need."

"It's not quite that simple. You have to know a thing or two about poison. There aren't any bottles here with labels saying what they contain."

"That's right. It was this lack of knowledge that gave a miner terrible trouble. Have you heard about his case?"

The botanist shook his head.

"No, I haven't."

"He spent his whole life underground and this led to a host of diseases. They might not have endangered his life, but they certainly made it miserable. He decided to end his life to spare himself further suffering."

"With poison?"

"Yes. He abhorred violent suicides. He wanted the whole thing to be easy and painless."

"Not all poisons work like that."

"He didn't know that. He thought all he had to do was go into the forest, eat the first mushroom he found and drop dead."

"That might have happened too."

"What happened was just the opposite."

"Opposite?"

"Yes. He ate a mushroom he found at the foot of an oak. Instead of poisoning him, while he was still in the forest he noticed that his attacks of asthma were subsiding. When he reached home, they'd stopped completely."

"Unbelievable."

"That was just the beginning. He went back into the forest day after day, determined to carry out his plan at all costs, but every time he came back with one disease less. In the end he recovered completely."

"Did he remember which mushrooms he had eaten?"

"No. They all looked the same to him."

"Too bad. He might have hit a goldmine."

"The money wouldn't have done him much good."

"Why?"

"He was poisoned soon after he got well."

"What poisoned him?"

"Mushrooms were to blame after all, but not those he'd found in the forest. He bought them at the supermarket. A very poisonous one had found its way into the package. He died as soon as he took a bite."

"He could have been spared such a fate if he'd known more about mushrooms."

"Not even those who know all the secrets of the plant world are spared from affliction. An herbalist, for example."

"What could happen to an herbalist?"

"He was famous for his longevity tea. All those who drank it truly lived to a ripe old age."

"I can believe that. Herbalists know how to make miraculous teas."

"The tea was indeed miraculous, but it had a dark side."

"What kind of dark side?"

"The herbalist discovered it by accident. He kept on experimenting, adding new ingredients to make the tea as effective as possible. He would always try it first."

"Not all herbalists would do that."

"This one was honorable. It was his honor that finally did him in."

"How could he be harmed by honor?"

"After he put the new herb in the tea and drank it, he became very sleepy."

"That's not unusual. Some herbs put you to sleep."

"He had an unusual dream. The spirits of all those who'd died young appeared to him."

"Some plants cause hallucinations."

"These were very convincing. The spirits blamed him for their early death."

"How could he be blamed for that?"

"The time he gave to others with his tea had been taken away from them."

"Similar nonsense appears in dreams even without the help of plants."

"He believed this one. His conscience was unbearably guilty."

"I thought that herbalists were more level-headed."

"He thought he was very level-headed when he drank all the remaining stock of tea."

"What was that supposed to get him?"

"Isn't it obvious? Not to allow the longevity of some to be paid for by the foreshortened lives of others."

"It would've been better if he'd destroyed the tea. This way, he certainly must have been sick to his stomach if the stock was large."

"What happened to him was much worse than an upset stomach. The more tea he drank, the older he got. He died at a very old age as he drank the last cup with a shaking hand."

"Hogwash. That's impossible."

"If that seems far-fetched to you, what would you say to an even stranger case?"

"You mean there's something more far-fetched than that?"

"Oh, yes. Considerably."

"One would say that stories about suicide attract you."

"They're irresistible. Shall I tell it to you?"

The botanist looked into the hole, then at the surrounding vegetation.

"If you really want to."

∽ 9 ∾

The watchmaker looked through the window of the slow-moving city bus. The morning traffic jam was getting worse and worse. The trip from the stop near his apartment to the watchmaker's shop used to take just fifteen minutes. Now he was lucky if he traversed the same distance in three times as long.

Indeed, he didn't have to go to work in the morning anymore. He could wait for the rush hour to pass or not go at all. Eleven-and-a-half months ago he'd retired and sold his shop. Now it held a little café-bar. But he hadn't been able to change the habits of almost fifty years.

As though still going to work, he reached the café-bar a little before nine. There weren't many customers there at that time of day so the table in the corner where the shop counter used to be was usually free. He sat there and ordered the green tea he had always made for himself every morning as soon as he got to the shop.

He took a gold watch out of his vest pocket and put it on the table. He didn't do it to see the time since he was no longer in a hurry. But he would consider himself somehow incomplete if he didn't have a watch in front of him. Too bad there was no reason to open it up and tinker a bit inside. The watch had worked impeccably for decades.

He stayed in the café-bar until noon, reading the newspaper. Then he took a long walk. He didn't go home until the evening traffic jam was in full swing. He could have avoided it by heading back earlier, but habit prevailed there too.

His walks were not without purpose. He made the rounds of the watchmakers' shops in the center. He'd stop for a while in front of each of the eighteen shop windows and have a look. He didn't go inside. He used to know all the watchmakers in town, but as the years passed, his contemporaries became fewer and farther between, and he hadn't clicked with the younger generation.

In his day, watchmaker shop windows had remained unchanged for a long time, but now they kept up with the other windows. He noticed something new in them almost every day. Although he didn't approve of this faddishness, searching for the changes started to amuse him. He still had an excellent memory, so he had no trouble detecting them.

This game had recently spread to the watchmakers' shops outside the center of town. Owing to the slow movement of the bus, he had time to get a good look at four shop windows as he passed by.

The shops on the outskirts seemed to be even more impetuous in their window dressing. Objects appeared with increasing frequency whose connection to measuring time was difficult to grasp. What were they thinking of by putting a stuffed pheasant, snow shovel or pirate doll among the watches?

What he'd just seen outdid all the rest. Completely astounded, he decided to get out at the next stop, go back to the shop and sharply reprimand the owner. This wasn't just about him. He'd shamed the entire guild. Indeed, what would people think when they saw a large wine barrel in a watchmaker's window? Was the conclusion that they were all lushes?

Just as he started to get up, a sudden memory held him back. Many years ago, while he was still an apprentice watchmaker, he'd seen a barrel like that. But there hadn't been a drop of alcohol in it.

He'd stopped by a pharmacy to buy some cough syrup. The young pharmacy assistant asked him to wait a minute. He had to go to the basement storeroom to get some more since they'd run out upstairs.

Ten minutes later when the pharmacist still hadn't returned, he was uncertain what to do, since it didn't seem very polite just to leave. He was in a hurry, though, and couldn't wait much longer. In the end he decided to go and look for the pharmacy assistant.

He called out from the door that led to the basement, but no one answered. Slowly, he went down the stairs. The storeroom was well-lit, but there was no sign of the young man. He searched for a side room, but saw neither doors nor windows.

He stood at the bottom of the stairs for a while, puzzled, then shrugged his shoulders and started to go back up. Suddenly he heard some sort of mumbling behind him. He turned around, but couldn't figure out where the sound was coming from. After listening intently for a few moments, he stared at a barrel standing in the middle of the basement.

He went up to it cautiously, put his ear against the bulging slats of wood and then jerked back when he heard the assistant's voice. It was muffled, but didn't sound agitated. He seemed to be talking to someone, but the other person's voice couldn't be heard.

Questions started to swarm through his head. What on earth was the pharmacist doing in a barrel? Had something happened to him? Had he hurt himself and was now delirious? Although he would have preferred to make a hasty exit, he had to come to the man's assistance if he was in trouble.

He raised the lid cautiously and fixed his eyes on the impossible. The barrel was filled to the brim with thick brown syrup and the pharmacist was completely immersed in it. There was no way he could breathe, let alone speak, but now his words could be heard more distinctly.

Feeling every single hair on his body stand on end, he closed the barrel with a bang and rushed out of the basement, taking three steps at a time. He didn't stop until he was out in the street and had closed the door behind him.

He stood with his back to it as though he wanted to prevent anyone else from leaving the pharmacy. But he didn't stay there long. The sound of the door being locked from the inside made him jump back and dash down the street as fast as his legs could carry him.

He paid no attention to the curious looks of the passers-by, nor did he ever tell anyone what had happened in the pharmacy. Luckily, he didn't have to go back there again because he soon finished his apprenticeship and moved to the big city.

He hadn't thought of that event in a long time. Turning around, he took another look at the watchmaker's window, since the bus hadn't gone very far from it. There was still enough time to head for the door and get out at the next stop as planned, but a second look at the barrel brought another unexpected memory that kept him in his seat, as had the first one.

This was strange because he couldn't see any connection between the barrel and the incident in the elevator dating back more than a quarter of a century. But the paths of remembrance are sometimes hard to fathom.

He had several privileged customers whose expensive watches he picked up for their annual service and then returned in person. One was the president of a reputable pharmaceutical company.

He entered the elevator of the tall building that housed the company headquarters and pushed the button for the seventeenth floor. But he had only got as far as the eleventh when the power was cut. He was alone in the pitch blackness.

He wasn't too annoyed at this bad luck. The president wasn't waiting for him at any fixed time. He actually wouldn't even see his prominent customer. He would leave the watch with his secretary and take the money. It made no difference when he got there.

He expected the power to come back on quickly, but fifteen minutes later he realized that this must be a serious breakdown. He hesitated over whether to remain standing or sit on the floor, which seemed clean enough as far as he could tell. He was already starting to sit down when something happened that made him stand up straight.

At first he thought someone had turned on an auxiliary power source. But before he even managed to wonder why it hadn't been turned on as soon as the power was cut, he realized that it was something else. But he couldn't imagine what it was.

Numbers were flashing at head height. Their red glow seemed to cut through the soft darkness. He stared for several long moments before he realized what in other circumstances would have been immediately obvious.

Shining before him was the day's date. It was like looking at the large digital display on the main city square, but this date didn't alternate between the time and temperature. It was fixed, as though announcing something very important.

But its steady state didn't last long. First the numbers indicating the day started to change. They advanced slowly at first, then faster and faster. One change necessarily brought a second and a third as the days changed the months and the months changed the years.

The speed of the change soon made it impossible to read the numbers of the days. It was even hard to follow the changing months. He concentrated solely on the years because that change was the slowest. He stared spellbound, without even trying to understand.

The red calendar stopped as suddenly as it had started. The date that it now showed was almost twenty-six years in the future. He had no chance to try and decipher the new riddle because the numbers started to fade and then disappeared almost completely. He didn't know for sure whether they were still there or whether what he could still see was their afterimage.

He started when he suddenly heard voices in the elevator. He looked intently at the opposite wall from which they were coming, but couldn't see anything. Not knowing what else to do, he began to listen.

The younger man, who was nervous, was rushing to an important meeting. The older man tried to calm him down and suggested that he sit next to him on the floor while they waited for the power to return. The younger man refused, not wanting to soil his expensive suit. The older man then offered to tell him the story of a similar incident in the dark. The younger man grudgingly agreed.

The watchmaker didn't have a chance to hear the story too because the calendar suddenly flashed again and the older man's voice went silent at the same moment. The red glow softly illuminated the only passenger in the elevator.

The numbers changed again as before, racing towards the future, and then started to slow down. Soon the days could be distinguished. The watchmaker was suddenly filled with fear at the new halt.

But there wasn't any. The lights suddenly came back on. At the same time the elevator shuddered and continued its climb. The watchmaker stared blankly ahead all the way to the seventeenth floor. Although nothing remained in the space that had just held the calendar, it seemed that the last date still hung there.

When he soon handed the watch to the secretary, he told her he was sorry but he would no longer be able to pick it up and deliver it personally. He'd be happy to keep on servicing it if someone brought it to his shop. He felt easier when the dispassionate woman didn't ask for an explanation.

The fear that had crept into the watchmaker in the elevator settled in his soul for good. He told himself soberly not to attach any importance to what he'd seen, that various apparitions can seem to manifest in the dark, but this did not dispel his unease. The last date on the calendar before the power returned and scattered it hung over him like an ominous cloud.

The cloud didn't plague him during the day, but it pressed against him periodically when he woke up in the middle of the night. That is when dark thoughts usually visited him and refused to let him go back to sleep until dawn. It wasn't so much the thought that the last date could be his last date too. There had to be some last date, after all. What caused his anxiety was the feeling of helplessness in the face of predestination.

He felt he had been snared by fate with no choice but to wait for the last date to arrive, like someone sentenced to death waits for the sentence to be carried out, not counting on a last-minute pardon. While that date was far away, the anxiety had been easier to bear. The closer it got, the harder it became to be wakened before dawn.

And then, as he was still looking out the bus window, it suddenly crossed his mind that there actually was a way out of the trap. A very simple way. How strange that he hadn't thought of it before.

He touched the small revolver in the carrying case under his arm. He'd bought it back when two shops in his neighborhood had been robbed. Luckily, he'd never had to use it. Watchmakers' shops weren't very high up on robbers' lists. He had had no reason to carry it after he retired, but habit prevailed there as well.

This was the only way to turn the tables on predestination. Even if nothing were to happen on the last date, suicide still made sense. What was the use of spending such monotonous, empty days, with no hope of anything changing in the future? He'd been trying in vain to revive the past that was gone for all time.

He didn't think twice about where he'd shoot himself. His old shop was the perfect place. He'd drink some green tea, read the newspaper a little, then go to the men's room. He felt sorry for the new owner who'd been attentive towards him from the very beginning. A suicide would certainly be no recommendation for his café-bar. But it would soon be forgotten. Life has no time for death.

He raised his head and looked forwards. He'd always put up patiently with the bus's slow progress through the traffic. Now, for the first time, he was filled with impatience.

"Traffic jams like this make you want to kill yourself, don't they?"

Staring out the window, he hadn't noticed the passenger sitting next to him. He glanced hastily at the elderly woman in a green coat and pillbox hat of the same color.

"I suppose more serious reasons are needed for suicide," he replied, turning forward again.

"Not necessarily. People kill themselves for all kinds of reasons. Not all of them are serious. What would you say, for example, about a colonel in the medical corps who decided to kill himself because while he was on maneuvers, his orderly lost a rabbit he was particularly fond of?"

"He should have killed the orderly."

"He sent him before the military court. But that didn't bring the rabbit back. He couldn't get over the loss. Suicide was the only way out. It turned out, however, to be a hard thing to do."

"What's so hard about it? At least officers are armed."

"Yes, they are, but the colonel was a poor shot and plagued by bad luck."

"Even the poorest shot wouldn't be able to miss himself."

"Ah, you're wrong. The colonel managed three whole times. The first time he put the gun to his temple, his hand was shaking."

"A real colonel, that's for sure."

"Most of the medical corps is like that. They rarely handle arms. The bullet took off half his right ear."

"I guess he was more skilled at medical work than shooting."

"That's right. Even though he was wounded, he gave himself first aid. On the second try, the bullet got stuck in the barrel. The gun went off, however, as he was clumsily trying to dislodge it. The bullet hit him in the heel."

"He really was out of luck."

"Wait until you hear what happened the third time. He'd caught cold on maneuvers and sneezed at the very same time he pulled the trigger. He missed his head but blew apart his favorite canary in its cage."

"Someone should've taken away his gun after that. He was a danger to everyone around him."

"He wasn't for very long. In the mental derangement that followed the loss of yet another pet, he went out of the medical corps tent and headed across the field aimlessly. After wandering around in the dark a quarter of an hour he ended up at the training ground where they were practicing nighttime artillery shooting. All they found of him the next day was the bloody dressing he'd used to bandage his ear and heel."

"He should've relied on the artillery right away instead of fooling around with something he wasn't good at."

"Well, if we could only know the outcome in advance. A sergeant taking part in the same maneuvers, for example, couldn't even imagine. His duty was to command the firing squad during executions."

"A military executioner?"

"You might say that. He didn't show the slightest compassion for those who were sentenced to death. He wouldn't give them a last cigarette and always made a scornful remark as he was putting the blindfold over their eyes."

"A real sadist."

"Even more than one would expect from a sergeant. To top it off, he had his picture taken with each of the condemned before he shouted, 'Fire!' He'd put his arm around their shoulders and grin from ear to ear."

"Why did he have his picture taken?"

"As a souvenir. He had an album where he kept the pictures from the executions. He'd bring it out all the time during drinking binges in the officers' mess. He was as proud of the pictures as if they were decorations."

"What a pervert."

"But he got the punishment he deserved. After the twelfth execution, he stopped showing off the album."

"Why's that?"

"No one found out until his suicide note. After pasting in the twelfth picture, his face apparently started to disappear from the previous ones. It disappeared from one picture every day, and his malicious smile shifted to the face of the condemned."

"How can that be?"

"No one ever found out. The album disappeared without a trace. The last paragraph of his letter said that he had to go to the execution wall. That's where he was to meet those he'd sent to their death."

"He'd clearly lost his mind. Maybe his conscience was pricking him?"

"Whatever it was, they found him dead next to the wall. The military investigating commission concluded it was suicide."

"Then that cleared up everything."

"Not quite. It remains a mystery how he could hit

himself in the heart twelve times from a rifle that wasn't even next to him. But the case was closed nonetheless. The army isn't disposed to complicated explanations."

"Unbelievable."

"That's nothing. Some suicides are much more unusual. Would you be interested in hearing about one?"

"No, thank you, I'm getting off at the next stop."

The bus suddenly started braking as it entered an intersection. The next moment a crash rang out from the front.

The woman looked down the aisle between the seats.

"I'm afraid it will be some time before we get to the next stop."

"What happened?" asked the watchmaker, craning his neck to see over the heads of the other passengers.

"We collided with a truck transporting poultry. So, would you like to hear another story about suicides?"

The watchmaker gazed at the smiling woman for a few moments.

"Let's hear it."

The Fourth Loop

I entered the concert hall.

Only the stage was lit, but in the gloom I saw that the seats were empty. There was no one in the audience.

The concert had already started. The conductor was in full swing as he led the symphony orchestra. The hall had very good acoustics. Even here at the entrance I seemed to be in the midst of the musicians.

I dropped into the nearest seat. I might have moved up closer if I'd gotten there on time. I usually try to sit as close as possible to the stage at concerts, but even from this position I would hear quite well.

Just as I sat down, the conductor signaled the musicians to stop playing. The hall was filled with silence. The conductor turned around, shaded his eyes with his hand and looked in my direction.

"Oh, madam, you're here! Wonderful, wonderful!"

Thundering applause accompanied him as he descended from the podium, crossed the stage and headed towards the stairs in the corner, then walked briskly up the aisle.

He stopped in front of me and the applause ended that same moment. As I rose from my seat, he stretched out his hands towards me, palms up.

"Welcome! Welcome!" he said, smiling broadly.

I took his hands in mine and returned his smile. We stood there without moving for a few moments, beaming into each other's eyes.

Then the conductor let go of me, stepped back a little and crooked his right arm. Joining him in the aisle, I took his arm. As he led me towards the stage, the musicians stood up and started clapping again.

He gallantly helped me up the four steps, then mounted them in two light bounds. He hastened ahead of me and when we reached the podium, beckoned me up. I had never been up there before; it felt awkward with my back turned to the empty auditorium.

Smiling all the while, the conductor gestured towards me with both hands.

"Our dear guest has finally arrived," he told the orchestra.

The strings began to tap their bows on the music stands while the other musicians stamped their feet on the wooden floor of the stage. The conductor waited a while, then raised his hand and everything quietened down again.

"First we should introduce ourselves, should we not?"

He indicated the closest violinist who stepped forward a little.

"This is our first violin," said the proud conductor. "A real virtuoso."

The violinist bowed.

"Our conductor praises me much more than I deserve. After all, I am just an ordinary surgeon."

"Oh, his well-known modesty! I assure you that he is anything but ordinary. Can you imagine how many successful operations he's performed?"

I shook my head.

"No, I can't."

"Four hundred and sixteen!"

I looked at the violinist in admiration.

"Congratulations!"

The first violin bowed again.

"Thank you!"

"He is particularly skilled at operating on the casualties of traffic accidents. It almost makes you want to have an accident just to come into his hands."

"It's always good to be in the right hands."

"One of his accomplishments has found its way into surgery textbooks. He saved someone who was seriously injured in the collision of two subway trains. It looked like a lost cause. Many surgeons wouldn't have attempted anything. But he did the impossible."

"Excellent."

"Of course, a good professional must have good assistants. Please let me introduce three more of our strings."

Two women and a man stepped before the podium. The conductor indicated the brown-haired woman first.

"Our second violin. Let me tell you openly: if luck hadn't brought us the surgeon, she would already be first violin. It won't be long before she reaches his maestro status. It's rare to see such talent."

"I'm flattered by the conductor's compliments, but am well aware of my faults. I need a lot more time to perfect my technique."

"It's just a question of diligence. And our second violin has no shortage of that. It's thanks to her diligence that she became a brilliant doctor who uses every opportunity to gain precious experience. As a young intern, for example, she assisted the surgeon during that difficult operation."

"She was able to learn a lot there, I'm sure," I said.

"Indeed she was. And these other two strings were also assisting."

His smile embraced a dark-haired woman with a violin and a tall, balding man with a cello.

"She was the nurse and he was the anesthetist."

"So that means the whole team is here," I commented.

"Actually, everyone who was in the operating room is here. Including the patient."

"Including the patient?"

"Yes. There he is."

He indicated a stout musician holding a contrabass. He was considerably shorter than the instrument he played.

"How nice."

"When you assemble an orchestra, you have to pay careful attention to the synchronism of its parts. The strings' previous successful teamwork was certainly a recommendation."

"Nothing without synchronism."

"They are also connected by the fact that they experienced something unusual."

"Come again?"

"Yes. It would take too long, of course, to tell you everything, but perhaps you'd like to hear what the contrabassist saw while he was under anesthesia?"

"Aren't patients completely unconscious then?"

"I assure you I did nothing wrong," said the cellist anxiously.

"No one is accusing you," replied the conductor. "You can't be responsible for what happens in a patient's head during the operation. What's important is that he doesn't feel any pain."

"And that he regains consciousness," I added.

"That's the most important thing," agreed the conductor. "So, would you like the contrabassist to tell you what happened to him while he was on the operating table?"

"I'm dying to know."

The little man lowered the neck of the bulky instrument onto a chair, stepped forward a little and bowed. The orchestra clapped briefly and I joined them.

"When I was put to sleep, I found myself on a boulevard lined with chestnut trees. There were a lot of passers-by. I was walking quickly, as though rushing somewhere, but I didn't know where. I might have reached that unknown destination if a man coming from the opposite direction hadn't caught my eye. He had to, of course, since everything he wore was white. Can you imagine that?"

"Was he wearing a white suit?"

"Not just his suit. His hat, bow tie and shoes were white too. Even his shoelaces. In addition, he had silver hair under his hat brim and a gray mustache. He even looked a little pale, like he'd used some white powder."

"He'd gone all white, no doubt about it."

"That's right. When he passed by me, I couldn't resist the temptation to turn around and stare. And then before I realized what I was doing, I headed after him. Please don't get the wrong idea. I'm not in the habit of following strangers."

"I would never dream of such a thing."

The contrabassist smiled.

"Thank you. The man in white didn't look like someone taking a leisurely walk. He ignored the shop windows and advanced with brisk, but not exactly hurried steps. It wasn't hard to follow him. After a while, though, something seemed strange. You'd expect his whiteness to attract attention, wouldn't you?"

"White is a conspicuous color."

"That's right. But I seemed to be the only one to take notice. The other pedestrians walked by him unaffected, as though there was nothing unusual about his attire."

"People usually mind their own business in the street. You might have acted the same way if you hadn't been given a narcotic."

"It's not my fault," wailed the anesthetist softly.

"Now, now," replied the conductor. "No one's blaming you."

"Certainly not," agreed the contrabassist. "Anyway, we passed two intersections like that and then the man in white stopped in front of a teashop. He straightened his bow tie a little and went inside. I only hesitated a moment when I reached the entrance. I went in after him, although I rarely go to such places. I'm not a tea enthusiast."

"I, on the contrary, love it," interjected the conductor. "I can't even do rehearsals without it. I keep a thermos right here, by the podium," he said, pointing under my feet, "and drink a little during every break. Unfortunately, that's impossible at the concerts."

"Inside I was greeted by intoxicating smells and a reddish gloom. It took a few moments for my eyes to adjust. I caught sight of the man at a distant table in the corner. Now everything white on him was drenched in pink. An older woman dressed in turquoise was sitting next to him. At least that's what it looked like in that lighting. Its real color might have been blue or green. She was wearing a cute little matching pillbox hat."

"That's why the man spruced himself up. Age is no obstacle to love," I commented.

"That's what I thought at first too. I was just about to leave so as not to bother them, since they certainly wanted to be alone. There were no other customers in the teashop. But then it occurred to me that I'd look suspicious if I did that. Who ever goes into a teashop and then leaves right away?"

"A spy?"

"Precisely. I certainly didn't want the man to conclude that I was tailing him. I decided to stay there briefly. I would have a quick cup of tea and then leave. I don't like tea, but I had to suffer the consequences."

"Worse things can happen."

"This one passed me by. I never had a chance to order any tea. No one came to wait on me. I sat there in vain at a table by the door. My patience was already starting to wear thin, when the couple from the other side of the teashop stood up, as though they too were fed up with the intolerably poor service."

"Teashops usually have exemplary service. It must have been because of the narcotic. . . ."

The anesthetist opened his mouth to say something else in his own defense, but the conductor stopped him with a sharp slash of the hand.

"Before they left," continued the contrabassist, "they bent down and picked up a wooden chest with metal studs. I hadn't seen it before because it was hidden by their table. It seemed heavy and bulky, but the two old folks carried it without any effort, holding it by the side handles."

"Even older people can be strong."

"Be that as it may, they headed for the door but didn't go out. They stopped at my table and put the chest on the floor."

"Did they say anything to you?"

"Not a word. They just smiled. Not knowing what to do, I got up. We stood there like that for a moment and then the man bent down and opened the chest."

"What was inside it?"

"I don't remember."

"You don't remember?"

"No. All I know is that I stared inside and something fascinated me. But I've forgotten what it was."

I sighed.

He shrugged his shoulders as though to exonerate himself.

"When I finally tore my eyes away from the chest, I saw that the man and woman were looking at me attentively, as though expecting something from me."

"Expecting?"

"Yes. It took me some time to figure out what it was. I was supposed to put something into the chest."

"What?"

The contrabassist did not reply immediately. He looked at the conductor for permission. When the man nodded, he went up to the podium and beckoned to me to lean closer. I had to bend down completely at the waist to bring my head close to his. His lips almost touched my earlobe as he whispered.

"That's what you put in it?" I asked in disbelief, after straightening up.

"Yes," he confirmed timidly, blushing.

"How admirable."

He bowed, then returned to his instrument.

"Then what happened?"

"Nothing. That's when I regained consciousness."

The anesthetist didn't even have time to open his mouth.

"How many times must I repeat that no one's blaming you?" snapped the conductor, sending him a piercing glance. Then he turned towards me and spoke gently. "You can't imagine how much we envy you. None of us knows what the gentleman put in the chest."

I looked at the contrabassist questioningly.

"I hope you can keep a secret," he said with concern.

"To be sure."

"All right," said the conductor. "Let's continue introducing the orchestra, if you agree."

"Please do."

He indicated a younger, slender man at the harp.

"Here is another true maestro on a stringed instrument. You should hear him in the solo parts. He simply mesmerizes the audience."

"The conductor knows my weak points as well," said the harpist softly.

"They are quite negligible. Like a tiny cloud in an otherwise perfectly clear sky. It will soon scatter. But music isn't our harpist's only redeeming quality. Do you need legal assistance, by any chance? Particularly patent protection and copyrights in general?"

I gave it some thought.

"I wouldn't say so."

"Too bad. I've never met a better lawyer. To date he's lost only two cases."

"Nothing's over yet," said the harpist, this time in a louder voice. "The high court has yet to rule on my appeal. I'm an optimist."

"You see," said the conductor with a broad smile. "He's full of self-confidence. This is no less important in our work too. You can't be a good musician if you're not self-assured, right?"

"Certainly," I agreed.

"And here is the most self-assured member of our orchestra."

A large man by the drums bowed curtly.

"It could not be otherwise," continued the conductor. "Imagine if we had some Mr. Milquetoast on the drums? How would that seem?"

"Quite inappropriate."

"When he starts to boom, the drums almost explode, and the audience gets goose bumps. Just look at those arms."

The drummer raised his arms and proudly displayed his biceps.

"Amazing."

"The only place to get that kind of strength is behind the wheel."

"Behind the wheel?"

"Yes. The drummer is a truck driver. An unfailing professional. If you need a reliable transporter on the longest hauls, there's no one better. He can go two nights in a row without sleeping. I especially recommend him for shipping poultry, where he's unrivalled. He's had only one accident to date."

"Caused by a bus driver."

"That goes without saying. You know what the drivers are like on public transport nowadays. Nervy and negligent."

"I know."

"Now let's move on to the wind section. Talk about cohesion! It's no wonder, when you consider what connects them."

"Connects them?"

"I doubt that you can guess what links our virtuoso on the horn to the other wind players. Here, take a good look at him."

I scrutinized the older, heavy-set musician with bright cheeks, then shrugged.

"Just by the look of him you'd say he had to be a great player, right?"

I nodded.

"You wouldn't be wrong. He's not only the mainstay of the wind section, he breathes heart and soul into the entire orchestra. When you hear his instrument, everything suddenly takes on a spiritual quality. He's able to elevate the most commonplace composition. That's when religious rapture imbues even hardened atheists, whether they admit it or not. How else could it be when a priest is playing the horn?"

"Really?"

"Yes. He performs all the rites, of course, but prefers weddings, which is only natural. It was he who married his colleagues."

I looked at the wind section in disbelief, and the conductor hastened to explain.

"Don't be confused by their difference in age. The oboist and clarinetist were the first to be married by the priest, and the flautist and maestro on the bassoon were the last. There are decades in between."

"Oh, I see."

"This has its advantages in the orchestra. The oboe and clarinet sound mature and composed, while the flute and bassoon are airy and unbridled, youthful. It's just the combination we need."

"How fitting."

"One other thing connects the couples. They dreamed something strange on their wedding night."

"All of them?"

"That's right. All four. They agree, however, that the oboist's dream is the most unusual. Would you like to hear it?"

"Yes, I would."

"Wonderful!"

The conductor approached the oboist and guided her to the podium.

"I suggest that the two of you withdraw to the back of the auditorium," he said, extending his hand to me.

"Why?" I asked as I stepped off the podium.

"Why, you don't expect her to talk about her wedding night in front of everyone, do you?"

"Certainly not," I replied in confusion. "It's just that I thought . . ."

"Although there would be eager ears here . . ."

The conductor looked reprovingly at the drummer, who lowered his eyes.

"You'll be comfortable there," he said, addressing me again. "Sit wherever you like. We'll play softly. Listening to dreams is nicer with music."

I helped the elderly oboist off the stage, then offered her my arm as we went down the aisle.

I sat down on the same seat as when I'd first entered the hall, and the elderly woman sat next to me. The orchestra started up while we were still walking.

We looked at each other in silence for a few moments, and then she smiled and began.

I walked onto the soccer field.

The bright floodlights made me squint. They all seemed to be pointed at me. When my eyes adjusted, the first thing I noticed was the stands. Alternating rows of red and black seats surrounded me without a single spectator.

The national anthem was playing solemnly from a multitude of speakers. Eleven players proudly raised their heads and their mouths opened as though they were singing. Although I was just a few steps away from them, I couldn't hear a thing.

Ten of them were wearing yellow, purple and gray striped jerseys, orange shorts and green boots. The only exception was the goalkeeper in his heavy brown monk's habit and leather sandals.

I too was standing quietly. Just as I thought how awkward it was to be the only one who didn't know the words, the anthem ended. The soccer players applauded tumultuously. Then the goalkeeper stepped out of the ranks and headed towards me with outstretched arms.

He gave me a fatherly hug. When he stepped back, his hands lingered slightly on my shoulders. His face was beaming with affection, particularly his watery eyes.

"Finally, my child! You got here in the nick of time. We were already afraid that you'd be late."

"Here I am," I replied with a smile.

"Wonderful! Let's go. The soccer players can barely wait for me to introduce them."

He went first. When we reached the row of players, he went back to the head of the row.

"I humbly hope you won't hold it against me for starting with myself. It has nothing to do with vanity. I'm not only the goalkeeper but captain of the team as well. Those are the rules. The oldest one is the leader. And in that respect I have no equal. How old do you think I am?"

"Around fifty," I said hesitantly.

Someone at the other end of the line giggled. The goalkeeper leaned forward and looked sharply in their direction.

"How kind of you," he said, once his face had regained its mild expression. "Why, I can't remember when I was only half a century old. But don't let my age deceive you. Age is certainly no hindrance to a goalkeeper. Quite the contrary. Do you know what instills the most confidence in the person guarding the net?"

"No, I don't."

"Experience. Nothing without that. And can you gain the necessary experience if you're not old enough?"

I shook my head.

"Of course not," continued the captain. "You'll never guess what experience helped me become almost invincible in goal."

I shrugged my shoulders.

"What I gained through my hobbies. I love to fish and play chess. I can see by your face that you wonder what they have to do with soccer."

"I do wonder."

"Let me explain. It makes no difference if your opponent is a fish, a chess player or a center forward, you have to outwit them all. And you can only do that if you are experienced."

"Oh, that's it."

"Yes. An experienced goalkeeper can even use something to their disadvantage, while greenhorns are bothered by the slightest detail. Here, take this, for example."

He grabbed hold of the broad sleeve of his habit.

"You'd say, wouldn't you, that this is the most unsuitable attire for the person standing between the goalposts."

"That's how it looks."

"But appearances can be deceptive. You can't imagine how many goals have been defended simply because the attackers botched it when they came eye to eye with me. It isn't easy to keep your composure when confronted by a man in a habit. That's when a lot of suppressed questions cross your mind. And a good chance suddenly disappears forever. Even the atheists get confounded."

"Even them?"

"Believe it or not. A habit is also handy from a purely practical viewpoint. When I spread my arms and stretch it out, I cover almost half the goal."

I looked at him dubiously.

"Is that going by the rules?"

"It's not explicitly prohibited. Provided, of course, that you're decently dressed underneath. And I certainly am. Here, see for yourself."

He started to untie his belt, but I hastened to stop him.

"It's not necessary. I believe you."

"Thank you." He tightened his belt again. "Even the hood comes in handy."

"Really?"

"One time everyone thought the ball was already in the net. I made a spectacular move, but it slipped through my hands. It didn't end up in the goal, though, but in my hood. You should have heard the ovations I received. Even the referee congratulated me."

"Quite a feat, there's no doubt about it."

The priest stepped out of the line.

"All right, that's enough about me. You might get the impression that I'm the most important member of the team, but it's not like that at all. I'm just first among equals. All my skills would be for nothing if I didn't have a solid defense in front of me. Please let me present our two fullbacks."

He indicated the first two players. They were younger than him, but had passed the half-century mark too. They stepped forward and bowed, and then we shook hands.

"When you see them like this in uniform, it must be hard to imagine what they do when they're not playing soccer. What would you say?"

I stepped back a little and took a good look at the fullbacks. One was tall and slender with stooped shoulders and the other had a red nose, ruddy cheeks and resembled a barrel.

"I wouldn't know."

"Both of them are priests."

"Is that so?"

"Don't be surprised. What's more natural than to find men of the cloth among the closest defense? The goal is like a little death. We know best how to keep it away and are also here to offer consolation if it happens nonetheless."

"Twice as useful."

"Quite so. But these aren't ordinary priests. That wouldn't be enough. They wouldn't do such a good job in defense if they didn't have hobbies of their own."

"Do they fish and play chess too?"

"No. They don't have to outsmart their opponents but surpass them in speed and agility. And what better hobbies develop these characteristics than pinball and bird photography?"

He indicated the tall fullback first, then the fat one. I gave this some thought.

"It's clear to me about pinball; you need quick reflexes and skill. But I don't understand the bird photography."

"Have you ever taken a picture of birds above a church?"

"No, I haven't."

"If you had, you'd know how fast you have to react. If you don't grab your camera and shoot, they've already passed. Our left fullback might appear sluggish, but that's just a misconception. He's photographed three hundred and twenty-seven flocks to date."

"That many?"

"He's like lightning. You won't find a single opponent out there who's faster than he is. It's mostly thanks to him that they rarely score any goals."

"I'm not worthy of such flattery," said the fat priest sheepishly. "I caused three penalties."

"Believe me, there were no grounds to award them," said the goalkeeper. "He wouldn't hurt a flea, let alone foul someone, and certainly not in the penalty area. The referees had it in for him just because of his stout figure. And ostensibly they want to do away with any sort of discrimination in soccer."

"How two-faced," I commented.

"You said it," replied the goalkeeper. "But we got the best of them. I repelled all three penalty shots."

"Congratulations."

"Thank you. Admittedly, those who kicked them complained that I'd hypnotized them."

"Hypnotized them?"

"They claim that as they ran towards the ball, they suddenly seemed to be underwater and couldn't surface. That's why their kicks were so bad. Not even the referees believed such rubbish, even though they were openly in their favor."

"They could have come up with something more convincing."

"With their thick skulls? That's why they're picked to kick penalties. They think that all they have to do is cut loose on the ball. But let's forget them for now. If you agree, we'll move on to our halfbacks. They are worthy of your attention."

"Please do."

The next three players stepped forward and bowed. They all had a firm handshake. They were middle-aged, of medium build and medium height and what differentiated them the most was their hair. The player with a number four on his shorts wore it in a braid that hung down his chest. Number five's hair looked like a yellow scrubbing brush and number six was almost completely bald, but he compensated for it with a long beard.

"Do you know the most sought-after virtue in a half-back?" asked the goalkeeper

"Teamwork?"

"That too. But there's something more important. The readiness to die for every ball. Sometimes even literally."

"Literally?"

"Yes. Do you know how many soccer players die on average every year?"

I shook my head.

"Sixteen-and-a-half. But that fact is concealed to keep the spectators from getting upset. It isn't supposed to be gladiatorial combat, after all."

"How dreadful."

"Yes, dreadful. We live in a rough-and-tumble world. And most of those who get hurt are halfbacks: seventy-two percent."

"Poor halfbacks."

"We all feel sorry for them. You can't imagine how hard it is for us to put someone in that position. It's like sentencing them to death. A parent would never be put there. Why should their children end up fatherless?"

"That would be intolerable."

"To be sure. That's why we try to get halfbacks without family obligations. And if possible with suicidal tendencies."

"Suicidal?"

"That's the most suitable. If someone has to die, it's better to be someone who will easily accept it. In addition, a man who's ready to commit suicide won't be afraid of exposing himself to danger, which often happens in the middle of the field."

"Isn't it roughest in front of goal?"

"It might look like that from the stands. But it's only when you're down here that you see where danger really lies. We're really lucky that all our halfbacks have suicidal experience."

I looked at them once again.

"They don't look that way."

"What suicide looks like a suicide? But you'll see for yourself when I introduce them to you. Here, let's start with the right halfback."

He indicated player number four who gave a bashful smile.

"He's not afraid to put his head where many would fear to put their feet. Where do you think he got such courage?"

I shrugged my shoulders.

"He dove in despair off a dresser onto the fragments of an expensive vase that his cat had broken. After that, how could he shrink from the other team's studs? To him that's like someone tousling his hair. And his hair softens the blows. Just see how thick it is."

The right halfback threw the braid over his left shoulder.

"Lots of women would envy him that."

"You said it. While we're on the subject of hair, do you think it's by chance that our center halfback has spiky hair like a hedgehog's bristles?"

He indicated number five who stood at attention almost like a soldier.

"I suppose not."

"Of course not. Everything on him is stiff and firm just like the stone that he carves. You should see him cut tombstones, the air sizzles all around him. He's the same on the field. A real bruiser. He engages in combat as though he cares nothing for his life."

"Isn't that going too far?"

"Of course it is. No one expects quite that much sacrifice from a halfback. But it's hard to talk him out of it. Ever since he tried to take his life after carving an early date of death on a tombstone, he pays no heed to danger."

"Do the referees allow that kind of play?"

"Of course not. They penalize him when he fouls and when he doesn't. They've stopped giving him yellow cards; he gets red ones right away. He's had so many that I wouldn't be at all surprised if his blond hair soon turns red."

The center halfback ran his fingers through his crew cut.

I tried to imagine him a redhead.

"It wouldn't look bad."

"Do you think so? In any case, unlike the center halfback, our left halfback is not plagued by the color of his hair."

"Maybe he could do something with his beard?"

"Not on your life. As it is, the opposition constantly derides him for his bald head. You can't imagine all the names they call him. If he dyed his beard, he wouldn't survive their taunts."

"That's not at all nice."

"Actually, envy is behind it all. They can't stand the fact that he's better than they are. Particularly when they have to jump on the ball. That's when he simply flies."

"Flies?"

"Yes. He has lots of experience. It comes from trying to kill himself by jumping from greater and greater heights. He got all the way up to the sixth floor."

"Unbelievable."

"That's nothing compared to what happened next. Would you like to hear about it? You won't regret it."

"With pleasure."

The left halfback stroked his beard and cleared his throat.

"Well, I jumped into the void."

"Weren't you afraid your heart would stop? I've heard that people's hearts burst before they hit the ground."

"I have a strong heart. If that weren't so, I wouldn't have survived all those falls. But I always faint when I start to drop."

"That's the best thing to do in such circumstances. The less conscious you are, the less you worry."

"I didn't lose consciousness completely, it was more like being half asleep. I seemed to be walking down a street. There weren't a lot of people out because the sun was scorching. I was drenched in sweat; I can't stand the heat."

"Me neither. I try to stay indoors."

"I wouldn't have gone out either, if it were up to me. But who asks you when you're half asleep? To make matters worse, I had no idea where I was heading. I could have wandered about town like that indefinitely."

"Why didn't you go inside somewhere to freshen up?"

"Everything was closed. It seems it was a holiday."

"How inopportune."

"Quite. But lady luck suddenly smiled on me. I ended up at the entrance to the public swimming pool."

"You were delighted, I'm sure."

"You can just imagine. But two worries spoiled my happiness. The pool was probably crawling with people and I don't like crowds."

"I stay away from them too whenever I can."

"Sometimes they can't be avoided, unfortunately. Also, I didn't have any swimming trunks. But I hoped I'd be able to rent some."

"You'd put on swimming trunks worn by someone else?"

"What else could I do? Skinny dip?"

"They wouldn't let you."

"Of course they wouldn't, but I wanted so terribly to cool off."

I sighed.

"Sometimes you have to choose between the devil and the deep blue sea."

"Well, I was spared from making that choice."

"How?"

"First, the entrance was wide open. No one asked for a ticket to the pool."

"Maybe it was free that day?"

"That's what I thought too. And if it was free, then the whole town must have flocked inside."

"People like it when they don't have to pay."

"It's better than candy. But when I went inside, I had a surprise in store: the swimming pool was empty."

"Empty?"

"Not a living soul."

"How could that be if it was free?"

"Under any other circumstance I would have wondered too, but right then how could I look a gift horse in the mouth? Who cares if something is unusual if it's in your favor? What else could I wish for but to have the whole swimming pool to myself? Even the problem of swimming trunks was resolved."

"So you decided to skinny dip after all?"

"No. Just the opposite. I decided to swim in my clothes. They wouldn't have let me do that either if there'd been other swimmers."

"But you'd be sopping wet when you got out."

"So what? I'd dry in no time under the blistering sun. And my clothes would prevent me from getting sunburned."

"So, you did jump in your clothes?"

"I don't know."

"Why don't you know?"

"Just listen. You'd have expected me to get into the water right away, wouldn't you?"

"I would have in your place."

"Well, people don't always do what's expected. When I saw the diving tower, I couldn't resist."

"That's not so unexpected given your affinities."

"I'm glad you understand. I was sorely tempted to jump from the highest point. What more could I have wanted, particularly since I knew that this time I wouldn't fall on something hard."

"It would be a nice change."

"Refreshing. But I had a new surprise in store at the top of the diving tower."

"It was forbidden to dive from that height."

"That wouldn't have stopped me. There was someone up there I couldn't see from down below."

"A lifeguard?"

"No. Two people. An older woman in a green suit and an older man dressed completely in white."

"What were they doing there?"

"At first I thought they wanted to be alone."

"At the top of a diving tower?"

"Even stranger places are chosen for trysts."

"Didn't you say they were old?"

"Age is not an obstacle to love."

"At their age they should have found some place in the shade."

"They probably would have if love was the point of their meeting."

"But it wasn't?"

"It wasn't. Who would haul a heavy chest with metal studs to a tryst?"

"A chest? How did they get it up there?"

"However they did it, they must have had a really tough time."

"Why on earth did they need it?"

"As soon as I got up there, the man opened it and the woman pointed inside. I bent over and took a look."

"And what did you see?"

The left halfback's shoulders slumped in remorse.

"I've forgotten."

Another giggle came from the end of the line. The captain shot an angry look in that direction once more.

"All I remember is that something mesmerized me. I wouldn't have taken my eyes off it if the woman hadn't pointed into the chest again."

"Why?"

"I wondered too. It took a full minute before I understood. I had to make an offering. Otherwise they wouldn't let me jump."

"It wouldn't have cost you a thing if you'd stayed away from the diving tower."

"What can you do? Passions don't come for free."

"So how much did you pay?"

"Nothing. I gave something."

"What?"

The left halfback looked timidly at the captain who hesitated briefly, then nodded. Number six came up to me, cupped his hand over his mouth and whispered two words in my ear.

"You didn't get off cheaply," I said after the player had gone back in line.

"Not at all. But nothing less would have been accepted."

"I hope the jump was worth it."

"I hoped so too as I fell towards the water. But instead of going under, I crashed onto the ground. My, but six floors is high."

"I don't envy you in the slightest."

"At least something good came of it. I gave up trying to kill myself by jumping from a great height."

"Smart thinking."

"And useful too," said the goalkeeper. "The world lost a suicide but gained a wonder midfield player."

"The captain knows my shortcomings. I've got to improve my interaction with the other halfbacks."

"That's a weak point among all those who try to take their own lives. They go it alone. But over time they adapt to the collective game," said the goalkeeper.

He looked at me inquisitively for a few moments without speaking. When he spoke, his voice was soft.

"I don't suppose you'd tell us what he put in the chest?"

"Don't you know?"

"He wouldn't have whispered to you if we did."

I threw the left halfback an inquiring look.

"I told you in the strictest confidence," he said disconcertedly.

"Rest assured. No one will get a single word out of me."

The captain shrugged his shoulders dejectedly and sighed.

"I guess that's that. Let's continue. It's time for the offense."

He indicated a middle-aged woman with a full figure and extremely large breasts. Her conspicuous makeup didn't exactly go with the soccer uniform.

"Our outside right. She might not look like one to you."

"I somehow imagined outsides otherwise," I replied uncertainly.

"No-one would blame you. Indeed, who would expect an opera singer in that position?"

"Not many."

"The opponents' backs are actually the most surprised. While they're coming to their senses, she's already whizzed by them. In spite of being slightly overweight, she's as fast as the wind. No one can catch her."

"Maybe I could lose a bit of weight," said the singer in a high-pitched voice.

"Only if you don't put your wonderful voice at risk. Did you know that it also helps her in the game?"

"Really?" I asked.

"If she comes across an overly resistant back, one who likes to play rough, our diva belts out an aria while running full steam ahead. Then the whole stadium goes silent and the back simply freezes. Her *coup de grâce* is to give a high C-note. Not a single opponent can withstand that."

"Who could stand a high C?"

"She used to have trouble with long through balls. She simply couldn't send them in the right direction. But ever since she learned when she's going to die, she's like a new person. Now she kicks the ball straight at our forward's head. She's completely thrown off the uncertainty that cramped her style."

"It's not easy to play when you're uptight."

"Our inside right could testify to that."

The player with a number eight on his shorts was also middle-aged with a pot belly. He had ruddy cheeks and bright eyes.

"He is otherwise an excellent actor. But for a long time they made him play parts in the theater that didn't suit him. Can you imagine him as a ladies' man?"

I scrutinized the inside right.

"Hardly."

"Thank you," replied the chubby man with a broad smile.

"But ever since he became a comedian, he's come completely into his own."

"He's got just the face for those rôles."

"It's enough to look at him and you feel like laughing, right?"

"That's it."

"Something similar happened to him in our team. He tried out for several positions but nothing worked. Even as goalkeeper. We finally understood that he was a born inside player. That's where his talent as a comic makes itself felt."

"Who would have thought?"

"He discovered it by accident. We'd been giving everything we had to score at a match, but the opponent's defense was unbeatable. And then, just a few minutes before the end, our comic had a flash of inspiration about how to get the better of them. He started to make them laugh."

"And it worked?"

"Sure did. While they were dying of laughter, we scored two goals. The referee was laughing himself silly too and there was pandemonium in the stands. Spirits were running high."

"Of course," said the inside right, "the same tricks don't work every time. Who would laugh at the same joke twice? I have to get new ones ready for every match. And it's not all that easy."

"It's not easy to be witty," I agreed.

"Our center forward has a completely different approach. There's nothing funny about him and his teeth are constantly bared. What else, indeed, could a dentist do?"

The center forward was slim with thinning sideburns, a full mustache and very hairy legs.

"Bares his teeth?"

"Quite literally. Here, take a look."

The dentist bared his teeth. I was blinded by a flash of perfectly white teeth.

"Dazzling."

"You should see what it does to our opponents. That dazzling smile makes the entire defense want to sink into the ground from shame. They all cover their mouths with their hands so no one can see their teeth. It's no fault but their own. They find time for everything but going to the dentist for a checkup."

"It's a pity that people are so unconcerned about their teeth."

"Our center forward owes one more soccer quality to his profession. Do you think they call him The Drill for no reason?"

"Certainly not."

"He penetrates through the toughest defense like a dentist's drill. He makes holes in the tightest set-up. Although not without qualms."

"It's easier with my patients," said the dentist. "I give them a local anesthetic so they don't feel a thing. But you should see the faces of the defense players as I break through them. They're all contorted. It wears me down more and more."

"He proposed giving our opponents a local anesthetic too, but this proved unacceptable. Anti-doping regulations are very strict."

"All they can do is grin and bear it," I said.

"And here's our inside left."

The slim young man seemed weak and frail. He had beautiful, almost feminine features and long, curly hair.

"You haven't failed to notice his delicate build?"

"If he wasn't wearing a soccer uniform I'd think he was a poet."

"And you wouldn't be far wrong. He is a great lover of the arts. The theater in particular. He has permanently reserved the third seat in the right front row."

"Quite the enthusiast."

"Only partially, unfortunately."

"Partially?"

"He always leaves after the first act."

"Why's that?"

"I can't stand the dénouements," said the young man sheepishly, head bowed.

"It's the same with soccer. He's brilliant in the first half. He makes up for his lack of strength with an agility that's almost balletic. His pirouettes and leaps take your breath away. But he's nowhere to be found in the second half."

"Do you replace him?"

"Oh no, certainly not."

"Even though you don't get much use out of him?"

"Not in the game, but in the stands. You can't imagine how many female fans come just because of him. They completely fill the northern stands. You should hear the shrieking and screaming when he runs out onto the field. They don't care how he plays just as long as he's before their eyes. There would be riots if we left him in the locker room."

"But with him it's like having one player less in the second half."

"We get by somehow. Ticket sales are what counts."

"Profit comes first."

"Such are the times. All right, to finish, please let me introduce our outside left."

The slender, attractive blonde giggled flirtatiously. The captain spread his arms.

"What's there to say? You've heard what she's like. She makes fun of everyone. But we pay no attention because of her qualities."

"Do you mean the fact that she looks good?"

"Looks aren't important, although our opponents often have trouble taking their eyes off her legs. They vie over who's going to guard her. But whoever it is, they're powerless before her dribbling."

"It's good to have a skilled dribbler on the team."

"She learned the ropes in the theater. She simply captivates the audience with her convincing roles. The fullbacks go ballistic too when she kicks the ball between their legs."

"No one would like that."

"Her game isn't without drawbacks too, unfortunately. Every once in a while she falls asleep."

"Falls asleep?"

"Yes. That happens to her on stage as well. It's like her thoughts wander off. The play was almost interrupted two or three times because she'd tuned out."

"That's not at all nice."

"What can I do when a memory suddenly comes to mind," said the actress coquettishly. "It completely consumes me."

"Luckily," continued the captain, "the game suffers less than the play. We can do without the outside left for a while. Once, though, she really went too far. She tuned out for a full seventeen-and-a-half minutes."

"That long? Had something come to mind then too?"

"Oh, no. That time I really went to sleep."

"In the middle of a match?"

"The noise in the stadium didn't bother me at all. I fell soundly asleep and even had a dream. Would you like me to tell you that dream? It's quite unusual."

I looked at the captain.

"It really is amazing. I heartily recommend you hear it. Why don't you go to the western stands where you have the best view of the field. You'll be able to watch us while you listen."

"I hope I won't keep your outside left too long."

"We'll get by somehow. We're already used to her leaving us from time to time. As long as she's all revved up when she joins us, everything will be all right."

He pointed to a gate in the metal fence on the edge of the stands. We climbed all the way up to the top, hesitated a moment where to sit, then settled on either side of the steep aisle. The actress giggled merrily once again before she started.

◇ 3 ◇

I entered the restaurant kitchen.

Four connected stoves stood in the middle of the large room. Worktops with sinks extended along three walls. Refrigerators and freezers covered the entire fourth wall.

A number of cooks seemed very busy. They were all dressed in light brown: their shirts, vests, bow ties, skirts and pants, and even their shoes. Only their toques were yellow.

"Come in, come in!" said the cook whose toque was twice as tall as the others'. He moved a transparent dish off the burner and came towards me with a smile.

My hand disappeared into the strong clasp of his two hands.

"You're just in time. Most of the dishes are just about ready; you'll be able to taste them in a moment. I hope you haven't eaten anything recently."

I pondered briefly.

"No, I haven't."

"Wonderful! It's best to go to a tasting on an empty stomach. That's when your sense of taste is the sharpest."

"I didn't know that."

"Here, see for yourself."

He indicated the spot where he'd been standing. When we reached the stove, he took a spoon wrapped in a brown napkin out of his upper vest pocket. He scooped up a bit of white mash from the transparent dish.

I took the spoon, but didn't put it in my mouth right away. The substance looked like sour milk and wasn't the least bit enticing.

"Don't be repulsed by what you see. It's true we also eat with our eyes, but sometimes the appearance improves in the mouth."

I cautiously put the tip of the spoon to my lips. I rubbed my tongue against my palate, waited a bit, then quickly put in all the rest.

"What did I tell you?" said the cook, seeing the look of bliss on my face.

"Outstanding!"

Sweet and sour fought for supremacy while some ingredient in the background gave everything a hint of bitterness.

"Do you know what that is?"

"No. I've never tried this before," I replied, giving him back the spoon.

"That's not surprising. You'll only find the firefighter soufflé in a very few restaurants."

"Firefighter?"

"Yes. It's made according to a secret recipe of the firefighters' guild."

"It's clearly not a secret to you."

"How could it be? I was a firefighter for many years."

"Oh, I see."

"The recipe dates from way back when fires weren't put out quickly like they are today. Even the small ones would smolder for a long time and firefighters had to be on duty to make sure they didn't burst into flame."

"You can never be careful enough with fire."

"Many people don't realize that until it's too late. While they were waiting, firefighters passed the time thinking up new dishes. Why not take advantage of idleness and free heat?"

"No one could hold that against them."

"An amazing number of new dishes were invented.

Unfortunately, we aren't given credit for most of them. No one paid attention to copyrights back then and history has a poor memory. Everyone stole our recipes, particularly the barbers' and hairdressers' guild."

"Were they interested in cooking too?"

"Yes, although they didn't have any talent. The only thing they were good at was copying others. Take barber topping, for example. Have you tried it?"

"No, I haven't."

"You really must, it's wonderful. And why wouldn't it be since it came from us? Its original name was firefighter foam."

"I have a weakness for topping."

"Me too. It's the same with shaggy sauce. They're so proud of it and all they did was add a little cinnamon and cloves to our famous fiery sauce. And that ruined it. They don't have a clue about putting tastes together."

"That's the most important thing."

"They tried to take over our soufflé too. Luckily, they weren't able to get hold of the recipe, even though there have always been bribable people in our ranks. Unfortunate but true."

"Every fold has its black sheep."

"Not every one. The lighthouse keepers' guild, for example, is not affected."

"How do you know that?"

"I held that job for a long time too."

"You've done a variety of things in your life."

"That stood me in good stead for becoming head chef here."

He indicated his toque and bowed slightly.

"I didn't think that lighthouse keepers were drawn to the kitchen."

"One of the misconceptions about us is that we supposedly live on dry food. But why would that be so? We have even more spare time than firefighters, plus an inexhaustible source of inspiration—the sea."

"I love seafood."

"Every lighthouse has its specialty. Recipes are not exchanged so no one is tempted to sell someone else's. Lighthouse keepers aren't saints either. That way, each one keeps only their own secret and there's no temptation."

"Clever."

"The lighthouse where I worked was famous for its stuffed coral."

I frowned.

"Is coral edible?"

"Of course! It's the ultimate delicacy, but it has to be properly prepared. The procedure is very long and complicated because the coral has to marinate nine-and-a-half years in order to soften enough. You can see why it's by far the most expensive item on our menu."

"I doubt whether I'll ever have the chance to try stuffed coral."

"You will this very instant."

The chef put on oven mitts, opened the oven and took out an oval ceramic dish. When he lifted the lid, my head started to spin.

"Enchanting?"

"Irresistible!"

"Just wait until you put it in your mouth."

This time he took a wrapped fork out of his vest pocket. If my nostrils hadn't been filled with the divine smell, I would have hesitated again. My eyes told me I was being offered a rotten piece of wood wrapped in something slimy.

The chef looked at me impatiently, waiting for my

comment, but it seemed blasphemous to talk until the last trace of the mouthful was gone. I licked the fork thoroughly before giving it back to him.

"Well?"

"Might I have a tiny bit more?" I asked, handing him the fork. I wasn't aware that I was capable of asking for something so pleadingly.

He took the fork but didn't reach into the dish again.

"No, unfortunately. It wouldn't be fair to the other cooks. I'd love to oblige you, but your palate doesn't belong to me alone. They can barely wait to tickle it too."

He took my arm and led me to the next stove. I had a hard time taking my eyes off the stuffed coral.

The woman was short and quite well along in years. There was a smell of burned food about her.

"Here's our goulash expert," said the chef. "You can't imagine how many fans she has."

"I love goulash too."

"How nice," replied the elderly woman with a smile.

"Did you catch the smell?" asked the chef.

I sniffed around as though I hadn't already noticed it.

"What smell?"

"Like something burned."

"Something is always burning in a kitchen."

"Here it's done on purpose. Take a look."

The woman took a round metal dish out of the oven. A carbonized surface could be seen under the raised lid.

"That's really . . . well done," I said, backing away a little.

"Her goulash wasn't always like that. It looked nice, but the taste was ordinary."

"How did she come up with this idea?"

"By accident, as is often the case in the culinary art. We would have been deprived of this excellent dish if she hadn't been through a fire."

"A fire?"

"Yes. Her house burned to the ground. There was nothing we could do."

"How terrible."

"Every cloud has a silver lining. I was the one who personally brought her out of the garret that was already filled with flames."

"Congratulations."

The chef bowed.

"And then when the fire was finally extinguished, in the ashes of the kitchen our cook found the remains of a goulash she'd just prepared. If it hadn't been protected by the oven of the old-fashioned stove, it would have been completely ruined."

"What luck."

"It was totally black. She was just about to throw it away when she decided to try it first."

"That never would have crossed my mind."

"Such inspiration comes only to the few. She was extremely surprised to find that the goulash tasted wonderful."

"Unbelievable."

"You have to try it too and see for yourself."

The old woman took a knife and fork out of her skirt pocket and handed them to me. I had considerable trouble cutting off a piece and was none too pleased to put it in my mouth.

"Unbelievable!" I repeated after the piece simply melted on my tongue.

The chef and cook beamed at each other.

"It's called parakeet goulash," he said.

I was so enraptured by the exquisite taste that the meaning of his words didn't sink in right away.

"You don't mean to say . . ." I began, then quickly placed the knife and fork on the edge of the range and brought both hands to my mouth.

"Rest assured," said the chef, allaying my fears. "That wasn't parakeet meat, although real gourmets have no prejudices. This is where the name came from."

The old woman looked left and right, then raised her toque. A little white parakeet fluttered on her head, but before it could fly off, she put the toque back in place.

"He was the one who warned her of the fire. It's not certain she would have reached the garret in time if it hadn't been for him. It's natural that she should want to repay him, don't you think?"

"Quite so."

"We're not allowed to keep birds in the kitchen, of course. At least not live ones. But I had to turn a blind eye. I hope we can count on your discretion?"

"Unconditionally."

"Excellent! Let's continue."

The cook at the third stove was plump and graying, with watery eyes and bright cheeks. He was stirring something in a large pot, but his eyes were turned toward the book in his other hand.

"Here's the best-read cook I've ever known. He uses every chance to bury his nose in a book."

"There's so little time," sighed the cook.

"And so many books," I agreed, sighing too.

We smiled at each other understandingly.

"Don't think that his cooking suffers from this affinity for reading."

"I never questioned it."

"Quite the contrary, one might say. It's all to the good."

"Really? How's that?"

"He always reads something out loud to the food before he uses it to prepare a dish."

I threw the cook a skeptical glance.

"Why?"

"Meat becomes juicy and tender, and frozen vegetables completely regain their freshness."

"It can't be!"

"Of course, it depends on what you read. The other cooks have tried in vain to copy him and even got the opposite of what they hoped for. You have to be a connoisseur of literature and none of them are."

"Nothing without knowledge."

The chef leaned towards me and his voiced dropped.

"Can we take you into our confidence?"

"Of course," I replied softly.

He nodded to the cook with the book who drew a little closer to me. We looked like conspirators.

"I read the meat excerpts from historical novels, in particular descriptions of great battles. The vegetables adore elegies and are simply revitalized."

"I never would have guessed," I said.

"You'll see how fitting this is as soon as you try it."

The chef nodded again. The cook picked around the bottom of the pot with the spoon and scooped up something that looked like a boiled rag. He put the book between his knees, then took a fork out of the inside pocket of his vest and wrapped the rag around it.

I took the fork but held it a distance.

"What's that?" I asked, unable to hide my revulsion.

"Tripe."

I frowned in disgust and held the fork out to the cook.

"I hate tripe."

"You'll love this," said the cook, refusing to take it back.

I looked to the chef for help. His smile said it all: Have I let you down this far?

I recoiled as I brought the rag to my mouth, closed my eyes and then nibbled the tip. My eyes remained closed even after the rest of the morsel soon ended up in my mouth. The frown on my face turned to an expression of delight.

"Literature works wonders, doesn't it?" said the chef when I finally opened my eyes.

"Wondrous."

Now the cook had to wrench the fork away from me.

"All right, now we can continue."

I followed the chef grudgingly towards the last stove. A thin, graying cook stood there, holding an opened pink envelope and a letter.

"This is where surprises are prepared," said the chef.

"What kind of surprises?"

"We never know. Would it be a surprise if we knew?"

"No," I agreed.

"Not even the cook knows what he'll prepare until he opens the letter."

"Does he correspond with someone who recommends what to cook?"

The chef cleared his throat.

"It's not exactly about correspondence."

"So what is it about?"

The chef and cook exchanged conspiratorial glances.

"It's a delicate matter. We might have serious problems if the word gets out."

"My lips are sealed," I hastened to assure them.

"Thank you. Well, he works as a mailman in the

morning. Perhaps these two professions seem unrelated?"

"I can't see much of a connection between them," I had to admit after thinking it over a little.

"They are more closely related than they seem, as you will soon discover. Our cook delivers lots of letters every morning."

"That's what mailmen usually do."

"To be sure. What's not so well known is that a full fourteen-and-a-half percent of the letters contain recipes."

"That doesn't surprise me. The world is full of gourmets."

"Indeed. And some of the recipes are real culinary gems."

"I can just imagine. But how does the mailman know which letters they're in? You don't mean to say that he opens them all?"

"Certainly not. That would take too long."

"So what does he do?"

"He relies on his cat."

"Cat?"

"Yes. Once he had seven cats. Now he only has one left, but with a special ability. If it starts to grind its teeth after sniffing a closed envelope, that means there's a recipe inside."

"I didn't know that cats could be trained."

"They can't. This talent is innate."

"How convenient."

"It eases our cook's life considerably. Instead of a hundred, he only opens about fifteen envelopes a day. Done in no time."

"I hope he's careful about it."

"He's quite skilled. After choosing the most attractive recipe, he seals the envelopes in such a way that the recipient never suspects a thing. Let's hear what he's made for our pleasure today."

The cook waved the pink paper.

"This could only be found in a private letter. I love the culinary underground, the sky's the limit there."

He raised the lid of a shallow rectangular dish with something simmering inside. My nostrils were filled with the smell of strong spices.

"Skunk entrails."

"Skunk?" I said, horrified.

The chef and cook laughed heartily at the face I made.

"I'd say you never tried skunk," said the chef.

I shook my head briskly.

"Heaven forbid."

"You've missed out on a lot. But now's your chance to make up for it."

The cook rescued me from my predicament.

"Not this very moment, I'm afraid," he said. "It has to simmer a bit longer. It took me some time to find a skunk. But it will be ready by the end of the tasting. Please don't hesitate to come back again."

"Certainly," I lied without blinking an eye. I didn't wait for the chef to guide me, but headed towards the nearest cook at the worktop.

"Ah, here's our salad expert," said the chef, joining me next to a tall, heavyset man. He was tossing various vegetables in a large bowl.

"I'm crazy about salads."

"Then there's no reason to hesitate. As far as I can tell, it's ready."

With a bow, the cook took a small bowl from the shelf, filled it and handed it to me along with a fork.

The tomato, celery, carrot, pepper, cucumber and lettuce were very fresh. Black pepper enriched the flavors, lemon sharpened them and parsley gave them a velvety touch. I liked the small round pieces of cheese in particular. I wouldn't have minded if there were more of them.

"Divine."

"Many people visit us only because of the hanging hook."

"Hanging hook?"

"That's what the cook calls the salad."

"Why?"

"He tried to kill himself a full seventeen times because of unrequited love. He invented it in-between two unsuccessful attempts to hang himself."

"If the salad arose in the midst of a love story, he could have chosen a more romantic name."

"Cooks are rarely romantic. In addition, the salad was not inspired by love but by something much more prosaic. A pigsty."

The bite I'd just swallowed got caught in my throat.

"Excuse me?"

"He raised hogs. He fed them nothing but vegetables. These very ingredients," he said, indicating the bowl, "produced the best meat. It was natural to think they would be suitable for humans too."

"Should something be suitable for us if pigs like it?"

"That's right. Perhaps you weren't aware, but of all the animals, pigs are the most closely related to us in terms of diet. We like the same vegetables in particular."

"All right for the vegetables, but do they eat cheese too?"

"They rarely have the chance. The small rounds of

cheese were added to the hanging hook later, in commemoration of a painful event. A golf ball accidentally hit him in the temple."

"That could be dangerous."

"Not only dangerous. After he lost consciousness, the cook experienced something unusual."

"Can you experience something when you're unconscious?"

"But of course. If you like, he'd be happy to tell you about it."

"I'd like that."

The cook placed the tongs in the bowl and cleared his throat.

"After the ball hit me, everything went black for just a moment," he began in a deep voice. "Then a bright streetlight dispelled the darkness. I was on an unfamiliar boulevard. There were lots of people everywhere enjoying the summer evening."

"It's nice to go for a stroll when the heat subsides."

"Yes, if you're not in a hurry. But I was in a real hurry."

"Where were you going?"

"I didn't find out until I saw the main post office. The large clock on it said that only two minutes were left before closing time. I ran the rest of the way. There was something I simply had to send that day. The next day would be too late."

"You shouldn't leave things till the last moment."

"I agree. I was really embarrassed about the delay because I normally do everything on time. Here, our chef can confirm it."

"I believe you. Did you get there in time?"

"At the last moment. The elderly doorman dressed all in white had just closed the door. He let me in with a chiding look."

"I didn't know that post office doormen wore white."

"Me neither. I hurried to the window to send my parcel. There were three people in front of it, but I wasn't bothered by the wait."

"What's important is that you got inside."

"That's right. The doorman let people out when they had finished their business, but he didn't let anyone else inside. About ten minutes later it was my turn. I was the last customer in the post office."

"It's nice when problems are happily resolved."

"Mine had just started."

"What do you mean?"

"An older postal clerk in green was sitting behind the window. She was wearing a matching pillbox hat."

"She was probably all ready to go out for a stroll too."

"Probably. She smiled at me, waiting for me to give her the parcel. But I just stared at her in confusion."

"Why?"

"I realized that very moment that I didn't have the parcel."

"Had you forgotten to bring it?"

"I'd forgotten more than that. I couldn't remember what it was and who I was supposed to send it to."

"How strange. So what happened?"

"The woman stopped smiling. She got up and signaled to the doorman to come to us. I wanted to sink through the floor in embarrassment."

"Why didn't you just say you were sorry and leave?"

"I might even have just rushed out of the post office without a word of explanation, but the door was locked and the doorman had already joined the clerk behind the window. They looked at me frowningly."

"They had nothing to hold against you. A little forgetfulness isn't the end of the world."

"Even so, I felt I was to blame. I just stood there frozen to the spot."

"How about them?"

"They didn't move either for a while. Then they bent down and lifted a wooden chest with metal studs onto the counter."

"They kept mail inside it."

"No, they didn't."

"So what did they keep inside?"

"I've forgotten that too."

"You have a real problem with your memory."

"It's all because of that golf ball."

"Well, all right, what did they want with that chest?"

"They just opened it. The expressions on their faces softened. It took a while before I understood what they wanted from me."

"What?"

"To put something inside."

"Money? Did they expect you to pay something for them to let you out? That would be blackmail. You should have threatened to report them."

"No, they didn't want money."

"So what did they want?"

The cook looked at the chef who opened his arms dejectedly and withdrew a little. The hog farmer came up to me and whispered two words in my ear. After he stepped back, I stayed there staring at him for a moment.

"And you gave it to them?" I asked.

"What else could I do?"

"I hope they didn't detain you in the post office after that."

"I don't know. As soon as they closed the chest, everything around me went black again."

"People should stay away from golf courses. There are too many clumsy players."

"Ah, if I'd known that before . . ."

Clearing his throat, the chef came up to us.

"We have to move on. We'll miss the right moments for tasting."

He took my arm and we moved off, but he stopped halfway to the next cook. He spoke to me in a whisper without bringing his head close to mine.

"Perhaps you'd care to tell me what he put in the chest?"

"I can't," I replied, also in a soft voice. "He told me in the strictest confidence."

"Not even for a full portion of stuffed coral?"

We looked each other in the eye for a few moments.

"I'll pretend I didn't hear that," I said at last with a heavy heart.

The chef kept his eyes on me a bit longer and then we continued to a short mustachioed cook with sunken cheeks and a wrinkled forehead. Everything around him was fragrant. He was cutting multicolored flowers with a broad knife and putting them in a large jar. It was almost full.

"We are especially proud of this: pickled flowers," said the chef.

"I didn't know you could pickle flowers."

"This is the only place it's done. I can barely wait for you to try it."

The cook had a bit of trouble stabbing a petal from the jar. He smiled when he handed me the fork. He had the yellow teeth of a smoker.

"Extraordinary," I said after holding the pickled flower in my mouth a while. "How did you ever think of this?"

"Thanks to this cook's dog."

"Rex," added the cook in a hoarse voice.

"Dogs eat flowers?"

"Only under special circumstances. Rex started to eat them during the war," said the chef.

"He couldn't stand the bombing," explained the cook. "You should have seen how he trembled."

"Poor thing."

"After a while," continued the chef, "as soon as he heard the air raid siren he'd jump on the table and start eating flowers. It calmed him down."

"Do flowers have a calming effect?"

"If they have the right additive."

"What additive?"

The chef and cook looked at each other.

"Rex probably discovered it by accident. Dogs are like people. Fear often makes them lose control of their bladder."

I shook my head.

"I don't understand," I said, hoping I hadn't heard properly.

"Before he ate the flowers, Rex would, excuse the expression, pee on them," said the cook, mortified.

My eyes opened wide in disbelief.

"You don't mean to say . . ." I said, pointing at the jar.

"Don't worry. It's ordinary vinegar with selected spices."

I gave a deep sigh of relief.

"Although some customers ask for Rex's additive" said the chef.

"Some people are really perverted."

"Don't be hard on them. We live in stressful times. People are ready to do anything to lower their tension."

"I'm glad I'm not that tense."

"You're lucky. Shall we continue?"

He offered me his arm and we headed for the next cook.

He looked like a boxer at the end of his career who was used mostly as a boxing bag. He had a smashed nose, low forehead and hands like mallets. On the worktop in front of him was a large crystal tray covered with tissue paper.

"I hope you like bite-sized pastry," said the chef.

"Is there anyone who doesn't?"

"There are some around."

"They don't know what they're missing."

"Some prefer cakes," said the cook grouchily with a hint of disdain.

"Bite-sized pastry is less fattening." I giggled. "Unless, of course, you overdo it."

"That's the very danger that threatens here," said the chef.

"They're that good?"

"Not just because of that."

He signaled with a nod and the cook took off the tissue paper. The entire alphabet seemed to be underneath it; the pastry was in the shape of letters.

"I've never seen any like this before."

"Only our cook here makes them."

"Is he also a literature aficionado?"

"Oh, no. Biologists don't exactly associate with books."

"So where did the letters come from?"

"Once he saw a message written under a microscope."

"What was the message?"

"He won't tell anyone, but he did offer a large prize to anyone who guesses it. All you have to do is eat the letters in the right order. Would you like to try?"

"Gladly."

The cook gestured towards the tray.

"Help yourself."

As I stared at the pastries, hesitating, the chef brought his head close to mine.

"I might be able to help you," he whispered, "for a little service in return. . . ."

We stared at each other fixedly again.

"I thought we'd already settled that," I said.

The chef moved away, shrugging his shoulders.

"You're missing a chance to get rich."

I concentrated on the tray again, then chose a pastry in the shape of an "m".

I realized by the simultaneous sigh of the chef and the cook that my very first move had been wrong.

"I've never been lucky with games of chance. I hope there's a consolation prize at least."

I raised the pastry slightly.

"Of course," said the cook with a smile. On his face it looked like a grimace.

My face twisted into a grimace too as soon as I took a bite of the pastry. Had there been a napkin nearby, I would have spat it out. I hadn't eaten anything as tasteless in a long time.

"You don't like it?" asked the cook, disappointed.

"It's a bit . . . strange."

"You don't have to excuse yourself," said the chef. "Not many customers like it. But they still order it. Actually, it's the hottest item on our menu. Gamblers are ready to put up with a range of adversities for the sake of a win."

"I'm glad I'm not in the grips of that vice."

"Those above reproach live longer, but, as you yourself said, they don't know what they're missing. Well, let's move on."

The tray in front of the short, stocky cook was empty. I caught my reflection in the polished silver rectangle.

I looked at the chef inquisitively.

"Our main dessert," he said, as though this explained everything.

"Where is it?" I asked in bewilderment.

He gestured towards the tray.

"On the tray, of course."

"I don't see anything."

"That's quite natural. A black hole is invisible."

"Black hole?"

"That's right. This cook is an astronomer. What would be more fitting than to make a black hole cake?"

"You don't expect me to believe that, do you?"

"Believe your sense of taste."

The chef nodded. The cook opened a drawer under the worktop and took out a silver spoon. Like a mime, he pretended to take something off the tray, then handed it to me.

I was hesitant to take the empty spoon. I never liked practical jokes, in particular those at my expense.

"Go ahead and try it," said the cook encouragingly. "You won't be sorry."

I looked at the chef once more before I took it. Feeling like an idiot, I raised the spoon slowly, then stopped. Finally, ready for an outburst of laughter, I put it in my mouth.

No one laughed, they just smiled. I soon joined them. My smile spread from ear to ear.

"Incredible," I murmured, saddened by the fact that I finally had to swallow the morsel.

"You'd like it even more if you could see it," said the chef.

"That's impossible. The laws of physics . . ." countered the cook, but the chef cut him off with a movement of the hand, then took me a little to one side.

"The laws of the kitchen are older here," he said softly. "Everything can be arranged."

"I'm not interested in what the black hole looks like," I replied after a moment's hesitation.

"Too bad. Then we have only one specialty left."

We headed towards a pretty redheaded cook at the end of the worktop. She was squirting whipped cream over chunks of fruit in a multitude of small bowls.

"What does this look like?" asked the chef.

I shrugged my shoulders.

"Fruit salad."

"That's right. But if you think it's ordinary, you're wrong."

"I don't see anything unusual about it."

"You don't see it, but you can hear it."

"Excuse me?"

The cook picked up one of the bowls.

"Listen."

I looked at her in distrust, then brought my ear closer. At first I thought it was a noise like that from a conch shell, and then I realized it was a woman's voice. Without the whipped cream, it might have been more distinct.

"What's this?"

"Whispering fruit salad."

"What's it whispering? I can't make it out."

"Excerpts from great plays."

"How nice. Is she an avid theatergoer?"

"She worked as a prompter."

"I envy you. You sit in the best seat in the house."

"That's right," replied the cook, "but being so close to the stage has its drawbacks. Unpleasant things can happen to you."

"Such as?"

"Being hypnotized, for example."

"Who could hypnotize you there?"

"An actor. Although he didn't do it intentionally. He was playing a magician who was supposed to put an actress to sleep. She just pretended to be hypnotized, but the acting was so convincing that I, who was watching everything up close, really fell asleep."

"That could have jeopardized the whole show."

"They managed without me."

"When did you wake up?"

"The applause at the end brought me round."

"You were unconscious until then?"

"Oh, no. I was dreaming."

"Really? What did you dream under hypnosis?"

"A very unusual dream. Would you like me to tell it to you?"

I looked toward the chef who nodded his head.

"It's certainly worth listening to. You won't mind, though, if I leave you now. There's a lot of work waiting for me and I know the story quite well."

"Of course."

I turned towards the cook as the chef walked away.

"I'm all ears."

∽ 4 ∾

I came out of the bathroom in the tail of an airplane.

An older man in a pilot's uniform was standing in front of the door. Everything he wore seemed custom-made except for his hat which was too big; it covered half his forehead and squashed his ears.

"Finally!"

If it weren't for his broad smile and bow, I would

have thought he was reproaching me for staying too long in the bathroom.

"I couldn't any sooner," I said nevertheless.

"You're not late. After you."

He indicated the forward section of the plane. Not a single seat was taken. A number of men and women were standing along the aisle. They wore identical blue uniforms, but their age and appearance differed: old, young, plump, slender, short and tall. They were all smiling and waving at me.

I waved back.

"Please let me introduce myself," said the pilot. "I'm your host, the captain of the plane."

"Nice to meet you," I replied.

"Don't think that I'm neglecting my duties. The plane is on autopilot. In earlier days, the captain had to be a skilled pilot. Today that's no longer essential; other experience is valued."

"What kind?"

"What recommended me for this job was the fact that I was first a seaman and then a hunter."

"What do they have to do with flying?"

"Nothing. But the passengers can benefit from them. For example, would you like me to show you how to tie boating knots?"

"What would I do with boating knots?"

"They can come in handy. You don't even have to be at sea, they're used on land as well."

"I don't have any rope."

"Rope is necessary, unfortunately. But no equipment is needed if you'd like to learn how to deal with seasickness."

"Why would I get seasick? We're not on a rough sea."

"We're not, but there isn't much difference between

a boat in the middle of a storm and an airplane going through turbulence. I'll adjust the automatic pilot a bit and you'll feel nauseous right away."

I shook my head briskly.

"I don't like being nauseous."

"Who does? All right, how about if I teach you how to throw a harpoon?"

"Here in the airplane?"

"Yes. We have a rubber whale. Not full-sized, of course, but big enough. With a little practice, it'll be hard for you to miss it."

"I wouldn't have the heart to stab even a rubber whale."

"I understand. That part of a seaman's training was hard on me too. Real whales are such wonderful creatures. Then let's try saving lives instead of taking them. I'd love to show you how to help a drowning person."

I looked down the aisle.

"No one's drowning here."

"We can take care of that in a jiffy. We have a little pool and two people experienced at drowning. Just in case. Many don't like to give artificial mouth-to-mouth respiration to a person of the same sex. Then there are those who actually ask for it. . . ."

"I'd rather remain unskilled at saving people of either sex."

The captain looked at me for a moment in silence, as though in two minds about something. When he spoke, it was in a lowered voice.

"We have a special offer for passengers who can't make up their minds. But it's quite unofficial. If the word got out, I'd have to deny that I said anything to you."

"I'm not a blabbermouth," I replied, offended.

"That's good. So, would you be interested in a course for pirates?"

I thought I hadn't heard correctly.

"For pirates?"

"Yes. Real pirates. We would train you in everything that has to do with the pirate's vocation. Finding your bearings at sea, chasing and attacking ships. Capturing and killing passengers and crew."

"Are you joking?"

"No. That's unavoidable. You can't be a pirate unless you're ready for everything. Whoever heard of a soft-hearted pirate?"

"I haven't the slightest desire to be a pirate."

The captain sighed.

"It seems there's nothing for you in my seaman's experience. Too bad. But perhaps you'll find something among my hunting skills."

"I doubt it. I'm no more ready to kill animals than people."

"Hunting isn't just killing. That can even be left out. It has other attractions. Tracking, for example. Your wits are constantly being tested. I could teach you how to distinguish between the tracks of living animals and even of those that are extinct."

"I don't know what would be the good of tracking the living, let alone the extinct."

"That knowledge once saved my life. I came across the tracks of a mammoth."

"Where did those come from? The mammoths are all gone."

"That's what everyone says. But the tracks were clearly visible in the snow. There was no doubt about it. If I hadn't recognized them, curiosity might have led me to follow them. I fled in panic instead."

"I would have fled if I'd seen rabbit tracks. That's why I stay away from game, so I don't have to recognize their tracks."

"How about if I teach you to sing hunting songs? They're very cheerful."

"I don't have the slightest singing voice."

"Neither do most hunters. But that's just what's needed. When they start to scream during the hunt, they flush all the animals out of their holes. Not even the roar of a pack of hunting dogs scares them as much."

"I'd rather not frighten the poor animals."

"How kind of you. Perhaps you'd like to perfect the skill of inventing hunting stories? That certainly won't harm any animals."

"I'm no good at making things up."

"It makes no difference. After our accelerated course, you'll become a first-class liar. And that can be of use not only in hunting."

I thought it over briefly.

"I don't really think I need that."

The captain shrugged his shoulders.

"Then all that's left is our special offer. Need I remind you that it must remain a secret?"

"Like I didn't hear a thing."

His voice softened again.

"I can train you to hunt people."

I stared at him in disbelief, then put my hands over my ears and shook my head.

"I didn't hear a thing," I repeated, my voice raised.

"As you wish. Although, you'd be surprised at how many devotees it has. . . ."

I continued to shake my head.

"All right. I'm sorry that nothing about the seaman's

profession or hunting suited you, but I'm sure we'll find something for you among my crew."

He gestured broadly at the row down the aisle, then preceded me.

The first in the row was a tall, handsome young man with gray eyes. His uniform fit him perfectly.

"This is our veterinary expert," said the captain, introducing him. "Even though he didn't finish his studies for quite justified reasons, he acquired valuable knowledge nonetheless."

"I'm not exactly inclined towards veterinary science."

"Just wait until you hear what he can teach you. Veterinary skills have a broad application."

"Passengers most often ask me to show them how to milk a cow," said the young veterinarian with a captivating smile. My eyes were fixed on him as though glued there.

"You have a cow on the airplane?"

Even as I asked this question, I realized how ridiculous it was.

He laughed.

"Of course not. But we have an artificial udder. It's made of plastic but it feels like the real thing. The milk, however, is real. It's even sweetened. You can drink it as soon as it's milked. Hot or cold, as you like."

"Unfortunately, milk disagrees with me and I avoid sugar."

"You can also milk buttermilk. It's quite dietetic."

"I don't like buttermilk either," I replied defensively.

The veterinarian appraised me briefly, then his smile softened.

"The udder doesn't have to produce a dairy product."

"So what does it produce?"

"Anything. Just about any liquid can be used to learn how to milk. Hard liquor, for example."

I frowned.

"That would be blasphemous even with an artificial udder. In any case, I don't drink."

"Of course. Let's see what else might interest you. Perhaps you'd like me to teach you to gobble?"

"Do you mean . . . like a turkey?"

Another stupid question. But I had to make sure.

He nodded and his smile broadened again.

"After practicing for just fifteen minutes, everyone who hears you will be convinced that you're a real turkey. You'd even deceive the males."

"What for? I don't want to deceive the males."

"You don't have to. You could compete."

"In gobbling?"

"Yes. There are international competitions. Many of our passengers have won valuable prizes."

"I'll go empty-handed."

The veterinarian looked at the captain who cleared his throat.

"I have a special offer here, too," said the captain in a low voice.

"Really?" I asked warily.

"A course on removing sea urchin spines," said the veterinarian.

I couldn't avoid another stupid question.

"Real ones?"

"Of course. No spine could be as sharp if it was made of plastic."

"Here in the airplane?"

"That's right. In a container of seawater. Ready for use."

"And how is it . . . used?"

Now the veterinarian cleared his throat.

"The passenger takes off their shoe and steps on the sea urchin."

"Are you out of your mind?" I asked, dumbfounded. "That really hurts."

"Yes, it's not painless. But I'm afraid there's no other way. Pain is the best teacher. When you become skilled at taking spines out of your own foot, others won't feel a thing when you take spines out of theirs."

"I don't want to take spines out of anyone's feet. My own or anyone else's. In any case, I only swim in a swimming pool and those who prefer the sea can make do themselves."

"That's not very charitable," said the captain, chiding me gently.

"It's not. But it doesn't hurt."

"So, shall we continue?"

Under other circumstances, I would have stayed a bit longer with the veterinarian. Even though he wasn't smiling anymore, it was still hard to take my eyes off his face. But I was chilled at the thought of the black spines.

"Let's."

Behind the veterinarian stood a thin young woman with large dark eyes and short hair. She had a tiny mole on the tip of her nose.

"Here's our hairdresser," said the captain. "She will offer you lots of useful advice from the profession."

I smoothed my hair.

"How nice."

"Would you be interested in commando haircutting?" asked the hairdresser in a squeaky voice.

"Commando?"

"Yes, just with a knife. It's amazing what you can do if it's well sharpened."

"But why would I cut my hair with a knife?"

"Because you don't have any scissors."

"My hairdresser always has scissors."

"You might be far away from a hairdresser. In the middle of the jungle, for example. The only equipment you have is a knife. What would you do then?"

"Nothing. I'd wait to return from the wild."

"But you won't have time for that. There's an urgent need to fix your hair."

"Why would I need to fix my hair in the jungle?"

"You never know."

"To impress an orangutan, maybe?"

"You should always look your best. In any case, it doesn't have to be the jungle. You might be in the desert. Or on some glacier."

"I don't go to places like that."

"How about if I teach you to give a dry shave?"

"To whom?"

"A man, of course."

"Why on earth would I shave him, let alone without water?"

"Because he won't like it one bit."

"Is there a reason to torture him?"

"Have you ever been insulted by a man?"

I didn't have to think twice.

"What woman hasn't?"

"Of course. And you'd like to take your revenge, wouldn't you?"

"Naturally."

"Believe me, there's no sweeter revenge than a dry shave. After that he'll never think of insulting anyone again."

"Maybe, but I doubt that he'd let me do it to him."

"You won't ask for his permission. The course on painful shaving includes instructions on abduction. Highly reliable."

Now I gave it some thought.

"I don't bear a grudge against men to the point of kidnapping them."

The hairdresser didn't reply. We stood there briefly in silence, and then the captain spoke up.

"The special offer . . ."

"Wasn't this it?"

"Learning to give a haircut and shave to the deceased," said the young woman in a low voice.

My eyes went back and forth from the captain to the hairdresser in astonishment.

"Do you have the deceased on the plane?" I finally asked, also softly.

"No, we don't. But our colleague does a wonderful job of playing the part."

He indicated the short, obese man behind him who was about forty. His three-day beard and long curly hair made his face look even chubbier. He smiled rather stupidly.

"When he lies down, crosses his hands on his chest and closes his eyes," said the captain, "he's the spitting image of a corpse."

"You can't tell he's breathing," added the young woman. "He even goes pale. He can stay like that for hours and we can take our time practicing."

"I haven't the slightest desire to practice anything on the dead," I said, almost shouting. "Fake or real."

"Of course, of course," said the captain soothingly. "Let's move on."

When we stopped in front of the fat man, I shot a piercing glance at the captain.

"If the only thing on offer here is pretending to be dead, we can move on immediately."

"Certainly not. That's only his hobby. Otherwise he's

a galley cook, a true master of his work. You want to lick your fingers after every one of his dishes."

I frowned at the thought of licking my fingers after a dish prepared by a hobby corpse. And from the unpleasant smell that surrounded him.

"You can learn various skills from a galley cook," continued the captain. "How to cook in the middle of a storm."

"How can you work in the galley on a rough sea?"

"It helps to put on a bit of weight," said the cook. "The heavier you are, the steadier you are on your feet."

"That's certainly no reason for me to put on weight."

"You have to be agile too, otherwise something hot will spill on you or you'll cut yourself while chopping."

"I'm hopelessly clumsy."

"After a short course you'll become a real juggler."

"I doubt that even a very long course would help me. But what on earth are you doing in the galley during a storm? Who feels like eating then?"

"You'd be surprised at the number of passengers who get the most pleasure out of eating on the high waves."

"My stomach would turn at the very thought of food."

"It's not all about food," noted the captain. "Our cook can also offer other things. No one has just one duty on a luxury liner. When he wasn't in the kitchen, he put on magic shows."

I jumped when the fat man suddenly cracked his knuckles in front of my eyes. The next moment a bouquet of violets appeared in his hand, seemingly out of nowhere. He bowed. Applause echoed down the aisle.

"I can show you how to do a variety of tricks. Such as how to cut a passenger in half."

"It wouldn't do any good. If I cut him in half, he'd never be put back together again."

"How about a passenger disappearing from a chain-bound trunk?"

"He'd never turn up again."

The cook looked to the captain for help. He cleared his throat again, but I beat him to it.

"Let me hear the special offer."

"A ship, you see, is like a miniature state. While you're on the high seas you can take care of legal matters. Get married, for example."

"I know that."

"What you might not know is that trials take place. And sentences are carried out."

"The convicted are sent to the ship's prison?"

"Most often. But sometimes the harshest sentence is handed down. . . ."

I stared at the captain.

"Do you mean . . ."

He nodded slowly.

"The cook is also the ship's executioner. Someone has to be, and he's the only one with experience in taking someone's life. If you want him to teach you the most painless way . . ."

"No thanks!"

"That's what I thought. Let's move on."

The next man was the exact opposite of the galley cook: strikingly thin, neat hair, freshly shaved, nice-smelling. His glasses had the very thick lenses of the extremely short-sighted.

"This man has done many jobs," said the captain, "so he has a variety of things to offer. Let's see whether we can find something for you here."

"Let's see," I agreed.

"What do you say about taming snakes?"

"Lizards give me the willies, let alone snakes. Don't tell me you have venomous ones on the plane."

"We have two wild cobras. But rest assured, their poison has been removed."

"With or without poison, just keep them as far away from me as possible."

"Certainly. I don't like reptiles either."

"You're wrong to feel that way," said the short-sighted steward. "Cobras are such dear creatures. When you tame them they become very sweet. Even more so than cats."

"I don't like cats either."

"And you can talk to them. They listen to you attentively and constantly nod their heads. They make the perfect pet for people who live alone."

"I don't live alone."

"Perhaps," interjected the captain, "you'd be interested in learning how to be a stuntwoman? Our steward here was famous for his madcap stunts. He was celebrated for fire scenes in particular. After his course you'll be able to burn safely for up to six minutes."

"Would you start a fire in here?"

"Carefully controlled."

"Still, I don't want to burn on a pyre, even if the fire is controlled."

We sank into silence for a moment. By the looks the captain and stuntman exchanged, I knew what was next, so I rushed to avert it.

"We can skip the special offer."

The captain smiled.

"There isn't any here. Instead, he would tell you about something he experienced under special circumstances. It would be an honor for him if you listened to his story."

"Gladly," I replied, thinking that there could be no harm in a story. All I was expected to do was listen, without undergoing any foolish training.

"Perhaps you'd like to take a seat," proposed the captain, indicating the empty seat behind me. "It's nicer to listen that way."

I sat in the middle seat and the stuntman took the aisle seat. The captain sat on the armrest of the seat across the way.

I thought the story would start immediately, but the captain spoke once again.

"Once he accidentally drank a full bottle of laxatives."

I made a face.

"How awful."

"He spent a day-and-a-half on the toilet seat. He was delirious for a while and saw an apparition."

"Visions often appear when you're delirious."

"This was really unusual," said the stuntman. "All of a sudden it seemed I was no longer in the bathroom but on a street, under an umbrella. It was raining cats and dogs."

"I don't like downpours."

"They don't bother me. I was holding a thick brown leather-bound book under my arm and was taking it back to the town library."

"You didn't have to go in a downpour."

"You don't really choose very much when you're delirious. There were hardly any passers-by."

"No wonder."

"I stayed away from the pavement so the cars wouldn't splash me."

"Drivers can be really inconsiderate."

"It wasn't until I reached the library that I realized I wasn't a member."

"Then how did you take out the book?"

"I don't know. But no matter how I took it out, I had to return it. I couldn't turn around and head back home with it, could I?"

"That wouldn't be smart even when you're delirious."

"I climbed the broad flight of steps to the upper floor and entered a long room with a high ceiling. There was a counter at the opposite end and the walls were covered with shelves full of books."

"As befits such a place."

"Yes. There were books of all shapes, sizes and colors. A real motley collection."

"It's nice when a library is well-stocked."

"But it didn't last long."

"How's that?"

"I headed for the counter. I'd barely gone two or three steps when I noticed out of the corner of my eye that something was happening on the shelves after I passed them."

"What?"

"I stopped and turned around. The motley collection behind me had disappeared. Instead of the variety of books, there were now identical brown leather bound volumes."

"Like the one you were holding?"

"Exactly. As I raised it to take a better look, I realized that I didn't know what book it was."

"What was written on the cover?"

"Nothing."

"Nothing?"

"There was no title. Or author's name. Nothing."

"Then it must have been written inside the book."

"It wasn't. Everything inside was blank."

"Blank?"

"That's right. Just white pages with nothing written."

"I've never heard of such a book."

"Me neither. I looked towards the counter, thinking of asking for an explanation from the librarian, but no one was sitting there."

"Librarians aren't very hardworking nowadays. So, what did you do?"

"I kept going, paying no attention to the shelves. I wanted to get rid of the book as soon as possible."

"I'd do the same thing. Who likes to be holding a hot potato?"

"I decided simply to put the book on the counter and leave as quickly as possible."

"No one could blame you for that. It's not your fault that no one was there."

"Someone did turn up, though, when I got closer."

"The librarian?"

"I don't know. They didn't seem to be."

"There were several of them?"

"An older woman in a green suit and pillbox hat, and an older man in a white suit. They came out of the back room behind the counter."

"What did they say to you?"

"Nothing. There was no need to say anything. Their faces said it all. They looked at the identical shelves behind me, then shot me a piercing glance as though I'd killed someone."

"Unbelievable. Their book did the damage, not you."

"That's what I wanted to tell them, but I didn't have the chance. They signaled angrily with their heads for me to follow them into the back room."

"Did you obey them?"

"Yes. What could I do? They were very threatening."

"They didn't mistreat you back there, did they? Bureaucrats are capable of anything."

"There wasn't any violence. The only thing in the little room was a table with an open metal-studded chest on it. They gestured with their hands for me to look inside."

"What did you see?"

"I was so surprised that I don't remember."

"Too bad. Is that the end of it?"

"Oh, no. They pointed at the chest again."

"Did they think you hadn't taken a proper look?"

"That's what I first thought too. Then I realized that they expected me to put something in it."

"The book?"

"If only it had been the book."

"So what was it?"

The stuntman looked at me probingly for a few moments, then brought his head close to mine and whispered something to me.

"What's that?" I asked to make sure I'd heard right.

He repeated it a little louder.

"That?"

He nodded.

"And you agreed?"

He shrugged his shoulders contritely.

"Brave, I must admit."

He smiled shyly.

"They let you leave afterwards, I assume?"

"It's still unclear. That's when I came out of my delirium on the toilet."

"What an undignified ending."

"There, you've heard the story," said the captain. "You also know what he put in the chest."

"Don't you know?"

"He would have told you out loud if we knew."

I looked at the stuntman questioningly.

"I hope that everything will stay just between us," he pleaded.

"Certainly."

The captain sighed.

"Then we can move on."

The stuntman quickly got up and made room for me to go into the aisle.

The middle-aged man behind him looked withered. He had sunken cheeks, large circles under his eyes, a pale face, and his left eyelid was trembling.

"Here's where you can get useful medical instruction. Everything from personal experience. He's had practically every disease that exists."

"He even looks frail."

"He was as fit as a fiddle until he started to take medicine."

"Why would a healthy man take medicine?"

"To ruin his health."

I looked askance at the sickly steward.

"Is that what medicine is for?"

"If you want to harm yourself."

"Who would want to do that?"

"A suicide."

"Is he a suicide?"

"Failed. He mixed and drank all kinds of medicine, in vain. He simply couldn't do himself in."

"It wasn't totally in vain," said the steward weakly. "At least now I know the best way to ruin each organ."

"Every cloud has a silver lining," I said.

"Your liver will fail you reliably from yellow and blue pills. Nothing will weaken your heart like red and green pills. Kidneys will fail in no time at all from brown and black pills. And for permanent lung damage there's nothing like purple and white pills."

"Nicely matched colors."

"He's an aesthete," noted the captain.

"Beauty can be dangerous nowadays. In any case, thank you for the advice. It will come in handy if I decide to ruin my health."

"My pleasure," replied the steward with the hint of a smile.

"That's not all," interjected the captain again. "He was also a policeman until he received a disability pension. He would love to instruct you in various skills from that profession. Is there something you'd like in particular?"

I shook my head.

"I've never been attracted by police work."

"Some things are useful to know. For example, he can show you how to find someone who's hiding."

"How could he show me that in an airplane?"

"There are lots of nooks here. If I was to hole up in one of them, you'd never be able to find me without comprehensive police training."

"I'm not at all fond of the chase."

"Very well. Perhaps you'd like the special offer? You can imagine what it is, can't you?"

"No."

The captain glanced at the retired policeman, who bowed his head.

"He could teach you how to beat someone up."

"Beat someone up?" I repeated, aghast.

"Yes. Very professionally. Not a single mark is left after his beatings. Nothing to charge him with. Here, look."

He opened his jacket and unbuttoned his shirt.

"Do you see any bruise or scar?"

I stared awkwardly at the naked, hairy chest.

"No. But I don't understand. Why should there be any?"

"Because he uses me in the training. He has to use someone and as the captain it's most natural for it to be me. It would be hypocritical to expect that from a member of the crew."

"And he really . . . beats you?"

"Mercilessly. Not only him, the passengers too. It's indispensable for the training. Practice is highly important when it comes to beating."

"But it must hurt. . . ."

"Of course it hurts. I often groan, but you mustn't pay attention. I'm well paid to put up with it. In addition, you'll never become a good goon if you're soft-hearted."

"The farthest thing from my mind is to become any kind of goon."

"Wouldn't you rather think it over a bit? It does have its charms. . . ."

"There's nothing to think over," I said sharply and headed for the next steward. When the captain rejoined me, his shirt and jacket were properly buttoned once again.

The young woman was diminutive but solidly built. Under her short brown hair was a broad, muscular neck.

"Do you go in for sports?" asked the captain.

"Not as much as I'd like."

"Here's a chance to rectify that. Our stewardess is an all-round athlete. She can coach you in a variety of disciplines. Her specialty is throwing events. Would you like to try shot-put?"

"Shots are heavy. I don't think I'd be able to pick one up. And where would I put it in here?"

"We have light shots for beginners and an airplane is a perfect place to train. You stand in the tail and put it forward. What do you think is the longest put?"

"I wouldn't know."

"Nine rows. One of the passengers put it all the way to here."

He indicated a seat in the ninth row from the back.

"But if the shot falls on the floor instead of a seat, it could make a hole. Even the lightest shot is heavy when it's put."

"The floor is sturdy, but the windows aren't. Luckily, not too many of the passengers are clumsy. Only once did a shot hit a window and break it. The decompression almost sucked the poor passenger out of the airplane."

"I'm not that skilled either. I wouldn't like to tempt fate."

"Maybe you'd prefer a hurdle race?"

"Hurdle?"

"Yes. The seats can be quickly arranged so their backs are the hurdles. And there's a prize waiting if you beat the record. The fastest passenger to date ran from the tail to the cockpit in five seconds and twenty-seven hundredths."

"I wouldn't even make it to the finish. I'd fall at the very first hurdle."

The captain glanced at me briefly in silence, then looked at the athlete.

"Not even sports are without their special offers," he said diffidently.

"I thought as much. I'd be quite interested to know what that might be in sports."

"Javelin throwing."

"I don't see anything special about throwing a javelin."

"You don't throw it just to reach the farthest point."

"But . . . ?"

"To hit the target."

"What target?"

"A live one."

"Live? You're not thinking of some poor animal again, are you?"

"Of course not. I may be a hunter, but I'm not a sadist. I was thinking of myself."

I was speechless for a few moments.

"I'm supposed to hit you with a javelin?"

"Yes. And you won't find a better teacher than her to do it."

"I have personal experience in hitting live targets," said the athlete. "You're sure to hit the captain with a bit of practice."

"But I don't want to hit him. How could I have him on my conscience?"

"Don't worry, you won't," the captain said. "A lot of people have hit me already and nothing happened. Here, would you like to check?"

He started to unbutton his shirt again, but I stopped him.

"I believe you. But how can that be? Does the javelin not leave marks like the policeman's beatings?"

"No such javelin exists. I wear a flak jacket. It hurts a little when I'm hit, but it's not even close to the blow of a night stick. You can target me with a clear conscience."

"Regardless of whether or not it hurts, my conscience would by no means be clear. Please, let's continue."

The captain sighed again.

"It's not easy to please you."

"It's not," I agreed.

The second-to-last in the row was a tall, blond young man. The uniform emphasized his athletic build.

"This is what someone looks like," said the captain, "who didn't wear a flak jacket when he was hit by a javelin."

I took another look at the young man and was just about to say that he looked better than the captain who had worn a flak jacket, but held back. The captain didn't deserve that, after all. He'd made a wholehearted effort for me. I just smiled and nodded, and he replied in kind.

"He was also an athlete, a long jumper. A recklessly thrown javelin . . ."

A whimper from the stewardess-athlete interrupted him. The captain looked at her gently, as though to console her, then continued.

". . . put an early end to his career. That's why he can't offer much instruction in sports, but he can offer many things from other fields. He held a variety of jobs after he left athletics. For example, he could give you a short course on dynamiting."

"Only theoretical, I hope," I said, sensing trouble.

"Not at all," said the young man. "You can't become a good dynamiter without proper practical training."

"So where does the training take place?"

He indicated his surroundings.

"Here."

The captain grinned, seeing my astonishment.

"Rest assured, there has already been lots of dynamiting in the plane. The explosion is carefully controlled. Only one seat is destroyed. Those around it are completely unscathed. Nothing would happen to you even if you were sitting in one of them."

"I wouldn't even like to be sitting in the cockpit with the door closed. I detest noise."

"Have you ever tried to be a lumberjack?"

"No, I haven't."

"There's nothing healthier. You're out in the fresh air and all your muscles are working. Just look at how well-built he is."

I had to agree.

"He's got a good figure."

"How else could it be after cutting down one thousand seven hundred and sixteen trees?"

I frowned.

"I'd feel bad about cutting down one single tree."

"You won't have to feel bad here. Strict ecological rules are in force on the plane. The beech tree used for training is made of artificial wood. You can chop it with a good clear conscience."

"Artificial or real, I'd still be heartsick. And I've never held an ax in my life. That's not for me."

"Then perhaps the special offer is for you?"

"If it's like the other ones . . ."

"Would you still like to hear it? You can never tell what you might like."

"All right, but I don't think . . ."

"Do you know the favorite pastime of lumberjacks after a hard day's work?"

"I haven't a clue."

"Sword swallowing."

"They could have found something less harmful."

"It's not at all as dangerous as it looks," said the young man. "People are quite amazed when they hear how deep a sword can go down the throat. What do you think, how deep could it go down yours?"

"Not at all. I have a very sensitive gag reflex. I can't stand to have anything in my mouth. But don't tell me you have cold steel on the plane?"

"Solely for this purpose," the captain assured me. "I guarantee that with a little practice you'll have no trouble swallowing a sword that's three meters and fifteen centimeters long."

"What's that? Where would it all fit?"

"There's a lot more space inside than you suspect. The record is over nine-and-a-half meters and it was swallowed by someone smaller than you. But even that is far from the end."

"Wouldn't the sword cut up my insides?"

"Quite the contrary. It has a very therapeutic effect. It's enough to insert it properly two or three times and duodenal ulcers disappear without a trace. It also cures gastritis and colitis. Even hemorrhoids, if it reaches them."

"Thank you very much. I'm not suffering from a single one of those ailments."

The captain opened his arms.

"We haven't had such a discriminating passenger in a long time. But don't lose hope. Few women can resist what we still have to offer."

He indicated the last person in the row.

I scrutinized the stewardess who was already past her prime. She was at least four or five kilos overweight, garishly made up and dressed in clothes that were too tight. Her bright-red lips were curled into a clown-like grimace of a smile. I returned just the suggestion of a smile.

"She is an experienced seductress," said the captain proudly.

"Really?" I replied caustically. "I never would have thought."

"Let me assure you. If you only knew about all those who she's seduced."

"I can imagine."

"She will let you in on her secrets of seduction if you wish."

I'd already started to shake my head when curiosity got the better of me.

"How would she do that?"

"Hands-on. Choose one of the stewards and in no time at all she'll teach you how to win him over. He won't be able to resist your charms."

"I don't need anyone's help for that."

"Perhaps you might like to seduce a stewardess?"

"What an idea!" I snapped.

"Please don't be offended. Passengers have even more unusual appetites. She has successfully shown how to charm an anteater, a wild boar, rubber doll, coat rack, dentist's chair. . . ."

"Enough!" I shouted. "I don't want to hear any more abominations."

"Of course, of course," replied the captain soothingly.

"You don't have to trouble yourself with the special offer," I hastened to add. "If the ordinary ones are like this . . ."

"Ah, you're wrong," interrupted the captain. "Her special offer is quite respectable. It's a story."

"A story?"

"Yes. She will tell you about a dream she had in a lifeboat. Strange dreams appear after five bottles of champagne in cramped quarters and total darkness in the middle of the ocean. Would you like to hear it?"

"Are there any anteaters and all the rest?"

"I give you my word as a captain."

"All right, although I don't approve of binge drinking."

"Me neither. But under such exceptional circum-

stances, it's understandable. I suggest that you sit here."
He showed me the middle seat in a nearby row. "It's not
a short story."

I sat there and the seductress sat next to me.

"Please excuse me now," said the captain. "It's time I
checked on the automatic pilot."

He bowed.

"Of course," I replied.

Before she started the story, she gave me another of
her clown-like smiles.

∽ 5 ∾

I entered the prison corridor.

There were four cells on either side. Thick white
bars stretched from floor to ceiling. Brightness poured
down from neon lights along the top of the corridor.
There was a small, high window at the corridor's end.

The nearest door on the left opened with a metallic
sound and a tall, slender, older man came out of cell
number one. His striped prison uniform was clean and
neat, accentuating his dignified appearance.

"Hello," he said to me in a deep voice. "We've been
expecting you."

"Hello," I replied, a little hesitantly. "Here I am."

"I'm glad. With your permission, I would first like to
introduce myself."

"Please do."

"I am a judge."

I looked at him, bewildered.

"Is prison a place for judges?"

"The place for judges is alongside those they have
sentenced. Should we turn our backs on them and
abandon them to their fate?"

"Certainly not. It's just that I didn't know. . . ."

"A sentence only has meaning if the convicted leave this place completely rehabilitated. And who can take better care of that than a judge?"

"No one, I presume."

"No one, of course. Only judges are prepared to devote themselves to the inmates twenty-four hours a day. The guards, psychologists and confessors spend just a short time with them, which is by no means enough."

"But then it's like you've been sentenced too."

"I am. I sentenced myself. If it weren't for that, I wouldn't be able to wear this uniform. And you can only establish trust with convicts if you are one of them."

"What did you convict yourself of?"

"There was a reason. No one's a saint. You'd certainly be found guilty of something too. If you want to join us, we can dig something up."

"No, thanks. So, what was your crime?"

"I abused my wives at night."

"How terrible. You don't look at all like a sadist."

"I'm not. My wives were the incidental victims of my insomnia. Have you ever suffered from that?"

"No, I haven't."

"You can't imagine how hard it is when your eyes don't get sleepy. You'd do anything to fall asleep."

"So, what did you do?"

"I tried everything. In the end I discovered that the only thing that helped was to leave the light on and play a recording of a storm with the sound turned up. That was the only way I could close my eyes."

"And your wives put up with that horror?"

"The first one did for seven-and-a-half months and the second one almost a year-and-a-half."

"Poor things. I would have left you after the third night."

"Don't think my conscience doesn't prick me. That's why I gave myself the maximum penalty. I didn't take into consideration any mitigating circumstances, even though there were some."

I opened my mouth to say that he didn't deserve any mercy, but then something crossed my mind. I glanced inside his cell. There was an iron bed in the corner.

"You sleep there, don't you?"

"Yes. I'm no different than the others. I'm here night and day."

"I hope you don't put yourself to sleep the same way you did at home. You'd be sending seven innocent prisoners to the madhouse. Unlike your wives, they can't leave when they've had enough."

"Rest assured. The light, though, doesn't go out at night. Those are the regulations, it doesn't depend on me. But I don't need to hear a storm anymore. I fall asleep soon after I close my eyes."

"How so? Perhaps being in a prison bed does you good."

"It doesn't do anyone any good. The mattresses are hard, the sheets are rough. It's something else: my hobby helps me."

"Hobby?"

"That's right. I keep bees."

"Where?"

"There."

He pointed to a tall metal cabinet across from the bed.

"I have two hives inside. I let the bees out every morning. They go out the window and then come back in the evening."

"Are you allowed to keep beehives in prison?"

"Officially no, but as a judge I have certain privileges. As do my wards."

"How nice."

"My bees produce excellent honey. Everyone here loves it. Would you like to try some?"

"No, thank you. I don't like honey."

"More's the pity, it's very healthy."

"But how does keeping bees help you sleep?"

"First I counted them. Like people count sheep. But it didn't work. And then I accidentally started to give them names. And that worked. Before I get to the seventh name I'm overcome by sleep."

"What a great idea you hit upon."

"Where there's a will there's a way. All right, now let me introduce you to the other prisoners."

We went up to cell number two. A short, older woman put the notebook in which she was writing down on the bed and came towards us. She was wearing an unusual prison uniform with wiggly purple and black stripes. In addition, she had a large brooch on the left lapel and a bright red belt. A brightly colored ostrich feather was stuck into her graying bun.

When she reached the bars, she nodded without speaking.

"This is my third wife," said the judge affectionately, as though we were on a promenade.

"You sent your wife to prison?" I asked, horror-struck.

"I had no choice. The law applies equally to us all. In fact, I gave her the maximum penalty too. So I wouldn't be accused of favoritism."

"What was her crime?"

"Spouse abuse."

I looked at the tiny woman in disbelief.

"She abused you? To me she looks more like the victim of your nocturnal eccentricities. How did she ever put up with them?"

"It was simple. She put on a sleeping mask, stuffed her ears with cotton wool and slept like a log."

"So where did she go wrong? Were you bothered by the fact that she was sleeping?"

"Of course not. Everything was fine at night. It was the days that became unbearable."

"How's that?"

"She didn't close her mouth from the time she got up to the time she went to bed."

"And that's why she ended up in prison? How extraordinary!"

"It's clear you haven't lived with someone who talks without letup. I put up with that torture for over two years and four months. Many people would have lost patience much earlier. Murderous thoughts crossed my mind after just five days."

"That's a terrible thing for a judge to say."

"Even a judge is only human. In any case, I managed to restrain myself somehow."

"Why didn't you put cotton wool in your ears too if it bothered you that much?"

"Because she became offended when I didn't listen to her. Women like for people to listen when they talk."

"Men aren't any better. But what did you gain by putting her in here? She's still in your vicinity. Although she doesn't look at all like a chatterbox. She has yet to say a word."

"That's because she's been ordered to keep silent while she's in prison. For her own good, as therapy."

"This is getting worse and worse. How merciless to put a plug in the woman's mouth. . . ."

"There are ways to talk even when your mouth is closed."

"Pantomime, you mean?"

"No. Writing. My wife never puts down her pen. She tirelessly fills notebook after notebook."

"Poor thing. Doesn't she get writer's cramp?"

"I'm the one you should pity. I had to read it all until recently. I didn't have time for anything else. It was worse than when she talked."

"You don't have to read anymore?"

"No. Thanks to her hobby."

"She has a hobby too?"

"Yes. Everyone here has one."

"What's hers?"

"She's raising a goat."

"Where?"

He pointed to the back of the second cell.

"In the cabinet, where else?"

"She keeps a goat there?"

"Don't worry, the goat's comfortable in the cabinet. There's enough light, fresh grass and water. It's almost like being in a meadow."

"But it's so cramped."

"Yes, a bit. That's why my wife lets it run around the cell when the guards aren't nearby. But even when they're here, they turn a blind eye. They're not at all as insensitive as people say."

"So how does the goat get you out of reading her notebooks?"

"It's not an ordinary goat. Once it accidentally ate half a poet's collection of poems and really liked it. Manuscripts turned out to be a real treat for it."

"Do you mean to say . . ."

"Yes. The goat eats everything my wife writes. It's

insatiable. She's unable to write as much as that animal can devour. It would eat up three times as much."

"But that is so humiliating. Writing for a goat to eat . . ."

"Not in the least. Everyone is satisfied this way. The goat enjoys its favorite food, my wife is happy because her immoderate talking finally suits someone, and I am completely spared from my former painful obligation."

"Looks like your third marriage will last."

"Quite so. When we get out of here, we'll take the bees and goat with us."

"When you think about it, it takes so little to live together in harmony."

"Very little, I agree. And now I suggest we move on. My wife has to go back to her writing. The goat will soon start to bleat from hunger."

"Of course."

The tiny woman nodded again, then rushed to the bed, and we headed for the third cell.

Standing next to the bars was a dark man in early middle age. The black stripes on his prison uniform were considerably wider than the white ones, but his large bow tie and the napkin thrown over his left forearm were radiantly white.

"He is a waiter," said the judge.

"May I offer you something?" asked the waiter. "Perhaps you'd like to refresh yourself with a drink? We have the choicest selection."

"I didn't know that alcohol was served in prison."

"Only to visitors. What would you like?"

"Nothing, thank you. I don't drink."

"Are you sure?" said the waiter dejectedly.

"Quite."

"That's good," said the judge. "He can barely wait to

open a bottle for a guest. Then he finishes it by himself. Although he might not appear so, he's quite fond of a good drop. He's always on the watch for a chance to pour it on."

"Was it the drink that put him in prison?"

"Oh, no. He used to be a paragon of sobriety. If he hadn't, he wouldn't have worked in a reputable restaurant. He only started drinking when he got here."

"It must have been tough on him."

"It's tough on everyone. I'm not happy to be in prison either, but I don't get drunk."

"Why is he behind bars?"

"Because he hates birds."

"Is that a reason to go to prison?"

"In particularly serious cases such as his."

"So how does he hate birds?"

"He paints them black."

"What's that you say?"

"He never went anywhere without a can of black spray paint. As soon as he caught sight of a bird, he'd hide and then spray it black."

"How awful."

"First he did it in the public parks. He turned almost every pigeon black."

"Poor pigeons."

"He even sprayed birds he didn't have to because they were already black. Crows and ravens, for example."

"That's really hard to understand."

"He was finally arrested after sneaking into the zoo one night. By morning everything with feathers was completely black. Even the down pillow of one of the guards was hit."

"It was high time someone put a stop to it. But why did he do it? What did he have against the birds?"

"He'd been traumatized when a woman brought an exquisite bird into the restaurant and ordered roast pigeon in wild strawberry sauce for it."

"Why, that bird was a cannibal."

"That's right."

"How awful. It's no wonder the waiter was shocked. Even so, taking revenge on all the other birds because of that one. . . ."

"That's why he had to go to prison."

"Wouldn't it have been better to put him in an institution where he would get treatment?"

"Oh, he's already been cured here."

"How?"

"His hobby helped. He's raising an ostrich."

I stared over the waiter's left shoulder at the metal cabinet at the back of the cell.

"You aren't going to tell me there's an ostrich in there, are you?"

"Only during the day, when it sleeps. It's a special type of nocturnal ostrich. It comes out of the cabinet at night and has the run of the cell. On the weekend, when there are fewer guards, it even walks in the corridor."

"But why expose the poor bird to such danger? It's like putting something flammable in a pyromaniac's cell."

"There isn't any match. He doesn't have any spray paint."

"Regardless, the ostrich must be a constant provocation for him."

"Yes, but you have to fight fire with fire, right?"

"So they say."

"Constant provocation was the only way to get rid of his bad habit."

"So how did he get rid of it?"

"He got his knuckles rapped. When he returned from a short leave, he smuggled a can of black spray paint into the prison. He waited for the ostrich to fall asleep in the morning, then opened the cabinet, ready to spray it. But the bird woke up and, seeing what was about to happen, pecked him so hard on the hand that the can flew all the way to my cell."

"Served him right."

"He wore a bandage for two-and-a-half months. Now he wouldn't even think of spraying the ostrich black. I offered to return the spray can as a temptation, but he refused."

"So, he's completely cured?"

The judge hesitated briefly before he replied.

"Not quite completely."

"No?"

"When he gets good and drunk, he starts to blather about finding some white spray paint."

"Then you shouldn't let him drink."

"We don't. You can imagine what a relief it was when you turned down his offer."

"Just have a small one," cried out the waiter softly.

I shook my head in reproof.

"Alcohol is really harmful. I think it's best if we continue."

"I agree," replied the judge cheerfully.

A tiny little old man was waiting for us behind the bars of the last cell on the left. He was barely a meter-and-a-half tall and couldn't have weighed more than forty-six-and-a-half kilos. Gray strands poked out from under his black and white jockey cap. He was holding a small whip at his thigh.

"This is our retired jockey," said the judge.

"I thought that might be so," I replied.

"He was long reputed to be unbeatable. He won every race he entered from age forty-three until he retired."

"He must have had an excellent horse."

"He changed horses. Whichever one he rode always came in first."

"Then over time he must have become a very skilled jockey."

"To be sure. But even so, winning every time . . ."

"Lady luck must have smiled on him."

"The racecourse management doesn't really believe in nonstop luck."

"Did they suspect foul play?"

"That was inevitable. At first they thought the horse was doped. That's what usually happens."

"So, did he dope them?"

"No, not the slightest trace of anything illegal was found."

"He was cleared of suspicion then?"

"No. They kept a close eye on him and shadowed him, hoping to find out what it was, without success."

"How did he end up here?"

"He revealed the secret himself after winning his last race."

"What was it?"

"When we were warming up before a race, I would whisper one of my dreams to the horses," said the jockey. His voice was discordantly deep for someone so small.

"Is that why they came in first?"

"Yes," said the judge. "Never underestimate dreams. They don't all have the same power, of course. Others would have had no effect on the horses, but his really stirred them up."

"I didn't know such dreams existed."

"Unfortunately, the law doesn't tolerate incitement by dreams. Their use puts all those without them in an unequal position."

"That's not fair. No one's to blame for their lack."

"Fair or not, a judge must abide by the law."

"Even so, condemning a man just for a dream that horses like . . ."

"They like it here too."

"Really? Do you organize prison horse races? That wouldn't really be abiding by the law. . . ."

"We don't, of course. But horses plagued by mental anguish are brought to him almost every day. You can't imagine how many there are."

"The life of a horse isn't easy."

"Not at all. But as soon as they hear his dream, they feel better. Afterwards they take a little nap in the cabinet."

"But how can you put a horse in the cabinet?"

"It's roomier inside than it looks and the horses don't stay long."

"Is one in there now?"

"Yes. A black stallion. It came here all bewildered and when it leaves it will be rejuvenated. Would you like for him to tell you his dream?"

"Tell me? I'm not a horse with mental anguish."

"You're not, but a little disencumbering is good for everyone. You'll see how good it makes you feel. Being in a prison isn't pleasant even as a visitor."

"I'd go crazy if you closed me up in a cabinet."

"That's not at all necessary. In any case, even if you wanted it, there's no room at the moment. You can sit with him on his bed."

"Well, I don't know. . . ."

"You'll like my dream," said the jockey. "It's very strange. I dreamed it in the hospital after they gave me a blood transfusion when I was in a traffic accident. Before that I heard my late wife's voice."

"My condolences."

"Thank you. Please come in."

He opened the cell door and motioned me in. I looked at the judge, hesitating.

"You haven't been inside a cell before?" he asked.

I shook my head.

"You'll see, it's not at all terrible. You'll quickly get used to it. And the world looks different from the other side of the bars. It's something to be experienced."

I walked inside slowly, then turned towards the judge.

"Everything's fine. Here, we'll leave the door open."

The jockey went ahead of me towards the bed, lightly tapping his thigh with the whip.

"Would you mind putting that down?" I asked after we had sat down.

"Oh, certainly."

He put the whip on the end of the bed.

"Are you comfortable?" he asked.

"As much as the circumstances allow," I replied after thinking it over.

"The bed isn't very soft."

"It doesn't matter."

"So, shall I begin?"

"Please do."

"Have you ever received a blood transfusion?"

"No, I haven't."

"When you receive a large amount of someone else's blood, you're dazed for a while."

"Really?"

"Yes. You have visions."

"What kind of visions?"

"In mine it seemed that I was on a street decorated with triangular blue and white flags everywhere. Music could be heard."

"It must have been a holiday."

"One would say so. And the passers-by were dressed up."

"As they should be on a holiday."

"That's right. Soon, however, I noticed something unusual. Everyone was headed in the same direction."

"What's unusual about that? There must have been a rally."

"That's what I thought. Then why was I the only one to be rushing in the opposite direction?"

"Maybe you didn't feel like going to the rally?"

"But I love celebrations."

"Then why didn't you join the others?"

"Something was pulling me in the direction I was headed."

"Where was that?"

"I only found out when I got there. The racecourse."

"Why, of course. What's more natural for a jockey than to go to a horse race on a holiday?"

"There weren't any races."

"What was there?"

"There weren't any spectators or horses. Everything was deserted. Even so, as soon as I got there, a call came over the loudspeaker for all the jockeys to take their place at the starting gate."

"So what did you do?"

"I stood in position number five, as usual."

"Without a horse?"

"What else could I do?"

"And?"

"I started to run when the gate opened."

"Do you mean, like a runner?"

"Yes, as fast as my legs could carry me."

"But who were you racing against?"

"No one. But to hear the loudspeaker, you'd think that there were lots of contestants and we were hotly competing with each other."

"Maybe you didn't see the others, if you were the leader?"

"I wasn't the leader. I reached the finish line last."

"Who overtook you?"

"All the others."

"What others, if there was no one?"

"I don't know. I was bewildered too. But that's what they announced over the loudspeaker."

"You should avoid transfusions."

"Sometimes that's impossible."

"All right, and that's how it ended, with you being last?"

"No, that was only the introduction to what happened when I crossed the finish line."

"What happened?"

"An elderly woman in green and an older man all in white were standing behind the finish line."

"So there was someone else at the hippodrome."

"I hadn't seen them before. An open chest with metal studs was on the grass in between them."

"How imprudent. You might have tripped over it when you ran across the line."

"I was staggering more than running, completely out of breath. Jockeys are not exactly renowned runners."

"But you do know how to drive a poor horse to exhaustion. Why did they bring that chest onto the track?"

"At first I thought there was a prize for me inside."

"For last place?"

"Sometimes you get a consolation prize for that."

"So did you get one?"

"No, I didn't. I understood from the old woman's and man's angry looks that I wouldn't get a thing and would even have to give something."

"Why?"

"As punishment for last place, I suppose."

"What did you give them?"

The jockey raised his eyes briefly to the judge, then moved closer and whispered two words into my ear.

"That's impossible" I exclaimed in amazement.

He nodded and sighed.

"This was for your ears alone," he added in a low voice.

"A secret is sacred to me," I said, hastening to reassure him.

"Thank you."

We got up from the bed at the same time and headed towards the judge. When I had left the cell, the jockey closed the door behind me.

As we approached the cells on the right, the judge spoke to me quietly.

"Lucky you."

"Why?"

"He confided in you, didn't he?"

I stopped. We looked each other in the eye.

"Yes," I confirmed.

"Would you perhaps . . ."

"Should I betray his trust?" I said, interrupting him.

"Having a judge in your debt can be useful."

"What use is a judge in prison?"

Before we continued, we eyed each other again briefly.

Behind the bars of cell number five stood a slender young woman with short, brown hair. She was wearing a clinging prison suit with short sleeves and pants to just below the knee.

"This is our long jumper," said the judge, introducing her. "A record-holder, although unrecognized."

"Why unrecognized?"

"She made the longest jump, but at practice, not at a competition."

"What bad luck. But that's not what put her in prison, is it?"

"No. What brought her here was her habit of taking showers whenever she could."

"Since when is personal hygiene against the law?"

"It is, if you overdo it."

"Who cares a fig how many showers she takes? She can stay under the shower permanently if she feels like it."

"She can in her own home. But she took showers in public places."

"How's that? There aren't any showers in public places."

"There aren't, but there is water. Whenever she saw water, she couldn't resist. She would stand under city fountains, douse herself with bottles of mineral water in the supermarket, pour drinks over herself that she ordered in bars. . . ."

"That is going a bit far," I had to admit.

"To put it mildly."

"How do you restrain her in here? I hope you don't deprive her of water completely. She would die of thirst, to say nothing of her hygiene."

"This isn't a torture chamber. Quite the contrary, she has enormous quantities of water at her disposal. She chose a water hobby, in any case."

"Water hobby?"

"Yes, she has a large aquarium full of fish."

"In her cabinet, I presume?"

"We barely got it in there."

"Isn't she tempted to jump in among the fish? Bathing is even better than showering."

"She has to resist temptation. If she succumbs, she'll pay for it with her life."

"She doesn't know how to swim?"

"All athletes know how to swim."

"Then what's standing in her way?"

"Piranhas."

I stared at the young woman.

"You keep piranhas?"

"People have the wrong idea about the poor piranhas," she said in a purring voice. "They're such sweet creatures."

"Until you're in their midst," noted the judge. "But there is some benefit to be gained from the piranhas too. She now takes a shower only where she should. In a shower."

"Every cloud has a silver lining."

"So it seems. Shall we continue our visit?"

I nodded, so we headed for the sixth cell. We were met by a stooped man with a pale and wrinkled face. The only hair he had left was above his ears. His striped uniform was at least one size too big and seemed to hang on him. Round wire-rimmed glasses were perched halfway down his nose.

"This is our librarian," the judge informed me, pointing to the back of the cell.

Between the bed and the cabinet rose a shelf full of books. The gooseneck lamp on the little metal table in front of it illuminated an open book.

"Nice, but what put a librarian in prison?"

"Unpaid bills."

"Librarians are known to be modest and upright people. They certainly pay their bills regularly."

"He did too while he could."

"Did he succumb to the thrall of an expensive vice and lose all his money?"

"No. It's all because of the color red."

"Red?"

"Yes. He gets nauseous whenever he sees it."

"What's there about it that bothers him?"

"It reminds him of blood."

"It reminds me of it too, but I don't feel nauseous when I see something red."

"He didn't either until he saw his own blood for the first time. He tried to cut his veins but fainted at the first drop."

"Finally something good out of having an aversion to blood."

"There was something harmful too. After that failed attempt, he collapsed whenever he saw something red."

"How unpleasant."

"It's not until you're in his shoes that you realize how much red there is in the world. At home he was able to get rid of everything that color, but as soon as he went out, he'd run into something red."

"That's inevitable."

"Unfortunately. And do you know how much it costs to have an ambulance come and revive you all the time?"

"Medical services are expensive."

"Not even someone who earns a lot more than a librarian could keep it up. Finally, when the bills amassed, he ended up here."

I looked around the area with the cells.

"It's good that you don't have anything re . . ."

I stopped in mid-sentence, taking hold of my left sleeve.

"My blouse," I added softly.

"It's all right," replied the judge with a little smile. "He no longer has any trouble with the color red."

"Prison cured him?"

"His hobby. He raises leeches."

I frowned.

"I find leeches disgusting, all black and slimy. . . ."

"I don't like them either. But they're good for him. He has a cabinet full of them."

"What does he do with them?"

"He lets them suck his blood. What else do you do with leeches?"

"Some people eat them," said the librarian in a hoarse voice. "Even alive."

"Phooey!" I replied.

"That's prohibited here," said the judge. "He only puts the leeches on his stomach. As soon as they're filled with his blood, all his troubles with the color red disappear."

"So that's why he's so pale."

"It's the small price he has to pay. It's better to be pale than faint all the time."

"Leeches get rid of other ailments too," said the librarian. "Fear of eggs, of buttons, of pacifiers, of wash-basins, of corkscrews . . . Perhaps you'd like to try them? It doesn't hurt at all."

I waved both hands dismissively.

"I'm not suffering from any phobia." I turned towards the judge. "I think it's time we continued."

"Of course."

Behind the bars of the seventh cell stood a tall, middle-aged man with coarse features. The tight prison uniform was covered in stains.

"Our plumber," said the judge.

"Finally someone who belongs in prison," I replied angrily. "If you ask me, every single plumber should be arrested. Whenever I call them in to repair something, all they do is take my money without fixing a thing."

"I can guarantee that he's an excellent repairman. Just wait for him to get out of here and all your plumbing problems will be fixed."

"An excellent repairman who ended up in prison."

"It wasn't because of his work but because of his passion."

"Oh, I see. Romantic?"

"No, gambling. He's an ardent fan of roulette."

"That's not a harmless passion. There's a lot you can lose."

"That's for sure. He lost everything he had."

"How awful. You couldn't keep it under control?" I asked him.

"Have you ever been in the grips of a passion?" asked the plumber in return. He had a deep, manly voice.

"I know how to stop myself in time."

"Then you don't know what passion is."

"He didn't completely lose his presence of mind either," noted the judge.

"How's that when he squandered everything?"

"He didn't get into debt because of gambling."

"How comforting. So how did he end up in prison?"

"He tried to steal a roulette wheel from a gambling house."

"Is that where he lost the most?"

"No. He got it into his head that the only way to discover the secret of roulette was with that wheel."

"Then this was actually doing him a service. While he's locked up here there's no chance for such notions to gain the upper hand."

"Oh, there are. His hobby helps. He raises frogs."

"What do frogs have to do with roulette?"

"He has thirty-seven frogs in his cabinet. Each one has a number on its back. At night he lets them hop around the cell and carefully notes down their hopping."

"Why?"

"Because it's as random as the movement of the ball on a roulette wheel," replied the plumber.

"So did the frogs help you get to the bottom of roulette?"

"Not yet, but I'm on the right path. It just might happen, though, that they let me out too early."

"Then what will you do?"

"I'll do something that puts me back in prison. At least that isn't hard."

"If that does happen," interjected the judge, "he'll certainly drop by to see you before he comes back and will fix all your plumbing problems once and for all."

"How kind. I only hope I don't drown in a flood in my apartment before you come."

"One should never lose hope," said the plumber. "You only learn that when you find yourself in the grips of a passion."

"A useful lesson, to be sure."

"We have one cell left," said the judge, motioning ahead.

A tall woman with a youthful appearance, although already advanced in years, was standing behind the bars of the eighth cell. The prison uniform looked elegant on her, accessorized with a yellow hat and colorful feather.

"Don't be deceived by her polished look. She's quite rightfully in prison."

"What was she convicted of?"

The judge turned briefly and indicated cell number three.

"This is the person who brought on the poor waiter's trauma. The owner of the cannibal bird."

"But it's not against the law to keep a bird that eats other birds. And there's even less reason to charge someone for the waiter's squeamishness."

"That's not why she's here."

"So why is she?"

"For a cunning hoax that she got away with for a long time. She and the bird ate for free in the finest restaurants."

"For free?"

"That's right. Waiters would always be nauseous when they saw one bird devour another. While they were vomiting in the men's room, she and her pet would finish their meal and disappear without a trace. The bill was left unpaid."

"That's not only cunning but vile."

"I agree. But she was finally cornered."

"She got the punishment she deserved."

"If you're thinking of prison, you're wrong. She gets her meals for free here too. The food might not be as good as in fancy restaurants, but we don't complain. Something worse than prison happened to her."

"What?"

"They took away her bird. The cannibal bird was convicted as an accessory and sent to animal prison."

"She could get another pet. Everyone here has an animal, bird or insect as a hobby."

"She didn't want any other. The cannibal bird meant

everything to her. It's like being separated from someone very dear."

"Well, then that's cruel."

"What's to be done? The law is the law."

I pointed to the cabinet behind the woman's back.

"So she's the only one without a hobby?"

"Oh, she has one, even though her cabinet is empty. But she isn't able to pursue it very often."

"Why's that?"

"There aren't any listeners. She loves to tell her dreams. Her greatest pleasure was telling them to the cannibal bird that listened to them tirelessly. That's why she misses it the most."

"Why don't the rest of you listen to them?"

"Regulations won't let us. Each of us may pursue our own hobby exclusively. I alone, during the trial, heard one of her dreams. It was truly fascinating. Perhaps you would like to hear it?"

"But regulations . . ."

"They don't apply to visitors."

"All right, if it will make her happy. . . ."

"Oh, it will, it will," she said, clapping her hands, then quickly opening the cell door.

"You go ahead and get settled inside," said the judge. "You already have cell-time experience. I won't be able to join you, unfortunately. It's time for me to get the hives ready. The bees will soon be back."

"Of course," I replied, then walked into the cell.

The woman closed the door behind me and motioned to the bed with a smile.

"Please sit down."

∽ 6 ∾

I stepped into the circus ring.

A fanfare rang out that same instant and a powerful spotlight beamed down on me. I shaded my eyes with my hand but everything was still blindingly radiant. Just as my eyes adjusted, the thunderous music stopped.

About a dozen people were lined up in the middle of the ring at short intervals. There wasn't a living soul in the stands, but tumultuous applause rang out of the loudspeaker. As though waiting for this signal, a middle-aged, balding man with a pot belly stepped out of the head of the line and came towards me with open arms. His checkered suit made me think he was a clown, but his round, ruddy face had no makeup or red ball for a nose.

I stood still and almost disappeared in his bear hug. His cloying violet aftershave lotion could not quite hide the smell of sweat.

"We've been waiting for you, madam!" he said, almost shouting.

"How nice," I said. Nothing more suitable came to mind.

"Please let me be the first to introduce myself."

"Please do."

"It's not because I feel that the director is the most important person in the circus. Oh no, not at all. To be honest, who in the audience even knows that there is a director? And if they do, they don't care a plugged nickel. They come to the circus because of the performers, not the director, right?"

"So it would seem."

"That's all fine and dandy while things are going

well. But when there's a spanner in the works, do you know who takes the blame?"

"The director?"

"The director, of course. If only you knew how much responsibility is on my shoulders. If a performer botches things, they quickly exit the ring and leave me to clean up after them."

"How unpleasant."

"Not only unpleasant, you can put your life on the line. You can't imagine what the audience has pelted me with, mostly just for something piddling."

"Tomatoes and rotten eggs?"

"Tomatoes and eggs would be a real godsend. Much more dangerous things have flown my way. A dead beaver, half a toilet, a bottle of rancid turpentine, a worm-eaten tree stump, a broken bakelite telephone . . ."

"How did all that get into the circus?"

"Spectators bring even more unusual objects."

"Why don't you take them away at the entrance?"

"We have to be understanding and humor the crowd, or else they'll turn their backs on us."

"I don't envy you in the slightest."

"It's nice of you to be so sympathetic. People are unconcerned for the most part about a circus director's problems. They say, who forced the job on him? Perhaps you also wonder why I chose this work?"

I gave it some thought.

"I do wonder."

"I made up my mind after an agonizing experience. I spent the whole night locked up in a ghost train."

"Who locked you in a ghost train?"

"Negligent employees. They thought there weren't any more visitors, so they left."

"How irresponsible. You certainly must have had a rough time."

"Yes, but I held up bravely."

Someone in the line cleared their throat.

The director looked sharply in that direction for a moment and then continued.

"When they released me the next day, I decided right then to be at the head of a circus."

I looked at him in bewilderment.

"What brought you to do that?"

"Have you ever been in love?" he asked in return.

"Who hasn't?"

"What would you say if someone asked why you'd fallen in love?"

I shrugged my shoulders.

"I'd say I didn't know. It just happened."

"Well, it was the same with me. I have no explanation. I simply wanted to be the director of a circus. Besides, is any explanation needed?"

"Of course not."

"I'm no exception in that regard. Many of my performers also made an unexpected decision to take up the circus trade. You'll see, some stories are more unusual than mine."

A new round of applause came from the loudspeaker. The director made a sweeping gesture towards the circus troupe.

"Let's go. We don't have much time."

The young woman at the head of the line was a real beauty with a dazzling smile and luxuriant, dark wavy hair. The tight lion-skin-colored costume emphasized her slender build.

"Here's our main star. Lots of people come to the circus just because of her."

"I'm not surprised."

"But she's unhappy about that."

"Really? Why?"

"Every young woman is flattered to be admired for her beauty, but sometimes beauty can eclipse other qualities."

"Such as?"

"Goodness, for example; magnanimity, a gentle nature. In this case her talent suffers from her beauty. She's an exceptionally gifted juggler."

"I've always admired jugglers' dexterity."

"Thank you," said the young woman with a bow.

"Do you know how many pins are in the air at the high point of her act?"

"No."

"Seventeen."

"That's unbelievable."

"But what good is it when the men in the audience don't even see the pins? They can't take their eyes off the one who's throwing them."

"Perverts. Luckily, there are women in the audience too."

"They aren't any better."

"Really?"

"Yes. They only look at the pins so they don't have to see the beauty underneath them. Envy."

"It's hard to please everyone."

"You're telling me! I'm afraid there's only one way to save the act. The problem is that it's drastic."

"Drastic?"

"Rather. But it might get the men to look at what's being thrown and the women to look at who's throwing it."

"Nothing is too drastic if you can manage that."

"Not even if we replace the pins with human skulls?"

"What?" I said, horrified.

"She wouldn't have any trouble with the change. She learned her skill by practicing with skulls."

I took half a step back, staring at the young woman in disbelief.

"Why, that's appalling."

"Yes, it is unpleasant, but not unusual. What's more natural for a gravedigger than to use skulls? Everyone uses what's closest to hand. In addition, when you learn how to do it with skulls, pins are child's play."

"She's a gravedigger?"

"Yes, and a very experienced one. Don't be deceived by her youthfulness."

"Experienced or not, juggling skulls is still disrespectful to the dead."

"We would pay special attention to their anonymity. In any case, who among the dead wouldn't like to come briefly to life, even if it's only in a circus act?"

I shook my head with a sigh.

"I don't know. It's still too drastic. And what brought a gravedigger here, anyway?"

"The first time it crossed my mind," said the young woman, "was after going to the circus when I was thirteen. I was mesmerized by the lion-taming act. I made the final decision at the end of the Funeral Association's annual costume ball when there was a small incident."

"You changed your profession because of a small incident?"

"Oh, no. It had nothing to do with that."

"So what did it have to do with?"

"Nothing. I just felt a sudden urge. Isn't that enough reason?"

I nodded.

"I suppose so."

The loudspeaker burst forth with thunderous applause once more.

"We have to go on now," said the director quickly, indicating the next circus performer.

The tall, well-built man in his late thirties with clear-cut features was dressed in a formal black suit with a white shirt. He also had a white bow tie, a red flower in his lapel and a seductive smile.

"I hope you like illusionist acts," said the director.

"I'm mad about them."

"He's a wizard, second to none."

"I don't doubt it in the least."

"His number with seven safes is really popular. Some people come to all the shows just to see it."

"I'm sure it's spellbinding."

"You can't believe your eyes. They tie him up in chains and then enclose him in a safe that's barely knee-high."

I eyed the large illusionist.

"How can he fit into such a small safe?"

"He's extremely elastic. Here, just look."

Without bending his knees, the performer lowered his head to the floor, pulled it through his legs and looked up along his back. The smile never left his face.

"Go ahead and touch him," said the director.

I hesitated a moment before placing my hand on the top of his thigh. I would have kept it there longer if it weren't for the multitude of eyes on me. I removed it reluctantly and then applauded. The illusionist stood up straight and bowed.

"The safe is then put into a larger one," continued the director, "and that one is put into an even larger one, all the way to the seventh safe, the largest."

"He could suffocate inside," I said with concern.

"That would indeed happen if he weren't very fast. After we throw the cover over the largest safe, he has to get out in less than a minute-and-a-half. That's all the air there is."

"But how does he do it?"

"No one knows his secret. Not even me. In any case, ninety seconds later the cover is lifted and the safes are opened one by one. When we get to the smallest one, only this flower is inside."

He indicated the illusionist's lapel.

"Amazing. I had no idea that safes could be opened from the inside."

"It's easier than from the outside," said the illusionist in a velvety voice.

"He knows all about safes. He was a bank robber," said the director.

"Oh, I see."

"Perhaps you think poorly of that profession?"

"Not at all. I think it's very romantic."

The illusionist bowed once again.

"You must pay him handsomely," I added, "since he left such a lucrative job for the circus."

"We pay him well, but he still made a lot more as a robber."

"So why did he come here?"

"He suddenly turned himself in to the police after a robbery. When he finished serving his sentence, he decided to devote his life to the circus."

"Did something happen in prison that compelled him to do it?"

"That's another secret. You can ask him, but he won't say a thing. He's a very mysterious person."

"Illusionists should be mysterious."

"We don't mind as long as the spectators are happy."

The happy spectators' applause echoed from the loudspeaker throughout the empty circus.

"Let's continue," said the director and headed towards the next performer.

Although the man in tight black pants, white t-shirt and slippers was middle-aged with thinning hair, he was as solidly built as a young sportsman. Everything on him was taut.

"This is our acrobat," said the director, introducing him.

The acrobat clicked his heels, bowed sharply and cleared his throat.

"When you watch his act, it's like gravity doesn't exist."

"I have a weakness for acrobats," I confessed.

"Do you know which somersault he does on the trapeze?"

"A triple?"

"Fivefold!"

"Impossible."

"It's not only possible, but in between the third and fourth turns he manages to blow a kiss to the prettiest lady in the audience. That drives the crowd wild."

"Unbelievable."

"Quite believable. You can work wonders with muscles like this. See for yourself."

He indicated the acrobat's left bicep. I went half a step closer and squeezed it.

"Like steel."

"But you should see him on the rope. That act gets him an ovation every time."

"Does he climb up quickly?"

"Like lightning. Using only one hand."

"Oh, come on."

"Wait. That's just the beginning. When he gets to the top, he stops holding onto the rope with that one hand."

"Then he has to fall. Gravity does exist after all."

"It does, but he manages to defy it."

"For how long?"

"The longest he's hovered is fourteen seconds."

"But how . . ."

"He mastered that skill, inspired by something that happened on an athletic sports field."

"He was an athlete?"

"No, he coached long jumpers. One of the women long jumpers came to practice sopping wet."

"Was it raining?"

"It was a sunny day. She headed straight for the track without changing into sports clothes. She started to run and when she jumped, it was like flying. Nothing seemed to be pulling her towards the ground. She finally landed considerably farther than anyone before her."

"How did she do that?"

"No one knows. She left the practice after that one jump and never appeared again."

"But why didn't he try to use that technique at competitions, since he'd mastered it? He would surely break the world record."

"It would go unrecognized. Athletics has strict regulations against everything that's not quite natural. That's why he came to the circus. We're much more indulgent. We don't mind how something is done if it's a crowd-pleaser."

I was just about to praise him for that opinion, but I was prevented by a new outburst of clapping from the loudspeaker.

The director indicated the next circus performer without another word. The young man was the exact opposite of the acrobat: short, skinny and pale-faced with thick hair. He was wearing a yellow suit, pink shirt, a green scarf around his neck and sandals. His eyes were closed.

"This is our butterfly tamer," said the director.

"Butterfly?" I repeated in bewilderment.

"Yes. If you think it's easy to tame butterflies, you're badly mistaken. Even lions are easier."

"I had no idea it was possible to tame them at all."

"We are the only circus to feature this act. The crowd simply adores it."

"What do tamed butterflies do?"

"They conjure up his poems."

"He's a poet too?"

"A very talented one."

"So, how do they conjure up poems?"

"They flutter in synchrony and build various shapes in space. These shapes are used to express every verse. Even better than with words."

"Amazing." I paused briefly and then asked in a low voice, "Why are his eyes closed?"

"He doesn't need them. He can see without them."

"Oh."

"He discovered it by accident after an unusual experience with butterflies in a park. It's a priceless ability. When he sees with closed eyes, things appear that cannot be seen with ordinary sight. Perhaps you'd like him to tell you about one of those apparitions?"

"If we have the time."

"It won't take long. Poets know how to be succinct."

Without opening his eyes, the poet turned his head towards me and smiled.

"Once I saw myself rushing to the movies. But I didn't know what film I was going to see."

"I usually go with nothing planned and choose the movie when I get to the theater."

"Suddenly I was in a traffic jam. I got off the city bus and walked the rest of the way. Almost running."

"When it comes down to it, you can only rely on your own two feet."

"I got to the movie theater just as 'The Mysterious Chest' was about to start."

"Exciting title. Is that what you wanted to see?"

"I wasn't sure, but I thought the title was captivating too."

"I like to watch movies I know nothing about."

"Me too. An older woman dressed in green with a pillbox hat was sitting at the ticket window. She gave me a knowing look when I asked for a ticket to 'The Mysterious Chest'."

"Was it an adult movie? They're often camouflaged with innocuous titles."

"I'm already adult enough. The older man dressed all in white who tore the ticket at the entrance to the auditorium gave me the same look."

"I didn't know ushers were dressed like that in movie theaters."

"I had a surprise in store in the auditorium. There wasn't a single other person."

"That didn't say very much for the movie. Did you leave? I probably would have."

"No, I didn't. I looked at the ticket and then sat on a seat in the front row."

"You could have sat somewhere else. Watching a movie from close up is hard on the eyes."

"That's true, but you have to follow the rules. What

would happen if people sat wherever they wanted at the movies?"

"All right, so how was the movie?"

"I don't know."

"Why don't you know?"

"I waited for it to begin, the lights even dimmed, but nothing happened."

"Was there a power outage?"

"No. A spotlight finally flashed down on the small stage in front of the screen."

"Commercials? They're the bane of our lives."

"There weren't any commercials. The woman in green and the man in white were standing on the stage and between them was an open chest with metal studs."

"A prologue to the movie? How clever."

"That's what I thought too. But it wasn't a prologue."

"What was it?"

"I sat there waiting for something to happen, but the old folks remained stock-still. I was already starting to get restless when they finally moved."

"Did they break into a jig? I wouldn't be surprised. Today there are entertainers of all ages."

"No, they beckoned to me to join them."

"Climb up on the stage? This is the first time I've heard of movie screenings where the audience takes part. What did you do?"

"I hesitated briefly and then climbed up."

"What did they want from you?"

"To look in the chest."

"What did you see inside it?"

"Nothing."

"There was nothing inside?"

"There was, but my vision suddenly blurred. That had never happened before."

"Maybe they used a special effect."

"It's hard to say."

"Did it end at that?"

"No, they pointed to the chest once more."

"To look inside again?"

"No, to put something in it."

"What?"

I jumped when the poet suddenly opened his eyes. Two black wells flashed from behind his eyelids. Only an instant passed before his eyes closed again, but that was enough. He didn't have to say a thing.

"And you gave them that?" I asked softly.

He nodded.

"My respects. Then what happened?"

"Nothing. My vision blurred again. This time for good. The chest disappeared along with the two old people and the movie theater. Everything."

I wanted to ask him something else, but didn't have a chance. We were drowned out by new applause from the loudspeaker. The director immediately took my arm and guided me forward.

"I envy you," he said in a low voice.

"What for?"

"You understood his look."

"Didn't you?"

"I'm only an ordinary circus director. I lack insight. But perhaps you'd enlighten me?"

"I don't think the butterfly tamer would approve."

"He doesn't have to know."

I stopped.

"Do you expect me to do something dishonorable?"

We looked at each other for some time.

"No, certainly not," replied the director at last and then continued towards the next performer.

I couldn't imagine what kind of act was put on by the man in a light-colored jacket and dark turtleneck. Stout and already advanced in years, he could hardly be capable of a physically demanding act.

"Our photographer," said the director.

"How nice," I replied. "People love to have souvenir pictures taken with circus performers."

"Well, he's not an ordinary circus photographer. Not everyone is brave enough to stand in front of his lens."

"He's that expensive?"

"His photographs are free."

"So why are people reluctant?"

"Because his photographs show what the spectators would most like to hide."

"An ugly profile or excess weight?"

"Nothing so commonplace. He photographs the past."

"What kind of past?"

"Unpleasant ones. Everyone has a stain on their past. That stain is shown on his photographs. For example, you went past a beggar and didn't give him anything. The photograph will emphasize your insensitive face."

"I always give something to beggars."

"Or you didn't jump into the water to save someone who was drowning. The photograph will show you turning your back on the drowning person."

"I've never seen anyone drowning. Besides, I don't know how to swim."

"All right, then you stole something from the supermarket. The photograph shows you slipping it into your pocket."

"I don't steal from supermarkets."

"Maybe you have a secret lover? You will be caught with him *in flagranti* on the photograph."

"I don't have either a secret or an acknowledged lover."

"Those who've committed a crime have it the worst. The photograph shows you waving a knife, pulling a trigger or pouring poison in a drink."

"What's come over you? I'm not a murderer."

"All right, you aren't, but who among us is sinless? Something would certainly be found in your past, even if it's inconsequential. No one has ever turned out lily white on the photographs."

"So why do people agree to have their picture taken?"

"People are forgetful. They repress what they find unpleasant. They convince themselves that they're saints. But our photographer changes their mind in a flash."

"Wouldn't his services be more useful in a police station than in a circus?"

"They would, but for some reason photographing the past only works here. He discovered that by chance when he came to a performance after a strange incident at a train station. He took a picture of himself at the circus and realized with horror that the photograph was accusing him of being negligent towards the gray hamsters he kept at home."

I looked at the photographer in reproach.

"I don't like people who act irresponsibly towards animals."

I thought he wanted to defend himself, but the applause from the loudspeaker beat him to it.

"We have to go on," said the director, "but rest assured. Now he's much nicer to his hamsters. Photographs of the past straighten out negligent people."

The man before us was in his late thirties, tall and thin with short unruly hair and a bushy mustache. He seemed good-natured.

"This is our railroad engineer."

"You have a train in the circus?"

"A miniature one, to be exact."

"Your small visitors must love it."

"Children are not allowed to ride. Only adults can go on it."

"It is that dangerous?"

"Not at all. It barely crawls around the edge of the circus tent."

"So why aren't children allowed to go on it?"

"We can't let them disappear."

"Disappear?"

"That's right. One of the passengers always disappears. That's the real thrill of the ride."

"How do they disappear?"

"When the train stops, there's one passenger less."

"Where are they?"

"We never know. They appear somewhere outside the circus. One, for example, ended up in a park fishpond."

"They must have been sopping wet."

"That's right, but no one gets upset at what happens to them. They take the disappearance at their own risk. There are worse places than a fishpond. You might end up at the top of a factory smokestack, for example."

"What if you're afraid of heights?"

"Then it's best to close your eyes. But that would take away all the excitement and that's what attracts people most to the miniature train."

"Does it have to be so high?"

"There have been very low places too. One passenger found himself in an underground crypt. I guess you can't get much lower than that."

"I would be terrified."

"It isn't always terrifying. You could end up in a public library."

"That would be for me. But what's so exciting about that?"

"The library is temporarily closed. You can't get out of it for three-and-a-half days."

"How disagreeable. But at least it wouldn't be boring with all those books."

"A lot of people would consider that punishment. Who reads anymore nowadays?"

"There aren't many of us. How does the engineer make them disappear?"

"That's a secret. Not even I know it. Before he joined us, he was a railroad engineer on a real train. All I know is that he came to the idea while eating fish in the locomotive."

"Pike perch," said the railroad engineer.

"It seems that pike perch stimulates inventiveness," said the director.

"I prefer carp," I said.

The director smiled.

"Me too. Carp is wonderful for the memory."

This eulogy to carp received a well-deserved round of applause from the loudspeaker.

"It's a shame we don't have more time," said the director, beckoning me to move on. "I love to talk about fish."

The next circus performer was of medium height and stocky, with his hair parted in the middle and small glasses in a rectangular frame. He looked like an archivist.

"Here is our clown."

"He doesn't look like one."

"That's because he's not made up. You should see him when he's all kitted out. He doesn't have to do a thing. As soon as he appears, the audience is in stitches."

"I love clowns too."

The clown bowed theatrically.

"His act with pudding is a particular favorite. Do you like blackberry pudding?"

"Very much."

"Imagine a tub full of blackberry pudding in the middle of the ring."

"You don't mean to say that he eats it all?"

"Oh, no. Where would he put it? He bathes in it. That puts the audience in a frenzy. The whole tent trembles with laughter."

"It must be an uproarious sight. Even so, wasting so much pudding . . ."

"Something has to be sacrificed in order to entertain the audience. And while the audience is being entertained, he does his other duty."

"He's not just a clown?"

"No. He's also the main circus inspector."

"Are clowns skilled in inspectors' work?"

"Only if they've been inspectors before, like him."

"Those two professions don't seem very closely related to me."

"On the contrary. An inspector has to be inconspicuous, doesn't he?"

"To be sure."

"And who would be the last person in a circus you'd suspect of carefully observing your every move?"

"A clown?"

"Of course. Just because no one suspected him, he's thwarted many crimes."

"Do crimes occur in the circus?"

"They certainly do. The circus is practically riddled with them. We seem to attract all types of ne'er-do-wells. Who knows why?"

"Who would have thought?"

"There's nothing to be done. But ever since he's been with us, many have been caught. He has thwarted one hundred and seventy-three cases of petty theft, twenty-eight cases of grand theft, forty-one burglaries, nineteen armed robberies, twelve kidnappings, five suicides, three murders and one terrorist attack."

"Even a terrorist attack?"

"Believe it or not."

"Congratulations."

The clown bowed in the same theatrical way.

"This is now a much safer place."

The invisible audience rewarded the increased security at the circus with thunderous applause.

"Here we are at the end," said the director after we'd stopped before the last person in the row.

The woman could have been in her early forties, although she appeared somewhat younger. She had short straight dark hair, a turned-up nose, freckled face, narrow hips and modest curves.

"Here is our tightrope walker," said the director, introducing her.

"Tightrope walkers leave me breathless."

She smiled and dipped lightly.

"The audience trembles too when she walks onto the wire stretched under the very top of the tent. And when they see all that she does on it, without a safety net, someone inevitably faints."

"What does she do?"

"First, she doesn't use a balancing pole."

"But that can't be done."

"It can. She learned the skill as an experienced skier. She always skied without poles."

"I fall all the time even with poles."

"I can't even stand on skis. The job she used to do helped her. She was a court recorder."

"How did that help her?"

"A court recorder has to have their wits about them at every moment so nothing is omitted. And presence of mind is crucial on the wire. The slightest inattention is enough to cause a dangerous fall."

"I'd get dizzy just looking down."

"She doesn't look at all. She wears a blindfold."

"That's even worse."

"In addition, she doesn't walk on the wire but hops on one foot."

"It's no wonder people faint."

"The high point of her act is when she reaches the middle of the wire."

"What reckless stunt does she perform there?"

"None. She stays there a full six-and-a-half minutes without moving."

"Standing doesn't seem like much of a high point after hopping."

"It's not ordinary standing. She goes into a deep sleep. Nothing can wake her up."

I shivered.

"How awful. How does she stop from falling while she's asleep?"

"No one knows. She somehow manages to keep her balance, even though she twitches all the time in her sleep. She always dreams the same exciting dream. Perhaps you'd like her to tell it to you?"

I looked questioningly at the closest loudspeaker.

"There won't be any applause if you sit in the stands. Please don't hold it against me for not joining you. A circus director is always up to his neck in work and I already know the dream by heart."

"Of course."

With a new smile, the tightrope walker pointed to an opening in the low railing around the ring and then went ahead of me with bouncing steps.

∽ 7 ∾

I entered a large hospital room.

I was eclipsed by the whiteness. Everything was white: the floor tiles, walls, ceiling, drawn curtains, five beds, bedside tables, empty vases, small lamps, sheets, two light fixtures and the screen at the end of the room. The patients' pajamas, each in a different color, were all that disturbed the uniform whiteness. The covers of the books they were reading matched their pajamas.

The patient in green pajamas in the first bed on the left quickly placed the thick green volume on the bedside table, stood up and came to greet me. He was solidly built with a square chin, closely spaced eyes and a low forehead.

"As the ward bellwether, I have the honorable pleasure of welcoming you, madam," he said cordially.

"Thank you," I replied a little uncertainly.

"Have you perhaps not heard of hospital ward bellwethers?"

"No, I haven't," I admitted with regret.

"It's no cause for reproach. Almost no one knows about us, although we have a very important job. If there weren't any bellwether, who would be greeting you now?"

I shrugged my shoulders.

"No one. You would be left to your own devices. Would you like that?"

"No, I wouldn't."

"Of course you wouldn't. Well, luckily the bellwether is here. You're in good hands."

"That's nice," I said with a little smile.

The bellwether smiled as well.

"Forgive me for not shaking hands. Those are the rules. Most contagious diseases are transmitted by shaking hands."

"Don't germs spread most easily from the mouth? Should I be wearing a gauze mask?"

"It's not at all necessary. I'm the best example of that. I've come into contact with all kinds of mouths and nothing happened to me."

I eyed him suspiciously.

"You did a lot of kissing?"

"Not only that," he replied, blushing slightly. "I put my head in a lot of dangerous mouths."

"How can you put your head in someone's mouth?"

"You can if they open their mouth wide enough."

"Your head isn't all that small. Who could open their mouth that wide?"

"A lion, for example."

"You put your head in a lion's jaw?"

"Yes, at the high point of my lion-taming act in the circus."

"Well, then, we're colleagues. I work in the circus too."

"We aren't anymore. I left the circus after my favorite lion died. He got his head stuck in the bars of the cage one night and suffocated while trying to pull it out."

"Poor thing."

"I was very attached to him. But the lion's wasn't the only mouth I put my head into."

"Did you tame other animals too?"

"No, but I ran into them. For a while I led a really adventurous life. Once, for a bet, I went into the wide-open jaws of an alligator almost up to my waist."

"That's more than adventurous. You must have been out of your mind."

"Not quite. I was roaring drunk."

"So how did you win the bet?"

"I tricked them. First I got the alligator drunk too."

"Do alligators like to drink?"

"They do, but they can't hold good liquor. It takes just a few shot glasses for them to become as gentle as a lamb. I could have gone all the way inside."

"Clever. But where did you get the propensity for putting your head where it has no place to be?"

"When I was young, I tried to pull myself through the small entrance into a temple in the middle of the jungle. The opening suddenly started to narrow and I pulled my head out at the last moment."

"Didn't that dissuade you from doing such rash things?"

"On the contrary. After that I never passed up a chance to put myself in danger."

"Who's to understand the male intellect? So how did you end up in the hospital if none of those dangerous things harmed you?"

"Because of a harmonica."

"Were you playing it?"

"I didn't even put it to my mouth. I only turned it over briefly in my hands at an auction. Unfortunately, I didn't wash them afterwards. It was full of germs. Who knows how many people had played it beforehand."

"I never buy used things. They're a breeding ground for infection. I hope your treatment is progressing well."

"Another one hundred sixty-three pages and I'll be completely healthy."

"What pages?"

He turned around and indicated the green book on the bedside table.

"That's my therapy. I leave here as soon as I finish reading. I have the least left, that's why I'm the ward bellwether."

"I didn't know books were therapeutic."

"There's no illness that can't be cured by the right book. When you meet the other patients, you'll see for yourself their medicinal value. Follow me."

He preceded me towards the first bed on the right hand side. When we got to the head of the bed, the man in red pajamas closed a book of the same color and put it on the bedside table. He was in his late thirties with a thin face, sunken eyes and dark curly hair. He smiled weakly.

"He's a saxophonist," said the bellwether.

"I love the saxophone."

The patient raised his head a little and bowed.

"He's a true maestro, but unfortunately, you won't be able to hear him. He still can't play because of his illness."

"Did his instrument harm him too?"

"Oh, no. He's put all kinds of saxophones in his mouth and nothing happened."

"Don't musicians use only one instrument?"

"Usually. He, however, tried to lay his hands on every one that was within reach."

"He didn't play on other people's, did he? That wouldn't be hygienic."

"On other people's and on those that were new and unused. In the end his saxophonist colleagues started to avoid him to stop him from jumping on their instruments and he was prohibited from entering music stores because he tried the instruments to excess."

"But why did he do that? Wasn't he happy with his own saxophone?"

"He was until he took a tourist trip to a desert country. When he got back, he imagined that his instrument no longer produced a perfect sound."

"Did a bit of sand get into the saxophone? It's everywhere in those places, you can't ward it off."

"Even if it did, there wasn't any sand in the other saxophones and not a single one was to his liking."

"Perhaps the strong sun was to blame? When it beats down on your head, you can go a little strange. Is he in the hospital for sunstroke?"

"No, quite the contrary. Because of a serious cold."

"He caught cold in the heat of the desert?"

"After he got back. When he realized that the saxophone was no longer for him, he shut himself in a refrigerator one night. In the morning they found him almost frozen."

"What was the purpose of doing that?"

"Probably to cool himself off. What else do you do in a refrigerator?"

I looked back and forth from the bellwether to the saxophonist.

"Men," I mumbled with a sigh.

"But he's making a successful recovery. Here, just look."

He picked up the red book from the bedside table and showed me the ribbon marking the place where he'd stopped reading. It was approximately in the middle.

"Nice," I said.

Escher's Loops

"The book is treating not only his cold but also the perception that his instrument isn't any good. He might go back to his saxophone even before he finishes the book. Then it will be more cheerful here."

"It's always nicer with music," I agreed.

"Shall we continue?" said the bellwether, indicating the middle bed on the opposite side.

I couldn't get a good look at the face of the older patient in blue pajamas. The oversized dark glasses hid a wide swathe around his eyes. His hairline was well receded and the upper part of his forehead densely wrinkled. Long bony fingers held an open book with a blue cover.

"Here is our retired bank clerk," said the bellwether, introducing him.

"How can he read through those glasses?"

"With great effort."

"Wouldn't it be easier if he took them off?"

"It would, but he doesn't want to."

"Why's that?"

"He likes to be in total darkness. If it were up to him, we'd turn off the lights here completely. Since that's impossible, he wears dark glasses."

"I've heard of various male quirks, but not about liking the pitch dark. Where did that whim come from?"

"It's not a whim but a trauma. As a young clerk he went through a bank robbery. He was closed in a bathroom for hours without any light. The robbers turned off the electricity in the safe deposit box room."

"Wasn't he able to free himself from that trauma even in old age?"

"It was repressed for a long time but flared up after he retired. You should have seen what he looked like when he came here. He kept his eyes tightly shut. He only opened them when he got opaque glasses. He first read using them."

"How can you read through opaque glasses?"

"With great difficulty. But he had no choice. Reading was the only thing that could cure him. Now the situation is better, although he has quite a ways to go until he's completely cured. He has the thickest book here and is still not far from the beginning."

"Wouldn't you have expected the opposite? If something unpleasant happened in the dark, you wouldn't want to turn the lights off at all."

"It wasn't completely unpleasant."

"What was it?"

"As he sat on the toilet lid, he had a vision."

"What kind of vision?"

"He saw a young woman plunge into the sea. After that he looked for her continually in the real world."

"Why, that's really sentimental. Did he find her?"

"No, unfortunately."

"How sad. And now he hopes she'll reappear as a vision? Is it working?"

"No. Instead of the young woman on a beach, he sees something else."

"What?"

"Perhaps it would be best if he told it to you himself."

"I wouldn't like to interrupt him while he's in therapy."

"I think that a little break will be welcomed. Eyes quickly tire from reading through dark glasses."

The bank clerk placed the ribbon between two pages, closed the book and laid it on his chest. He coughed, wheezed and then started.

"In the vision I saw myself in the morning going to work at the bank. I wasn't in a rush, because I always leave in good time."

"Only irresponsible people rush," I said.

"I was stunned, however, when I caught sight of a digital clock in a store window. I was thirty-seven minutes late for work."

"How could that be? Had your watch stopped?"

"No. I quickly double-checked and saw that it showed the same time as the clock in the window."

"How awful. How could that have happened?"

"I don't know."

"All right, that's not important. So what did you do?"

"I ran as fast as my legs could carry me."

"Of course. And what did they say to you when you reached the bank?"

"Nothing. When I ran in all out of breath, I had a surprise in store."

"I hope a pleasant one."

"A strange one. The bank looked different inside."

"How so?"

"Everything had changed. The position of the widows, partition walls, furniture, curtains."

"Had you entered the wrong bank? A person can make a mistake when they're upset."

"That crossed my mind too. I thought of going outside and checking, but didn't have a chance. An older man dressed all in white came up to me."

"Was he a bank clerk too?"

"I didn't know him."

"What did he want?"

"He took my arm without a word and led me."

"You went with him?"

"What could I do? I was completely confused."

"Where did he take you?"

"To the place where I normally work. The safe deposit box room."

"Had it changed too?"

"No. Everything looked like it always did. Except that an older woman in a green suit and matching pillbox hat was sitting at my desk."

"What was she doing at your desk?"

"I wondered the same thing."

"You should have asked her."

"I wanted to, but she pre-empted me. She got up, came up to me and held out her hand."

"To shake yours?"

"No. Her palm was turned up."

"What did she want?"

"I wasn't sure. I just stood there and stared at her."

"And?"

"Several painful minutes passed until the old man in white finally came up to me and, without a word of apology, stuck two fingers into my right vest pocket."

"How rude. What was he looking for?"

"The key to safe deposit box thirty-seven."

"Was that your safe deposit box?"

"No. I don't have a safe deposit box in my bank."

"Then how did you get the key?"

"I have no idea."

"How unusual. So then what happened?"

"He went to safe deposit box thirty-seven and unlocked it. He had considerable trouble lifting a chest with metal studs out of it."

"It must have been heavy."

"That's how it looked. The old man wobbled as he put it on the floor."

"He might have fallen. Why didn't you help him?"

"He didn't ask for help. In any case, when the chest was on the floor, the old woman in green bent down and opened it."

"Why?"

"I assumed she wanted to take something out of it. But she and the old man just looked inside."

"What did you do?"

"I stood a little to the side."

"Weren't you dying of curiosity?"

"Yes, I was. I was happy when they soon motioned with their heads for me to join them."

"And what did you see in the chest?"

"Something that made me stagger."

"What?"

"I don't know anymore. Ever since I started wearing dark glasses, my memory has darkened too. I've forgotten some things."

"Too bad. I'm really curious about what you saw."

"I'd like to remember too."

"I hope you didn't fall after you staggered."

"No, the old man held onto me. Then the old woman held out her palm again."

"For another key?"

"That what I first thought. I shrugged my shoulders, not knowing where to look for it."

"Perhaps in your left vest pocket?"

"The old man's hand was headed in that direction, but this time I was faster. I took out what was in my left pocket before he did."

"What was it?"

The bank clerk beckoned for me to bend down. Even though my ear was right next to his mouth, I barely heard what he whispered.

"That's impossible," I said in disbelief, straightening up.

The head with the oversized glasses nodded in silence.

"What did they want that for?"

"For me to put it in the chest."

"You didn't do it, did you?"

"I did. My head was still spinning. I wasn't quite aware."

"So then what happened?"

"Nothing. That's where the vision ends."

"At the most exciting moment."

"Maybe I'll see the whole thing by the end of my treatment."

"I wish you a successful recovery."

"Thank you," replied the bank clerk, then picked up the blue book.

We headed towards the next patient on the right, but I stopped in the space between the beds.

"Why did he whisper to me just now?" I asked the bellwether in a low voice.

"Because he doesn't want his secret to be revealed here," he replied softly.

"Is there some reason for that?"

"Certainly."

"What is it?"

"In order to figure that out, you'd have to tell me what he whispered to you."

We looked at each other in silence for a few moments and then I finally shook my head.

"A secret should remain a secret."

"If you should change your mind later . . ."

"I won't change my mind," I said and continued on.

The patient in the middle bed had a cheerful face and a pencil-thin mustache. His pajamas and book were yellow. He didn't close the thick volume but just raised his eyes and smiled.

"Here is the owner of a flower shop."

"I often stop by flower shops. Gladioli and orchids are my favorite."

"I'm allergic to magnolias and narcissus," said the bellwether.

"He must miss flowers here. Why aren't there any in the vases?"

"He's to blame for that. Each night he destroys whatever we put in them."

I shot an angry look at him.

"A florist who destroys flowers?"

"He started doing that after a great disaster befell him. He lost his whole library in a flood."

"That is truly a terrible loss. But why blame it on the poor flowers?"

"He had to vent his feelings on someone. Flowers were the closest to hand."

"A typical male reaction. I hope he'll soon be cured of such violence."

"He's not being treated for that."

"So what's he being treated for?"

"His propensity for swimming across every river he happens to find in the worst possible weather."

I gave the florist another angry look. He raised the book a little, as though to ward off my glare.

"That is really daft. I wouldn't venture to swim across a river even in the most pleasant weather. What drove him to such madness?"

"Also the loss of his library. He tried to drown in a river after that. In the middle of winter."

"And he failed?"

"Obviously, although he made a tremendous effort. Finally, instead of ending up on the bottom he ended up on the other bank."

"That would never happen to a woman. We carry out our intentions."

"Be that as it may, he was so proud of himself after

that feat that he kept an eye out for every chance to repeat it. He paid no attention to the weather conditions; the worse the better, actually."

"Men will remain an everlasting mystery to me."

"Although he's having no trouble with the reading, the doctors don't expect to cure him completely. They feel they will have achieved something if in future he only swims across rivers on warm, sunny days."

"As far as I'm concerned, he can swim across them whenever he likes. What's important is that he stops abusing innocent flowers."

"That should be taken care of by the end of the book. We too can barely wait for our vases to be filled. It's much more cheerful when there are flowers."

I turned to look around the uniformly white room.

"To be sure."

"Let's continue," said the bellwether, indicating the last bed on the left hand side.

The man in purple pajamas had a powerful neck and short cropped hair. His features were rough and his eyes harsh. He snapped the purple book shut when we approached him.

"Here is our wrestler," said the bellwether.

"Did he injure himself in a match?" I asked. "Wrestling certainly isn't a gentle sport."

"Not at all. You can even die on the mat. But that's not what put him in the hospital."

"What did?"

"An uncontrollable vice. He became addicted to gambling."

"That's not such a bad vice. I've always liked gamblers. What did he play?"

"Cards."

"How romantic."

"Do you think so?"

"Of course. Haven't you seen those exciting movies about gamblers? When they're in the throes of passion they're liable to gamble away everything they own. And there's always a romantic interlude."

"I'm afraid there's nothing romantic here. First of all, there was no woman for a romantic interlude. He played cards with other wrestlers."

I frowned.

"That's not exactly the most edifying company."

"No, and they didn't play for money."

"What did they play for?"

"The one who lost had to drink a glass of water."

I shook my head in reproof.

"Only men could think up such nonsense."

"Very imprudent, I agree. Water is extremely dangerous for one's health in excessive amounts. After the fifth glass you're ready for the hospital."

"Fifth? I'd feel sick after two."

"He drank all of eleven before he ended up here."

"Eleven? Where did he put it all?"

"Wrestlers are large, but it was too much even for him."

"I would have completely exploded. The very thought of water would be repugnant for a considerable time."

"That's what you think. You might not be aware, but water is addictive. We had to chain him to the bed to stop him from getting up and drinking his fill. He didn't hesitate to pounce on the other patients' water glasses."

"How awful."

"If he couldn't find water anywhere else, he'd simply open his mouth under the faucet of the bathroom sink. Once they found him unconscious on the floor. He was as puffed up as a barrel."

"Addiction is so degrading."

"Luckily, his therapy is working. After just half the book, they took off his chains. Indeed, the other patients still don't leave glasses on their bedside tables, but the wrestler has stopped getting high on water in the bathroom."

"That's already something."

"If he perseveres, by the end of the book he will be completely sober. He won't drink another drop of water for the rest of his life."

"But how can you live without water?"

"Easily. There are so many other drinks."

"Alcohol?"

"Hard drinks and soft drinks, he can take his pick. All right, we've spent enough time with the men. Now let's go see the only woman among us."

We stopped in front of a screen on the opposite side. The bellwether pulled a chain next to the metal frame. Ringing was heard inside.

"Come in!" said the voice of a young woman.

After the whiteness that had surrounded me, my head started to swim when I entered the explosion of color in the screened-off part of the hospital room. Nothing was of uniform shade. The surfaces were an irregular motley, like the work of a crazed painter: the two inner sides of the screen and two walls, the floor, ceiling, sheets and bedspread, and the bedside table. Even the bed frame. Only the young woman's pajamas and book were white. She had short dark hair and a cheerful face.

"This young lady is an adventurer," said the bellwether, introducing her.

"How exciting!" I said.

"As I told you, I used to love adventures too, so our

paths inevitably crossed. I've gone through all kinds of things with her."

"I can imagine."

"She was imprisoned in the same temple that almost did me in. We all thought it was over for her, but she managed to get out."

"Fantastic!"

"And the things she experienced all alone. You could write a wonderful book about them."

"Or make a movie."

"A movie would be better. Today people only read for the sake of their health."

"At least there's some benefit from reading."

"It would take your breath away regardless of whether you read it or watched it. Just imagine, for example, that a gorilla is chasing you through the jungle and you suddenly fall into a deep hole."

"I'm all goose bumps."

"Or that you're shut up in a bank vault as a hostage."

"I'm on pins and needles."

The bellwether looked at me in surprise.

"Doesn't getting caught in such predicaments seem reckless to you?"

"No, why should it?"

"What if a man were in her place?"

"That would be different. Men are unreasonable creatures. They get themselves into trouble, then can't get out of it. Women, however, find a way out of every predicament that befalls them."

"Not exactly every one. She ended up in the hospital too."

"Why?"

"She was living among wild tribes and caught sleeping sickness. She almost never woke up."

I looked at the patient compassionately.

"I like to sleep too, but you shouldn't spend your life sleeping."

"At first the doctors had to pinch her all the time to make her read. Her eyes would close as soon as she opened the book."

"I wouldn't like to be pinched. Not even by doctors."

"Now things are much better. Before she falls asleep, she manages to read a whole chapter, if it isn't very long."

"Without being pinched?"

"Without being pinched. The book is such good medicine against sleeping that after she finishes it she might go to the opposite extreme and suffer from insomnia."

"Extremes are bad."

"She would have an easier time putting up with sleeping sickness if her dreams had more variety. But she only dreams one dream."

"How tiresome."

"Perhaps you'd let her tell it to you? It brings her relief."

"I'd be happy to ease her affliction. I hope she won't fall asleep while she's telling it. I'd feel guilty for her deteriorating condition."

"Rest assured. The dream is very tense. Both of you will stay awake."

"I love tense dreams."

The bellwether indicated the end of the bed next to the young woman's feet.

"Please make yourself comfortable there. Unfortunately, we don't have any chairs, so the visitors don't stay too long. You, of course, are an exception."

I nodded briefly and sat on the edge of the bed.

"I will have to leave you now. It's time for my therapy. And even the tensest dream is wearying if you hear it too often."

He left the screened-off area and I raised my eyes towards the young woman. We exchanged a smile before she started.

∽ 8 ∽

I stepped out of the mining elevator.

Before me stretched a stone corridor. The walls were humid, the boards on the ground barely broke the surface of the muddy water and flickering light embellished with periodic drops of water came from three spots on the ceiling. Seven miners were sitting on footstools. They were wearing dark gray raincoats with the hoods up and knee-high rubber boots. Their helmet lights illuminated the part of the wall in front of them as they pounded with tiny toy-like hammers.

The closest miner turned towards me, stood up and headed in my direction. He was tall and muscular, although advanced in years.

"Welcome, madam!"

White teeth flashed in a face darkened by grime.

"Thank you," I replied with a reticent smile. I was afraid he'd offer me his dirty hand, but he was kind enough to refrain.

"Please don't hold it against us for not receiving you in better conditions. You know how it is in a mine."

"Of course."

Two drops fell on my head. I looked up, frowned and moved a bit to the side.

"It drips here without letup," said the miner as though exonerating himself. "It's best to wear a raincoat."

"I didn't bring one," I replied, slumping my shoulders contritely.

"Don't worry. We're prepared for unequipped guests."

He went back to his stool and returned with a large, brightly colored parasol. He opened it, raised it above me and gave me the handle. I took it, feeling a bit silly. It was better suited to a beach than a mine. But at least it protected me from the drops.

"There. Now you're protected. It's time I finally introduced myself. Although there's nothing to indicate it, I'm the shift leader."

"Nice to meet you," I said with a slight bow.

"I'm sure you wonder what qualifications I have for the position."

I hadn't wondered, but I didn't want to disappoint him.

"I'm quite curious to know."

"I'm the only one with mining experience. And what's more appropriate than to have the most experienced one among us as the head of the shift?"

"Aren't the others miners?"

"No. This is their first time in a mine."

"What brought them here? The high wages?"

"On the contrary. They were ready to pay quite handsomely to be here."

"Who would pay to work in a mine?"

"Someone who needs inspiration."

"What kind of inspiration?"

"Artistic, of course."

"Where do you get artistic inspiration under the ground?"

"The nature of inspiration is underground."

"In the literal sense too?"

"In the literal sense above all. There is ore underground and each of the seven arts has its ore with a highly stimulating effect."

"I didn't know."

"Not much is known about it. Artists keep it a secret to preserve the illusion of the sublime nature of creativity. People are biased against the underground."

"So how does ore inspire artists?"

"Inspiration comes as we dig it."

"But you won't dig much this way."

"The quantity isn't important. That's why there isn't any heavy equipment. These little hammers are enough."

"That tapping is really inspiring?"

"You said it. Without that I wouldn't dare hope ever to achieve anything."

"What kind of an artist are you?"

"What do you think?" he asked in return.

I moved back a little and looked him up and down.

"It's hard to say."

"I'm a sculptor."

"Of course. Strong arms are needed for that."

"And you get the strongest arms as a miner."

"It turns out that your profession is artistically privileged. A miner works at the very source of inspiration."

"Quite the opposite. I didn't sculpt at all when I was a miner."

"How's that?"

"Not every mine is a source of art."

"You don't say? Why?"

"All seven artistic ores have to be in the same shaft."

"Do such mines exist?"

"They are very rare. That's why it costs a lot to come here."

"So when did you start to sculpt?"

"Not until I left my mining job. The working conditions became too difficult. My health was in such bad shape that I decided to cut my life short. I went into the forest and ate the first mushroom I found."

"Mushrooms can be really poisonous."

"This one wasn't poisonous; it cured me of one of the multitude of illnesses I'd contracted underground."

"There are therapeutic mushrooms too."

"Yes, there are. I was persistent, however. I kept going back to the forest, but instead of poisoning myself, each time I came back with one ailment less."

"A real blessing in disguise."

"When I was finally completely cured, I concluded that I had to repay the mushrooms somehow."

"You really were in their debt."

"I got the idea of making an enormous statue of a mushroom."

"That would be the best way to immortalize them. What is more lasting than stone?"

"It will be made of zinc, not stone, even though it doesn't last as long."

"Why?"

"Stone mushrooms already exist, but no one has made one out of zinc. A sculptor should be original, right?"

"Not just a sculptor but every artist."

"In addition, zinc is the artistic ore of sculpture."

"Oh, I see."

He pointed to the wall of the corridor in front of his stool.

"There's a vein of zinc there. A little more digging and I'll be completely inspired. And then I'll go straight to the surface to get down to work. I can barely wait to get out of here. If art hadn't compelled me to do it, I never would have set foot in a mine again."

I looked at the top of the parasol where it was dripping.

"It really isn't pleasant here. But you have to put up with something for the sake of inspiration."

"Everyone here is ready to make sacrifices toward that goal. You'll see for yourself after I introduce you to the others. Shall we go?"

He went ahead of me down the corridor and we stopped at the next stool. The figure in the raincoat turned and nodded. Only the whites of the young man's eyes stood out on his blackened face.

"He is mining silver."

"My favorite metal."

"It's the ore of music."

"Music is the art I like most."

"He hopes to leave here with a symphony for harmonica."

"I haven't heard of any symphony composed for that instrument."

"You couldn't have. He will compose the first one."

"Wonderful. I greatly admire original composers."

"He doesn't have any experience in composition. To date all he's done is play the harmonica."

"What made him decide to try for himself? Wasn't he happy with the compositions he played?"

"He was happy with them as long as they helped him seduce women."

"Oh, he seduced women?"

"Quite successfully. He sat on a bench on the edge of a forest and played. Every young woman who passed would stop and listen and then every single one followed him into the trees."

"Nothing is more irresistible to young women than music. Particularly played by a handsome musician."

"One young woman, though, did resist his music, even though she went with him into the forest."

"Some young women are more resistant to seduction. He must have taken it hard. Ladies' men are very vain."

"He didn't take his failure easily, but didn't give up either. He decided to win her over regardless of the cost. He concluded that the best way to reach her heart was to compose an entire symphony for harmonica for her."

"That's very flattering. Only a hard-hearted young woman would be untouched by that. And such young women aren't worth seducing."

The young man's lips curved into a relaxed smile, then he went back to tapping and the shift leader led me to the next digger.

I couldn't determine the age of the short man wearing a raincoat at least two sizes too big. It was as though he was under a tent. The black dust had settled in particular on his bushy mustache.

"He's mining nickel," said the shift leader.

"How nice."

"Do you know which art it's associated with?"

"I can't imagine."

"Motion pictures."

"I never would have guessed."

"It wouldn't be easy for you to guess his profession either."

"He's not a director?"

"No. He has a car repair shop."

"And wants to make a movie?"

"Yes, about an exciting experience he had."

"Something to do with cars? I love watching chase scenes and tremendous crashes on the big screen."

"There's none of that, although the film will be based on his personal experience."

"What kind of experience do car mechanics have?"

"Stressful. He was in a bank once during a robbery."

"I like movies about bank robberies too."

"He spent several hours with a young woman closed up in a bank vault as a hostage. His life was hanging by a thread."

"That really is stressful. I haven't seen a movie like that before."

"It won't be easy to see this one either."

"Why's that?"

"The whole thing will be filmed in the pitch dark."

"Why?"

"Because the robbers turned off the electricity in the vault. He and the young woman couldn't see the nose on their faces."

"But it can't be like that in a movie. You have to see something."

"Why? Just imagine what an original movie it will be where you can't see a thing."

"It might be too original."

"You don't seek inspiration for ordinary movies in a mine. Those who come here are trying to push the boundaries."

"To me this looks like doing away with them."

"That's nothing. Wait until we get to the other artists."

When we stopped by the next figure in a raincoat, I smelled the lush fragrance of plants in the damp air of the mine corridor. The old man squinted at us through his smudged round-framed glasses.

"Here is an herbalist renowned for his medicinal teas," explained the shift leader.

"I drink tea on a regular basis even when I don't need medicine."

"His longevity tea is highly valued."

"I'm not surprised. Everyone wants to be long-lived."

"In addition, he's a literature aficionado."

"How precious."

"The ore he's mining is precious too. Gold."

"What a nice match."

"He's filling up on inspiration for a new type of book."

"New in what way?"

"It will be made solely of herbs."

"That's truly original. And how would one read an herbal book?"

"It wouldn't be read at all."

"What would be the use of a book that isn't read? How could you know what it's about?"

"By putting it in a teapot with hot water, waiting for it to dissolve and then drinking the tea."

"And that would be like you'd read it?"

"That's right. Just imagine how much time it would save. It takes a lot longer to read than to drink tea. You could drink a real little library every day."

"But reading is a pleasure."

"Isn't drinking tea a pleasure too?"

"They're not the same pleasure."

"This would be two in one. And with it comes the pride of being well-read quickly and easily."

I shook my head.

"I don't know. I'd have to try it."

"Unfortunately, that's not possible yet. It will be some time before tea is made of books."

I pointed to the gold vein.

"Doesn't inspiration help?"

"Inspiration helps, but you have to be patient with herbs. Various mishaps can take place if you're impetuous. He's already had bad experiences."

"Of what kind?"

"He has to taste new teas while he's making them and it's not without risk. Once he fell into a coma right after swallowing the first sip. He barely regained consciousness."

"The job of an herbalist is dangerous."

"His coma is the best proof. It wasn't the least bit usual."

"Are there unusual ones?"

"Usual comas are dreamless. His, however, went with a very strange dream. Perhaps you'd be interested in hearing it?"

"I wouldn't like to disrupt his inspiration."

"Oh, he'll enjoy a little break. Mining isn't easy even when you do it for the sake of inspiration."

Before starting, the herbalist took off his glasses and wiped them with the edge of his raincoat. The lenses weren't much cleaner afterwards.

"In my dream I was walking through town."

"Where were you going?" I asked.

"I didn't know. It was night and I usually don't go out late."

"Me neither. There are strange people hanging about the streets after dark."

"I didn't run into anyone. Everywhere was deserted."

"That's even worse."

"It didn't bother me. When you fraternize with herbs, you don't like crowds."

"And you were just walking alone?"

"Until I reached the botanical garden."

"Isn't it closed at night?"

"Yes, but the large wrought-iron gate was ajar."

"You didn't go in, did you? I would never have had the courage."

"It was lit up inside."

"Even so. What if it was some kind of a trap? The world is full of strange characters."

"That didn't occur to me in my dream. I took the main path."

"I would have been terrified."

"I soon saw that not all the lights were on. At the first fork, only one of the paths was lighted."

"You didn't take it, did you?"

"I did. I was curious to see why it was set up like that."

"I wouldn't have cared. I would have turned and run out."

"I kept on going. After another three forks I reached a side path that ended at a high garden wall. In the middle of it was an orange plastic enclosure."

"What did it enclose?"

"A large square hole at least a meter-and-a-half deep."

"What was a hole doing in the middle of the path?"

"Someone had dug it. But that wasn't the main surprise."

"What was?"

"An elderly man and woman were standing in the hole."

"Ghosts?"

"They didn't look like that to me. She was wearing a lovely green suit with a matching pillbox hat and he was in a white suit."

"What were they doing in the hole?"

"Nothing. They were smiling. When they saw me above the enclosure, they waved at me to look down."

"What did you see?"

"An open chest with metal studs."

"Full of treasure?"

"I'm not sure. There wasn't enough light."

"And then what happened?"

"They motioned with their heads for me to throw something into the chest."

"What?"

The herbalist stood up and approached me, cupped his hand over his mouth and whispered two words.

"No!"

He opened his arms and raised his dusty eyebrows, then returned to his stool.

"And you threw it in?"

"I thought of refusing, but that's when the nearest light went out."

"Dirty blackmail."

"I only gave in after they put out the fourth light."

"Did they turn the lights back on after they'd got what they wanted? You never know where you stand with blackmailers."

"The rest is unclear. That's when I came out of the coma."

"What luck. That was a very agonizing dream."

"It put me off trying unfinished tea. Now I just hold it in my mouth a bit and then spit it out."

"You can never be too careful with herbs."

"It's time he went back to his digging," interjected the shift leader.

"Of course."

We continued, but stopped before we reached the next artist.

"The others have offered the herbalist the moon," said the shift leader softly, "to tell them what he just whispered to you."

"Are they that curious?"

"You shouldn't hold it against them. Not many passions can be compared to curiosity."

"And he refused their offers?"

"To the last. And he could have chosen, for example, however much he wanted of whichever ore."

"Why does he need other ores when he has gold?"

"Perhaps you would accept? You like silver, don't you? What would you say to a day's production? Just imagine the music it would inspire."

We stared each other in the eye for a few moments and then I shook my head.

"It wouldn't be worth it. I love music, but I have a tin ear. Not even all the silver in the world would make me a composer."

"One of the other arts, then?"

"I haven't the slightest talent for artistic creation. Not even the greatest inspiration would help."

I thought he was going to propose something else, but he changed his mind.

"There's nothing to be done," he said, shrugging his shoulders, and then went on.

The dripping got stronger as we reached the next digger. He was taller and larger than the others. The grime only seemed to emphasize his solid, masculine traits.

"Here is our botanist," said the shift leader, introducing him.

"Nice to meet you," I replied with a coquettish smile.

"The reason he's here, though, is for the painter's inspiration. That's why he's mining iron."

"I always dreamed of being an artist's model."

"Unfortunately, he's only interested in floral designs."

"What else would interest a botanist?" I said sourly.

"It has nothing to do with his profession."

"What does it have to do with?"

"When he was young he had a vision of a magnificent purple flower while he was sitting in the dark."

"It would be more natural at that age to have a vision of a magnificent female nude."

"One doesn't choose one's visions. In any case, he wants to paint that flower."

"If he wanted to paint a pretty woman, he wouldn't have to toil in a mine."

"Paintings of women resemble one another, while the flower painting will be unique."

"Really? I find paintings of flowers to be all the same. What will make this one unique?"

"First of all, it will smell like a flower."

"It could smell like a woman. Don't women smell nice?"

"They do, but I doubt whether they would like to be on his canvas instead of the flower."

"Why?"

"Because the flower will be like a real one."

"Do you think women would have something against being in a painting as though they were alive?"

"I don't think they'd like to go through their whole life in one day in the painting like the flower."

"In one day?"

"Yes. That will be the most original thing about the painting. The flower won't always be the same in it. It will bud in the morning, blossom by noon and then start fading slowly. By evening it will be withered."

"Day in and day out?"

"Day in and day out. And what woman would like to have everyone watch her age rapidly every day?"

"Not a single one, of course. But maybe the painting doesn't have to be so original. It could show just the first half of the flower's life. Until it starts to fade. Who's interested in what old age looks like? Regardless of whether it's a flower or a woman?"

"Artists don't do things by half measures. With them it's all or nothing."

I sighed.

"It's not easy with artists."

"You're telling me!" said the shift leader, then indicated the penultimate stool.

The thin young man appeared sickly. Dust emphasized the exhaustion on his long face. He had a hacking cough and brought his clenched fist to his mouth repeatedly.

"This is our pharmacist's assistant."

"He could use some help from a pharmacy."

"If he'd at least brought some cough syrup. He makes it himself and the pharmacy is famous for it."

"It's always good to have some cough syrup handy. You never know where you might need it."

"In a mine, for sure. This is no place for someone in delicate health. But what he's digging is also dangerous for his health. Lead is the unhealthiest artistic ore. Luckily, small amounts are sufficient to inspire an actor."

"Oh, he's an actor."

"Not yet, but he's firmly resolved to become one."

"His looks would suit the role of lovelorn young men."

"He's not interested in that."

"Who would he like to play?"

"God."

"No less. He doesn't really have the stature for that role."

"Do you think that God is well-built?"

"Maybe not, but in any case he has to look healthy. What would a sick God look like?"

"Looks aren't important. He won't even be seen."

"He won't be onstage?"

"He will, but in a barrel."

"God in a barrel?"

"Isn't it original?"

"Very. I've heard of God being in a variety of places, but never in a barrel before. Why there, exactly?"

"He had an unusual religious experience in a barrel full of cough syrup."

"There should be some syrup in the onstage barrel too. It wouldn't do for God to cough."

"A barrel is useful from another aspect as well. He doesn't exactly have the voice one would expect of God."

"That much is obvious."

"But a voice in a barrel sounds much deeper."

"One might say there's no better habitat for God than a barrel."

"So it seems. And while we're on the subject of habitats, you'll soon see that there can be even stranger ones."

We approached the final figure in a raincoat. If it weren't for the long locks of gray hair, I wouldn't have known by the dirty face that she was a woman.

"She's mining copper, the ore of architecture."

"I envy her. I'm sorry I didn't study architecture too."

"She didn't. She's a doctor by profession."

"Then where did she get the affinity for architecture?"

"It came after she retired, while she was running an auction."

"Was some famous building up for sale?"

"No. It was a picture of a dirigible."

"I don't see the connection."

"That's because you think that architecture has to stand firmly on the ground."

"Doesn't it have to?"

"Not necessarily. She's gaining inspiration here to free it from its confines."

"Does she intend to make a building that will float like a dirigible?"

"Why not? That would be truly original."

"But it isn't original for a dirigible to fall."

"Even buildings with deep foundations collapse."

"Nonetheless, it would have been better if the painting had been of something closer to the ground."

"Not even ground-level scenes are risk-free."

"They're not?"

"No. Once she bought a painting at an auction that no one else wanted. It showed a staircase that seemed to be constantly rising and then in the end it was back at its own beginning."

"What's dangerous about that?"

"Everything was fine until she brought the painting home and hung it above her bed."

"Did it fall on her head while she was asleep?"

"No, but whenever she looked at it before going to sleep, she always dreamed the same disturbing dream."

"That she was walking on the impossible stairs from the painting? At worst that would make her head spin."

"No, there weren't any stairs in her dream."

"So what was it that disturbed her?"

"Perhaps the best thing would be if she told you the dream herself."

"I wouldn't like to bother her."

"You wouldn't be a bother. She can talk without stopping her digging."

"Her inspiration wouldn't suffer?"

"Not in the least."

"Then I'd love to hear it. Stories about dreams are my favorite."

"Wonderful. I'll have to leave you, though. Zinc is calling me and I've already heard the dream."

"Of course."

He headed for the beginning of the corridor and I turned toward the doctor. She wiped her dirty forehead with the back of her hand, then smiled at me. I returned her smile.

$\backsim$ 9 $\backsim$

I walked in front of the firing squad.

Behind me rose a tall brick wall painted with flowers of all shapes, sizes and colors. Five men and a woman were standing in single file ten paces in front of me. They were dressed in camouflage uniforms with wide legs and short sleeves. Their rifles were at their sides.

I gauged where the middle of the wall was and took my place there. The only soldier who was not bareheaded stepped out from the left hand end of the line. He was wearing an officer's service cap and the insignia of rank were on his shoulders. Since I have no understanding of military matters, I didn't recognize them.

The officer marched up to me. He was in his later years, thin, with graying hair and a pencil-thin mustache. He took off his cap, placed it under his arm, clicked his heels together, stood at ease and bowed briefly.

"Please allow me to welcome you, madam, in the name of the firing squad!" he thundered.

"Thank you!"

It wasn't until I shouted this that I realized there was no need for me to raise my voice too.

"It is my duty to introduce myself first," he continued to roar. "I am the commander of the firing squad."

I shook his outstretched hand. He had a firm military handshake that cracked my tiny bones.

"Nice to meet you," I replied in a more moderate tone, rubbing my hand.

The officer reached into the left pocket of his uniform coat and took out a black silk band.

"Would you like this?" he boomed again.

"No, thank you."

The tense lines on his face suddenly crumpled and when he spoke again his voice was gentle.

"Wise decision. How could you miss the most important event in your life? If you don't watch, it's like you haven't seen anything."

"One should always look truth in the face."

"I'm glad you see things that way."

"I never turn my eyes away, not even in worse circumstances than this."

"We rarely get any condemned persons with such a broad outlook."

"I'm not surprised. Those awaiting execution usually have narrow views."

"And when the blindfold narrows their field of vision completely, they go completely blind. It's like they can barely wait to close their eyes forever."

"Really shortsighted."

"Not only that but it deprives us of a chance to make amends."

"How inconsiderate."

"And we really care a lot about not making a bad impression."

"How a man looks in others' eyes does make a difference."

"People think the worst of firing squads, although we don't deserve it at all. We're just carrying out orders."

"Obviously."

"But there's something that can be said about each one of us that shows we're full of compassion for our fellow man. You would be doing us a great service by sparing us a little of your attention."

"With pleasure."

The officer smiled and bowed again.

"With your permission, I'll start with myself. Seniority is respected in the army."

"Please do."

"When I don't wear a uniform, I work as a pharmacist."

"That's a responsible job."

"Even more than this one. I have to pay close attention to what I do at the pharmacy. Just a tad too much or too little of some medicine and instead of improving, the illness is exacerbated. Or even worse than that. It's much easier here. A fatal outcome is inevitable, so there's no way I can make a mistake."

"It's certainly less demanding."

"I had an assistant for a while, an unusual young man. Withdrawn, silent, shy, but diligent and very talented at the pharmacist's profession. He was particularly skilled at making syrup. We made our name with his cough syrup. Are you plagued by coughing, perhaps?"

I shook my head.

"I wouldn't say so."

"Too bad. We would have taken care of it in no time." He tapped the right pocket of his uniform coat. "I always have a bottle with me."

"It's good to be ready for a cough."

"One day, however, something in my assistant suddenly snapped. You'll never guess where I found him."

"I'm not good at guessing."

"In a barrel full of cough syrup."

"He must have come down with a really bad cough if he needed such a dose."

"No, he was as fit as a fiddle."

"So what was he doing in the barrel?"

"Let's not go into an eccentric's reasons right now. But whatever the reason, he ruined all the syrup. And do you know how much a barrel of syrup costs?"

"No."

"A small fortune. What would you have done in my place?"

"Turned mean."

"Any other pharmacist would have made him pay for the damage, then fired him. He wouldn't have been able to find another job. So ask me whether that's what I did."

"Did you?"

"Of course I didn't. That's because, as I told you, I'm mild-mannered and full of understanding. I just gave him a fatherly reprimand."

"Did your kindness bring him to his senses? I hope he didn't do anything like that again."

"He didn't, but not because he'd come to his senses. He resigned and left the pharmacist's profession."

"How ungrateful."

The commander sighed.

"People are ungrateful for the most part. Each one of us was similarly repaid for their kindness. But before you hear the other stories, I'd like to offer you something."

"Go ahead."

"You have the right to a last wish. Would you like something from the pharmacy?"

After giving it some thought, I shrugged my shoulders.

"Nothing comes to mind."

"Perhaps something to ease the pain?"

"Nothing hurts."

"A tranquilizer?"

"I'm not upset."

"Against excessive sweating?"

"I don't sweat at all."

"Against diarrhea? So there's no embarrassment. That happens to a lot of them here."

I shook my head briskly.

"It hasn't happened to me."

"Something illegal, then?"

"Do you have that too?"

"Officially it's not allowed, but they turn a blind eye. This is a last wish, after all."

"I wouldn't like to ruin my health."

"I'm sorry that there's nothing for you in the pharmacy. But there will be other opportunities. Each of the soldiers has something to offer. I'm sure we'll find something."

"I'm usually not very picky," I said, trying to defend myself.

"Even if you were, who could blame you? You don't get a last wish every day. All right, let's continue, if you agree."

"Certainly."

The commander turned towards the squad and signaled with his hand to the second soldier in the line. The short, balding man with a conspicuous stomach waddled rather than marched towards us. He stood at ease, lowered the rifle butt to the ground and gave a weak salute, bringing his clenched fist to his temple. I replied with a light nod.

"Here is our butcher," said the commander, introducing him.

"How nice," I replied, refraining from saying that he looked like one.

"Perhaps you think that butchers are insensitive, considering the nature of their work?"

"A certain indifference is inevitable in their profession. How else could they do their job?"

"Perhaps with regard to animals, although they do feel compassion for them. But no one is as kind to humans as butchers."

"Really?"

"Here, you be the judge. He would often bid at auctions against one of my colleagues, a pharmacist from his hometown."

"I love auctions."

"At first it was coincidental interest in the same object, but soon the object of their bidding became irrelevant. As soon as one made a bid at the auction, the other would make a counter bid just in order to beat him."

"People are blinded by their passions sometimes."

"And then they pay no attention to the harm that's done. These two gave vast sums of money for almost worthless objects."

"Every pleasure has its price."

"Once they really went too far. An inexpensive harmonica reached a price it would only have fetched if it was worth its weight in gold."

"That really is excessive."

"He came to this realization at the end of the auction. He wasn't as sorry for the money he'd wasted as he was for the sorrow on his friend's face when he realized he'd been defeated."

"How compassionate."

"His guilty conscience led him to send the pharmacist the harmonica in a package tied with ribbon."

"How generous."

"Just wait until you hear what he got in return for such generosity."

"The pharmacist didn't thank him?"

"Even worse. He sent the harmonica back."

"How ungrateful!"

"That's not all. He'd smashed the little instrument completely with a hammer. It wasn't worth a thing."

"How monstrous. He should have smashed the pharmacist with a hammer."

"Please don't judge all pharmacists by that single one. There's a black sheep in every guild."

"That goes without saying."

"Our butcher is able to fulfill any last wish having to do with dishes made of meat. Do you like pork neck?"

"Not really."

"How about roast veal?"

"Even less."

"Lamb? Really fresh?"

"No, thanks."

"What about chicken? Breast and drumstick? It simply melts in your mouth."

"I'd rather not."

"Then game, perhaps?"

"Certainly not game."

"Something quite unusual?"

"What, for example?"

"Anything made of meat. Let your imagination run wild."

"I simply have no imagination when it comes to meat. I don't eat it at all."

"A vegetarian?" asked the commander, disappointed. The butcher's face saddened.

"Unfortunately," I said, with contrition.

"There's nothing we can do about it. Well, all right. We still have four more proposals."

He ordered the butcher to withdraw with a brief nod. As soon as he had waddled off, the next soldier in the file headed towards us. He was of average height and middle-aged, thin, with short dark hair and stooping shoulders. He wore oversized, very thick glasses. When he reached us, I noticed that he was missing half his right ear.

"This is a demoted medical corps colonel," said the commander.

"Why was he demoted?"

"He turned out to be a poor shot."

"Was it his punishment to be sent to the firing squad?"

"He has to practice somewhere."

"That is extremely inhuman. One would expect only the finest shots to be here."

"You have no reason to worry. He's still a miserable shot. He'll have a hard time hitting the wall, let alone you."

"The army is no place for people like that."

"He's not a real soldier in other respects too."

"How so?"

"He doesn't have the cruelty of a soldier. For example, he has a real weakness for animals."

I gazed kindly at the demoted colonel.

"My opinion of him has just gone up."

"Whenever he saw an animal in distress, he took it in."

"How noble."

"He had all kinds of animals. Not only the usual cats and dogs, but others that aren't kept in the house: skunks, salamanders, gnus, moles, bats, wild boars, water snakes."

"A real philanthropist."

"Yes, a philanthropist. And do you think his philanthropy was adequately repaid?"

"It wasn't?"

"It was as though the animals he was looking after were competing to see which one could do the greatest damage. An ostrich took it to extremes: it devoured whatever it found. More than half of his parade uniform, one-third of the manuscript of his memoirs, an expensive butterfly collection, the casing of a war-booty saber, even two pairs of binoculars. And to top it off, it polished off a large supply of antibiotics."

"It must have been poisoned."

"Not only did nothing happen, but it never got sick ever again."

"Animals seem to be just as ungrateful as people."

"Even worse. He almost lost his life on maneuvers because of a canary."

"How could an innocent bird harm him?"

"He harmed it. He blew it apart with his gun."

"Then he's not a bad shot. Canaries are tiny."

"He wasn't aiming at the canary but at himself. He missed himself but hit the canary."

"How sad."

"And he was overcome by great sorrow. Completely beside himself, he left the medical corps tent and headed across a field where the artillery was doing nighttime target practice."

"He could have been killed."

"At first they thought he was. It wasn't until the next evening that they found him buried at the bottom of a crater blown out by a grenade."

"Was he injured?"

"Not even a scratch."

"Plain dumb luck. Why did he stay underground so long?"

"He was completely dazed by the grenade explosion."

"It's easier to suffer misfortune when you're dazed."

"He wasn't entirely spared from misfortune while he was dazed."

"What do you mean?"

"He had a strange illusion."

"An illusion while dazed?"

"Yes. A rare phenomenon. If you're interested, he would love to tell you about the vision he had while lying in the crater."

"Of course I'm interested."

"It seemed like I was walking along the city marina," said the demoted colonel in a rather reticent voice.

"It's nice to walk along a marina. What was the weather like?"

"Completely clear. The sun was going down. There wasn't a ripple in sight."

"The nicest time of day. There must have been lots of people."

"Not a soul but me. Neither on the promenade nor in the anchored boats and small craft."

"How unusual."

"It surprised me too. But what could I do? In any case, I soon heard sounds from somewhere up ahead."

"Sounds?"

"Yes. Like something bulky being moved along floorboards."

"What was it?"

"A large chest with metal studs."

"Was someone dragging it?"

"Pushing it, actually. Towards a boat at the end of a side dock."

"Dockers?"

"No. Two well-dressed old people. She was in a cute green suit with a matching pillbox hat and he was in a completely white suit."

"Couldn't they have hired someone to do the job?"

"How could they when there was no one around?"

"Did you offer to help them?"

"Of course. I've always respected my elders."

"How considerate. Did you have a tough time?"

"The chest was really heavy. I barely got it to the boat."

"What was inside it?"

"I had a chance to find out after I helped the old folks into the boat. They opened it."

"Did they want to repay you?"

"That's what I thought at first. I'd already waved my hand in refusal, when they motioned with their heads for me to look inside."

"And what did you see?"

"Nothing. I was standing in such a way that the low sun completely blinded me."

"Couldn't you have moved a bit?"

"There was nowhere to move. It was quite cramped in the small boat."

"Did they take something out of the chest?"

"Just the opposite. They made it clear that I was to put something inside."

"What?"

The demoted colonel glanced briefly at the commander, then bent down and whispered something in my ear.

I shook my head.

"I can't believe it."

"Believe it or not."

"And what did you do?"

"I certainly didn't want to comply, but then the boat suddenly moved away from the dock."

"All by itself?"

"All by itself. I knew at once that there was something fishy going on."

"Why didn't you jump into the sea and swim ashore?"

"I don't know how to swim."

"A colonel who doesn't know how to swim?"

"Medical corps colonels are not obliged."

"So you gave it to them?"

"What choice did I have? Should I have sailed off into the unknown with two oddballs?"

"Did they at least take the boat back after they got what they wanted?"

"They did. Beforehand, the old man locked the chest and the old woman took a gold chain with an oval locket from around her neck and attached it to the large padlock."

"Real oddballs. You might have had a worse time with them. And then they say we should be accommodating to the elderly. That's when you came out of your daze, I hope."

"No. Why do you say that?"

"Well, it seems like the right place for someone to regain consciousness. You might have ended up losing something else."

"They didn't ask for anything else. I stood on the dock and watched them sail off. They even waved."

"How nice of them. Did you wave back?"

"I was tempted, but refrained. I just watched them until they disappeared beyond the horizon."

"They went out to sea in an ordinary boat?"

"That's what it looked like. The only land on that side was a small distant island with a lighthouse. But I don't know if they headed that way because I regained consciousness as soon as they vanished from sight."

I sighed.

"The best thing is to stay away from artillery training grounds. You can get into all kinds of trouble there."

"I know," replied the demoted colonel dejectedly, "but I was driven to distraction by the loss of my canary."

"He also has something to offer for your last wish," interjected the commander.

"What?"

"Although he's not a skilled shot, he's an expert at bandaging wounds. Just look at how nicely his right ear has healed. That's because he was able to give himself first aid."

"I don't think my ears are in any danger."

"It doesn't have to be your ears. He would be happy to teach you how to bandage any part of your body. You never can tell where you'll be hit: your head, chest, stomach, legs."

"I hope that the other marksmen are more skilled so that no bandaging will be necessary."

"That's what we all hope," said the commander, then signaled to the demoted colonel to withdraw.

As we waited for the next soldier in the line to join us, he addressed me in a low voice.

"I could make sure that they aim really well if you tell me what he whispered to you."

"That's not much of an offer," I replied softly.

"Perhaps really bad aiming would suit you better?"

I though this over briefly.

"It wouldn't be worth it. If you ordered the squad to miss me, the colonel would certainly hit me by accident."

He was just about to say something in reply, but there wasn't any time because a tall man in his late fifties had marched up to us. He had bushy sideburns, a receding hairline and small wire-rimmed glasses.

"Here is our watchmaker," said the commander, introducing him.

"I couldn't live surrounded by clocks," I said. "They would remind me of the fleetingness of time."

"You get used to it, then pay no attention. There are worse things about the job."

"What else makes watchmakers' lives miserable?"

"Primarily the customers' ingratitude."

"Who would have thought?"

"And from those one would least expect. For example, the president of a reputable pharmaceutical company."

"Do people like that need a watchmaker's services?"

"For years he went to the company in person and picked up the president's expensive watch and then returned it after completing its annual service."

"Commendably obliging."

"One day, however, he decided not to go to the company any longer."

"Why?"

"When he was taking the watch back, something traumatic happened in the elevator of the building where the company was located."

"All kinds of things can happen to you in an elevator nowadays."

"He offered to continue servicing the watch if it was brought to his shop, but the president took offence at this. He brought charges against him."

"What for?"

"Allegedly damaging the watch when he serviced it."

"An outright lie."

"A lie, of course. But it's hard to prove that in court when you have expensive lawyers against you. In the end, the innocent watchmaker lost the suit and had to pay enormous damages."

"That's not only ungrateful, it's mean."

"Luckily, not all people are like that. Some are the exact opposite. Here, he spared no effort to make you something commemorative for your last wish."

"Commemorative?"

"Yes. A watch."

"What do I need a watch for? My time is up."

"This is the kind you need. It starts ticking the moment you leave us. It keeps posthumous time."

"I didn't know such watches existed."

"They're without equal. Posthumous time has no end, so they must be of the highest quality and durable. You won't have to worry about the fleetingness of time anymore."

I shook my head.

"I'm even less worried about eternity than fleetingness. But thank you for the kind offer."

"You are welcome," replied the watchmaker with a bow, then headed back to the line, and the next-to-last soldier came towards us. He had broad shoulders and a mustache, a low forehead and short legs. His movements were brisk, as though he were younger than he looked.

"He is the most experienced among us," said the

commander. "As a sergeant, he led the executions for many years."

"It's nice to be in experienced hands," I said with a smile.

"That experience, however, has its price. When you hold this position, it's inevitable that bad rumors are spread about you. That undoubtedly lies in store for me as well."

"What could they hold against you?"

"Nothing, but they'll think up something. The story about him was that he made mocking remarks to the condemned while putting on their blindfold."

"He seems good-natured, not like a sadist."

"He's never even looked at someone askance in all his life. He's an extremely fine fellow. But what's the good of it when you're targeted by evil tongues? He was also falsely accused of depriving the condemned of their last cigarette."

"That wouldn't affect me. I don't smoke."

"That's wise. Smoking shortens your life. But if you were to change your mind right now, he would be happy to offer you a cigarette."

The sergeant quickly reached for the left pocket of his uniform coat and took out a silver cigarette case. I waved my hand dismissively before he had opened it.

"No, thank you."

"And the worst was the claim that he took his picture with the condemned, supposedly putting his arm around their shoulders and grinning from ear to ear."

"Well, did he have his picture taken?"

"Yes, but there was no mention of any grin. On the contrary, he had a very serious expression on his face."

"But why on earth did he have his picture taken?"

"As a reminder of every execution."

"Why did he need a reminder like that?"

"Because of his conscience. It isn't easy living with all those executed people on your conscience. It wants to repress them, to ease the pain, but the album is there as a constant reminder."

"That looks like masochism to me."

"Many firing squad commanders are real masochists. I, for example, collect the condemned's autographs for the same purpose. Would you care to give me yours?"

"Gladly."

He took a small notebook and pen out of his pants pocket and handed them to me. I signed the first empty page.

"Thank you," he said, all aglow.

"You're welcome. I hope that this will burden your conscience permanently."

"Rest assured, it will. And perhaps you would do something for the sergeant's conscience?"

"What?"

"Have your picture taken with him, of course. That is also what he has to offer as your last wish."

"To see a picture of my own execution?"

"That's right. The offer would be meaningless if you'd accepted the blindfold, but as a person of broad views you certainly want to see yourself in front of this wall. And that is also of service to the sergeant."

I thought this over a while.

"I'll have to disappoint the sergeant."

The two faces before me fell simultaneously.

"Might I ask you why?" said the commander.

"I didn't have a chance to put on any makeup. And I'm wearing something quite ordinary. How could I have my last picture taken without getting spruced up?"

This time they sighed in unison and then the sergeant turned and headed back to the line with stooping shoulders. The only woman among the soldiers headed towards us. She was short and stocky with short red hair and a round face.

"Here is our gardener," announced the commander.

"I like nicely tended gardens."

"Not everyone does."

"Do such people exist?"

"There are all sorts of people. She worked in a botanical garden. For months someone came secretly during the night and destroyed everything she'd put in order during the day."

"Who could be bothered by an orderly garden?"

"The last person you'd think. In the end she caught the vandal and was amazed when he turned out to be a retired botanist."

"Unbelievable. What had gotten into his head?"

"That the orderliness of the garden betrayed the natural chaos of the plant world."

"How idiotic. So why didn't he go out into the wilderness if he wanted chaos?"

"He had a weak heart, so he couldn't."

"Men are really unbearable when they become infirm. He got the punishment he deserved, of course?"

"No, he didn't. He was forgiven."

"How could she forgive such a destructive person?"

"She didn't have the heart to report him. She took pity on his old age."

"I would have reported him without a moment's hesitation. First I would have beaten him up, regardless of his age and whatever heart condition he had. Ruining someone's efforts like that for months."

"That wouldn't make you popular with the firing squad. We don't employ vengeful people."

"It looks like I'm not made for your compassionate service."

"Unfortunately. But that does not deprive you of your last wish. I must warn you, however, that this is the last thing on offer."

"I hope that something will finally appeal to me."

"Do you like dreams?"

"I love them."

The commander let out a sigh of relief.

"Finally! I was really starting to get worried."

"You should have given me the woman's proposal right away."

"She would tell you a dream she had after she fell into a hole in the jungle."

"How did she fall into it?"

"She and a girlfriend were being chased by a gorilla. The hole appeared as their salvation. While they were waiting at the bottom for the gorilla to leave, she fell asleep. Her dream is very unusual. I'm sure that you'll like it."

"I can barely wait to hear it."

"It's not exactly short. I propose that you sit on the ground while she tells it. You can lean against the wall. I'm sorry that I have nothing more comfortable to offer."

"Comfort doesn't really matter to me while I'm listening to unusual stories."

"Please don't hold it against me for not staying with you. The soldiers will disband completely if I'm not with them and what kind of firing squad would it be without discipline? In addition, I already know the dream quite well."

"Of course."

He put on his cap and marched off. The gardener and I settled next to the wall and exchanged smiles.

"Do you go to concerts?" she asked me in a gentle voice.

"Whenever I can."

"Then you'll like my story. I dreamed that I'd entered a concert hall. The concert had already started."

Contributors

About the author

Zoran Živković was born in Belgrade, Serbia, on October 5, 1948. Until his recent retirement, he was a full professor at the Faculty of Philology, the University of Belgrade, teaching creative writing. He is one of the most translated contemporary Serbian writers: by the end of 2019 there were more than 100 foreign editions of his books of fiction, published in 23 countries, in 20 languages.

Živković has won several literary awards for his fiction, beginning with the Miloš Crnjanski award in 1994 for his novel *The Fourth Circle*. In 2003, Živković's mosaic novel *The Library* won a World Fantasy Award for Best Novella; in 2007 his novel *The Bridge* won the Isidora Sekulić award; and in 2007 he received the Stefan Mitrov Ljubiša award for lifetime achievement in literature. In 2014 and 2015 he received three awards for his contribution to the literature of fantastika: Art-Anima, Stanislav Lem and The Golden Dragon.

Zoran Živković has been recognized with his selection as European Grand Master for 2017 by the European Science Fiction Society at the 39th Eurocon in Dortmund, Germany.

Živković is the author of 22 books of fiction:
    The Fourth Circle (1993)
    Time Gifts (1997)
    The Writer (1998)
    The Book (1999)
    Impossible Encounters (2000)
    Seven Touches of Music (2001)
    The Library (2002)
    Steps through the Mist (2003)
    Hidden Camera (2003)
    Compartments (2004)
    Four Stories till the End (2004)
    Twelve Collections and the Teashop (2005)
    The Bridge (2006)
    Miss Tamara, The Reader (2006),
    Amarcord (2007)
    The Last Book (2007)
    Escher's Loops (2008)
    The Ghostwriter (2009)
    The Five Wonders of the Danube (2011)
    The Grand Manuscript (2012)
    The Compendium of the Dead (2015)
    The Image Interpreter (2016)

About the artist

Youchan Ito was born 1968 in Aichi prefecture, Japan. She launched her career as a graphic designer in 1988, becoming a freelancer illustrator in 1991 and founding Togoru Co., Ltd. with her husband in 2000. In 2017 the company was reborn as Togoru Art Works. She works with a wide range of genres including cover art and design for science fiction, mysteries and horror titles, as well as illustrations for children's books.
www.youchan.com